RIVERS OF HELL

MARINA FINLAYSON

FINESSE SOLUTIONS

Cover design by Karri Klawiter
Model stock image from Taria Reed/The Reed Files
Editing by Larks & Katydids
Formatting by Polgarus Studio

Published by Finesse Solutions Pty Ltd
2017/04/#01

Author's note: This book was written and produced in Australia and
uses British/Australian spelling conventions, such as "colour" instead
of "color", and "-ise" endings instead of "-ize" on words like "realise".

National Library of Australia Cataloguing-in-Publication entry:

Finlayson, Marina, author.
Rivers of hell / Marina Finlayson.
ISBN 9780994239198 (paperback)
Finlayson, Marina. Shadows of the Immortals; bk. 3.
Fantasy fiction.

For my dear friends in the AC. You guys rock.

1

Soft grey light illuminated the dead as they filed off the ferry and tramped up the road toward the gate. The fake sunshine that lit the grounds of Hades' palace didn't shine here by the dark river. The rocks on which I sat were grey, the spindly grass at the side of the road was grey— even the dead themselves had a grey pallor to their skin that meant you could never have mistaken one of them for a living person. Everything was dull, misty, drained of colour. *Welcome to the underworld, guys. Hope you like grey.*

One of Cerberus's heads growled as a man in a business suit strayed from the path. Hurriedly, the man rejoined the stream of souls heading for the gate, and Cerberus laid his head back down on his massive paws. I'd followed him down here after another day roaming the palace on my own while Jake and Hades struggled with the problem of the collars. I leaned against the giant dog's side, his body warm and alive against my back. His fur was black, like the waters of the Styx before us, which, at least, was a change from the ever-present grey. I felt like a parrot in my blue and green T-shirt.

Of course, compared to that gate, my T-shirt was positively tame.

Apparently, back in antiquity, the gate to the underworld had been made of diamond, but Hades had been renovating, and the diamond gate had been replaced by a giant laughing clown mouth, with bright red lips and mad, blue eyes sparkling above. The souls of the dead passed under his giant teeth to enter the afterlife. Was that supposed to make them feel more cheerful about what eternity had to offer? Because looking at the dull faces of the people passing before me, I'd have to say it wasn't working.

The ferry idling at the wharf was massive. Charon had obviously moved up in the world since the days of legend when he'd ferried the dead across the Styx in a rowboat. This thing towered above the wharf, as big as one of Crosston's huge commuter ferries. The throb of powerful engines split the air and churned up the inky waters. At least the gate wasn't the only thing Hades had modernised. Charon's back probably appreciated it. He didn't have to make so many trips, either, as the huge ferry obviously held a lot more passengers than a rowboat.

Across the dark river, the other bank was lost in mist.

Legend said that the souls who couldn't afford to pay the ferryman lingered there for a hundred years before they could enter the underworld. Frankly, from what I'd seen of the underworld so far, they might not be missing out on much.

I'd followed Cerberus here across the Plains of Asphodel. They'd stretched as far as the eye could see, a field of waving flowers in every direction, but distance was a funny thing down here. The laws of physics didn't apply. We hadn't been walking very long at all before the massive laughing gate appeared out of the murk, with the dark river beyond it. I had the feeling that I could have walked for days without ever reaching it, if I'd been one of the dead. Fortunately, I was still alive, one of the few living people ever to visit the underworld. Syl and Jake were here, too, as well as Apollo, but since he was a god, that probably wasn't as impressive.

Of course, I almost *had* joined the ranks of the dead. It had been a close call in that cellar, surrounded by shadow shapers bent on killing us. If Cerberus hadn't turned up when he did, it would have been game over for all of us. Instead, we'd managed to send a few of them to meet the Lord of the Underworld all up close and personal, and I wouldn't be shedding a single tear over any of them.

I sighed, shifting a little on the rocky ground. I'd been sitting here for what felt like hours, peering into every grey face that passed, hoping to see one of the shadow shapers. I needed to find out what had happened to the key that unlocked the collars currently around my friends' necks. Call me vindictive, but I was really hoping to see that bitch, Mrs Emery, joining the ranks of the dead, and so far I hadn't got my wish.

Could she have lived through the collapse of that enormous house? Or the firestorm that Jake had unleashed on her? Apparently, the answer was yes—at least, so far. Hades said a few of the shadow shapers had arrived not long after us, that first night, but none since then. Bruno had run as soon as Cerberus appeared, so he'd probably lived to tell the tale, but Adrian should have been well and truly smooshed under the collapsing mansion, as should Mrs Emery and the so-delightful Irene.

Well, speak of the devil … I jumped up as a familiar figure stepped off the ferry. Finally! Irene wore a smart suit and high heels, but the confidence had gone out of her stride. She shuffled along in the line, as grey as the rest of the dead.

She smoothed her hair back in a gesture I recognised. Irene had never met anyone she loved more than herself, and it showed, even in death. I strode down to the water's edge to meet her.

"Irene," I said. "Nice to see you again."

A flicker of recognition appeared in her eyes, but she said nothing. Just stood waiting, staring at the grey rocks as if she didn't care who I was or what I had to say. As if nothing mattered—which I guess, to her, it didn't. None of the other shades paid us the slightest attention, intent on their slow march into the afterlife. I didn't know how Hades could stand hanging out with this bunch. Their silence was starting to unnerve me. Maybe that was why he spent so much time topside pretending to be a vampire named Alberto.

"So, how's your boss? Still fighting fit? Or did we manage to crush her like the bug that she is?" Actually, that was an insult to bugs. "What did your friends do with the key to the collars?"

She raised her head, her eyes glittering with malice. "Why should I tell you?"

I shrugged and pulled out a knife, testing the blade against my finger.

She laughed, sounding like the soundtrack to every scary movie I'd ever seen. The hairs on the back of my neck rose instinctively. Damn dead people were creepy-ass bastards. "Your knife is no threat. What are you going to do? Kill me again?"

Ah, if only, Irene. Some people really deserved killing twice.

I feinted at her with the knife, and she leapt back, though the blade went straight through her raised hand.

"Nah, I just wanted to see you jump." I laughed at the

vicious frustration on her face, one of those *I'd strangle you with my bare hands—if only I had hands* kind of looks. "But, you know, I'm kind of tight with the boss of this place. If you don't tell me what I want to know, I'll just drop a word in his ear. He can make your life hell. Literally."

Rage flashed across her face, and she lunged at me, hands outstretched to claw my face. I danced away, but not before her spectral fingers passed right through my head, sending an icy tremor through my skull. Cerberus appeared at my side, snarling, and she hurriedly stepped back into line.

She glared at both of us for a moment, but her expression soon collapsed into the same apathy shown on every other grey face that passed us as the line moved inexorably onward. "It doesn't matter anyway. Mrs Emery will defeat you in the end."

"So she's going to live?" Damn, that was disappointing, even if it wasn't entirely unexpected by this stage. Poor Irene must have lingered in hospital for a few days. It was too much to hope that Mrs Emery was in the same sad situation. She was like a cockroach, that one—hard to kill and liable to scuttle back into the light when you least expected it.

Irene moved on, following the grey backs in front of her, and I let her go. If she knew anything useful, Hades would get it out of her. She wouldn't be able to refuse the Lord of the Underworld.

"You won't get what you want by interrogating the dead," a voice said behind me, and I jumped.

She lounged half on the riverbank, half in the black water, and her hair was so long and black its wet strands looked like the river itself flowing from her head. Her skin was pale, but not the grey of the dead surrounding us—more like someone who didn't spend any time soaking up the Vitamin D.

"Won't I?" I didn't appreciate being sneaked up on like that. My heart was still pounding. "How do you know?"

"Let's just say I've been around this place a while." She laughed, exposing a mouthful of pointed teeth like a shark's. "I have some experience with dead people."

"Who are you?" I didn't like the look of those teeth, but it was kind of hard not to stare. She looked like an emo cannibal. What was there to eat around here that required teeth like that? Casually, I glanced around for Cerberus. He was close by, still intent on the line of souls streaming into the underworld.

"I'm Styx," she said, "and this is my river."

Some kind of nymph, then. "It's very … black," I said, since she seemed to expect a response.

"It's coloured with the hate and fury of souls in torment," she said, and the water swirled around her hips as if in agreement. Nice. I bet she was great fun at parties. Faces appeared in the water, all screaming mouths and bulging eyes, and in between them, hands that reached out toward me. I backed up a step or two, checking again that Cerberus was nice and handy.

Behind him, two men appeared through the grinning gate, one tall and dark-haired, the other short and stocky: Jake and Hades. Hades pulled Irene out of the line and stayed by the gate, chatting to her, but Jake strode down the path toward me.

"That's a fine specimen of manhood," Styx said, flicking her long hair over one shoulder.

I wanted to shove her back into the river for saying it, but I had to agree. Jake smiled at me, a smile that lit his blue eyes with warmth, and then more warily at the water nymph.

"What are you doing down here?" he asked.

"Checking on the new arrivals," I said. "Any progress yet?"

I didn't have to be specific; the collars were virtually the only thing any of us talked about—those of us who were still talking at all. Syl had become more and more withdrawn as time passed with no solution, and Apollo alternated between tantrums and sullen silences.

His smile faded. "No change."

Styx leaned forward, thrusting her boobs at him. "Fancy a swim, gorgeous? You look like you could do with a break."

"No, thanks. The water looks a little dangerous for swimming."

"I'd take care of you, sweetheart." She grinned, showing those horrifying teeth again. Maybe she meant to be alluring, but the effect was creepy as hell. I'd sooner snuggle up with a shark. "Wouldn't let any harm come to a hair on your pretty little head. Of course, I might wear out a few other parts."

He took my hand in a firm grip and tugged me away from the riverbank. "Sorry. Maybe another time." A hint of red bloomed in his cheeks and Styx chuckled as he hurried me back up the path.

"You're blushing," I said. "That's so cute."

"Wait until some monster is trying to crack on to *you*," he muttered, once we were a safe distance away. "Let's see who's laughing then."

I glanced back. Styx was still watching him, a hungry gleam in her eyes that sent a chill down my spine. I was glad to join Hades at the gate and leave the pointy-toothed bitch behind.

❧

We walked back to Hades' palace through the fields of flowers. They were white and delicate, and if there'd been some sunlight on the scene, it would have been very pretty. Instead, we moved through a constant twilight, and shadows flitted like bats through my peripheral vision, leaving me constantly on edge. I did *not* like feeling as if something was sneaking up on me.

"What *are* those things?" I burst out finally, after one had swooped so close I'd automatically flinched away. Hades didn't seem bothered by them, so I figured they weren't dangerous, but they were still unnerving.

"Souls of the dead," Hades said. "They're attracted to us because we're alive—drawn to our vitality like moths to a flame."

That made it worse. I was being swarmed by dead people?

"The souls getting off the ferry weren't like this—they looked just like people."

"That's because they're newly dead. Some of these have been here for millennia, and they've faded." He smiled at the look on my face. "Don't worry, they're perfectly harmless."

Unlike some of the other denizens of this place.

"Did you get any info out of Irene's shade?" I rubbed at my face, remembering the chilly sensation of her fingers passing through my head. "The bitch tried to attack me. Cerberus chased her off."

The giant dog was padding at my side, and I reached up to give his shoulder an affectionate pat. The nearest head bent and licked my hand.

"No, she didn't know anything. But you should be more

careful. Someone like Irene couldn't have hurt you, but there are plenty of others here—dead and alive—who could. It's not wise to leave the palace grounds without either Cerberus or me."

I wiped my hand on my jeans. Cerberus's odd affection for me usually seemed to involve me getting slobbered on. "Like Styx? Is she a nymph or a monster?"

He laughed. "Maybe a bit of both? Actually, she's a goddess. A daughter of the Titans, like many of us. Earned her place here instead of languishing in Tartarus because she kept her oath to support Zeus. Her word is her bond— though it always pays to check the fine print with her. She'd leave some of your human lawyers for dead as far as sneaky sub-clauses go. But she's tame compared to some we have here. Monsters, heroes—and now even a few gods—mostly itching for a fight."

"The gods come here, too, when they die?" Jake asked. "That doesn't seem right."

Hades cocked a grey eyebrow up at him. In this form, he was pretty short, and older looking than when he masqueraded as the vampire Alberto. If you saw him in the street, he wouldn't rate a second glance. Maybe the ordinariness was meant as a comfort to the newly dead. Jake, striding at his side, looked far more godlike, with his height and his striking good looks, but there was an air of deference in his attitude to the shorter man. Jake had believed in the gods for a lot longer than I had. Actually talking with them and interacting with them on such a personal level like this must be surreal for him.

"Where else should they go?" Hades asked. "Dead is dead."

"So Hephaistos is here now?"

Ah. Smart boy. Now I saw where he was going with this. We had planned to visit Hephaistos's forge, in an effort to find some way to break these damned collars, but the location of the forge was a secret apparently only known to the god himself.

"We could ask him where his forge is." I grinned at Jake. Good looks and brains, too—the complete package.

"We might not even need to. He might be able to help us himself. He's the greatest smith who ever lived."

"The key word in that sentence being 'lived'," Hades said. "Being dead will certainly limit how much help he can offer. But I have to warn you, he's not adjusting well to his new situation. He may not be at all cooperative."

"He's been dead for a year, hasn't he?" I asked.

"A year isn't a long time when you've lived for millennia," Hades pointed out. "Particularly when you never expected to die at all. It's a bit of a shock. I've tried to make him comfortable. The gods have a special section of Elysium, and of course they're welcome to visit in my palace, too, but it's not the same."

"Can we go to see him?" Hades seemed unnecessarily negative. Surely Hephaistos would want to help us find a way to defeat the power of the collars. Without them, the shadow shapers would have a hard time controlling the gods they captured. Didn't he want to bring down the people who had killed him? I sure as hell would, in his place.

A light appeared on the horizon, like the sun peeking over the rim of the world. But it wasn't the sun, only the glow of the palace grounds, which were somehow lit with fake sunlight during the "day". Whatever day *was*, in an underworld that never saw the sun and probably didn't even exist in the same physical plane as the daylight world. I tried not to think too much about it, because it made my head spin. *Just write it off as "magic" and leave it at that.*

"I'll take you tomorrow," Hades said. "I need to head topside tonight and put in an appearance as Alberto."

"I'm sure Harry could manage the bar without you." Harry was a bit unreliable in his private life, but he took his work at the pub very seriously. Probably because his boss was a vampire.

"I'm sure he could, but I want to check in with my contacts, see if there's any fallout I need to contain."

"What kind of fallout? You think there's going to be some kind of diplomatic incident because we killed a few humans in their own territory? The shadow shapers can hardly go complaining to the human government."

"No, I was thinking more of our clash with Anders, and what the Ruby Council thinks of having the avatar of Apollo stolen out from under their noses."

Oh, right, that. Events were moving so fast I'd almost forgotten about that.

Cerberus galloped ahead as we neared the walls, barking with all three heads. Whether in response to that, or at some signal from Hades, the gates swung silently inwards. Magic again. I shrugged, and followed the giant dog through the gates.

Hades' palace was far more traditional country mansion than a true palace. He'd gotten sick of the awe-inspiring look and had remodelled to something a little more homey, if a fifty-room house could be considered homey. The long drive curved up toward the house on its rise, over a small stream and past some natural-looking copses that in the real world might have sheltered foxes or perhaps pheasants for the gentlemen of the estate to hunt. The house was an impressive sprawl of honey-coloured stone, the rather sinister gargoyles on its roof the only hint that its occupant wasn't the country gentleman he appeared.

Inside, under the soaring ceiling of the grand entrance hall, portraits of the famous and infamous stared down from the walls. Zeus was there, stern and bearded, as was his wife, Hera. Apollo was there, too, posed with his sister Artemis, all gold and shiny sun god compared to her silvery moon goddess. In fact, all the major Olympians were there—Aphrodite and Athena, Aries, Dionysius, Poseidon, and the rest. Basically, it was the equivalent of the photo wall in my mother's house, writ large. These were Hades' family snaps.

Apollo's voice echoed from the gallery above, and another familiar voice answered him. In a moment, they came into view at the top of the stairs, Apollo's golden head bent to Syl's dark one, an attentive look on his face. He stopped when he saw us in the foyer.

"I was just giving Syl the grand tour," he called down. At least he seemed more cheerful. Hades was always telling me how gods didn't notice the passage of time the way humans did. Maybe he'd finally decided to take a chill pill and trust that we'd find a way to get the collars off the two of them without him nagging at Hades every minute of the day.

He took Syl's elbow and guided her to the top of the staircase as if she were some delicate creature who might not be able to manage the descent without his help. She didn't take his hand off at the wrist, which showed more than anything how unsettled she was by everything that had happened. She might not be the most physically brave person I knew, but she had a mouth on her, and normally she wasn't afraid to put people in their place, god or not.

"Did you show her the Helm of Darkness?" Hades

asked. "I love that thing. Nothing like it to impress the ladies."

Now Syl rolled her eyes, but she kept her mouth shut. As she came down the stairs, the silver collar around her throat glinted in the light of the massive chandelier that lit the foyer. It was inscribed with symbols that almost looked like writing, except neither Hades nor Apollo recognised the language, and it was actually quite beautiful—as long as you overlooked its purpose. Apollo had his covered with a high-collared shirt, but occasionally, his fingers drifted to the lump it made beneath the shirt.

"No, I didn't know where you were keeping it these days."

"Follow me," Hades said.

With nothing better to do, we all followed him down a hallway and into another wing of the house. He opened a set of double doors with a dramatic flourish and gestured us through.

"Behold, the Helm of Darkness!"

Beyond the doors was an enormous library, its ceiling at least three storeys above us. Spiral staircases at each end of the room accessed the galleries that ran around the walls at each level, all completely filled with bookcases. It was a booklover's dream, and I stood in awe for a long moment, drinking it in, before I realised that the others were staring at a suit of armour opposite the door. It stood alone on a plinth in an alcove between shelves.

Jake crossed the room toward it, his feet making no sound on the deep carpet. "I always thought this was just a story." There was an almost childlike wonder on his face as he gazed up at the armour and the massive helmet perched on top of it. "Does it really make you invisible?"

"Absolutely," Hades said, grinning. Apollo was also watching Jake with a smile on his face.

I was no expert, but I'd never seen such a fancy suit of armour before. It was so covered with engraving and whorls and fancy sticky-outy bits it seemed to me that you'd do yourself a serious mischief just trying to put the thing on. The helm itself was the most outrageous part, sporting two giant golden horns that curled out like ram's horns. It must have weighed a ton, and looked more like a joke than an actual piece of armour.

Though I guess if you saw that coming at you in a battle, it might be a different story. The horns certainly looked sharp. But the menacing effect was kind of ruined by the fact that someone had decided to use the helm as a hat stand. A faded old baseball cap hung from one of the horns.

Jake frowned. "It seems a little disrespectful to hang a battered old thing like that off the Helm of Darkness."

"That's the joke," said Apollo, still grinning. "That battered old thing is actually the Helm."

Jake looked to Hades for confirmation. "Seriously?"

Hades nodded. "It used to be a right monstrosity.

Weighed half a ton and gave me the most crushing headache every time I wore it. So I had it modified."

Jake gestured at the suit of armour with its elaborate helmet. "Then what's this?"

"Nothing. Interior decorating. Just some old thing I had hanging around." Jake still looked unconvinced, so Hades stretched up and took the cap. "Watch this."

He put the cap on. The moment it settled on his head, he blinked out of existence. No fading or gradual disappearance, just one minute there, and the next, gone.

I sighed. Oh, the things I could do with a cap like that. Hades reappeared, the cap now in his hand. "What happens if you're touching someone else while you're wearing it?" I asked. "Do they disappear, too?"

"No. It only covers the person wearing it—plus their clothes and anything they're carrying. No two-for-one deals."

Jake shook his head. "And even though it looks like that, you still call it the Helm of Darkness?"

"The Baseball Cap of Supreme Sneakiness doesn't have quite the same ring to it, does it?" He put the cap back on its glorious hatstand. "Some of the old traditions are worth keeping."

My brain was running like a hamster on a wheel. I could sneak back into Newport with the Helm and the border guards would never know I'd been there. I could find the shadow shapers and roam among them at will, searching for the lost key. I could—

"No," said Hades.

"What?" I asked, confused.

"I can tell what you're thinking by the way you're looking at the Helm, and the answer is no. You can't take it to go hunting for the key."

"Why not? It would be perfect—"

"Nonsense. That key is probably buried under tons of rubble. Being invisible won't make it any easier to search through the mess, or any less obvious that that's what you're doing. People are going to get damn suspicious if bricks and beams start lifting themselves into the air, you know. Assuming you could even lift them."

"Then I'll find the shadow shapers and spy on them."

"Good luck with that," Apollo said. "They'll have gone to ground now, after the scare we gave them. They may not even be in Newport anymore."

I shot him a frustrated glance. Why wasn't he backing me up here? He had the most at stake of any of us, since the collar kept his powers locked down. I'd expected him to be all over my plan.

"He's right," Hades said. "We might as well accept that the original key is lost to us. It's not worth putting yourself in danger searching when the chances of finding it are so small."

"But you're not getting anywhere without it!" I burst out. Syl stood listening in silence, staring down at the carpet, her shoulders slumped. Maybe I was wrong about Apollo having the most at stake. I couldn't bear the change in her since she'd been collared. My sassy friend had disappeared with the loss of her shifting ability, and I was determined to get her back. I was scared of what she might do if I didn't.

"We'll go see Hephaistos tomorrow, and see what counsel he has for us."

I yawned, trying to hide it behind my hand. It was still light outside, but my body felt as draggy as if I'd pulled an all-nighter, still coming down from the stressed alertness of the last few days.

"Looks like you could do with an early night," Hades said. "I'm heading topside to the pub—I'll see you in the morning. Try not to get into any trouble while I'm gone."

Ha. He should have known me better than that.

2

I ended up crashing before dinner and sleeping the night away. When I woke in the giant four-poster bed, morning sunlight was streaming through the window as another picture-perfect day dawned over Hades' palace. Did he ever make it rain? Or snow? Or was every day a summer's one for the Lord of the Underworld? I stretched in front of the window, taking in the sight of dappled sunlight through the trees, and the water of the small stream bubbling clean and clear over the stones of its bed. No wonder Hades had never minded missing the days when he played the role of the vampire publican. We all thought he was sleeping the day away in a coffin in the cellar, when in fact he'd been coming home to this.

I hurried downstairs, eager to find Hades and get this day started. The schedule was pretty packed: visit Hephaistos, get his help removing the collars, then home to Berkley's Bay in time for tea. Okay, so maybe it would take a little more effort than that, but all the more reason to get this show on the road.

I passed the library and, just beyond it, the discreet elevator tucked away behind wood-panelled doors which Hades had used the previous night. I'd seen the outside of the house and there was quite clearly no elevator shaft extending into the sky above it; nevertheless, the next stop was apparently the pub's cellar. Another one of those magical explanations for things that it was best not to think about too closely. I suppose if I could accept that the gods were real and the underworld was an actual place, magical elevators weren't too much of a stretch.

Syl was already seated in the "small" dining room where we took most of our meals. I hadn't seen the "large" dining room yet, but it must have been pretty big if this was the small one. The table had room for thirty people, and she sat in the middle looking lost, her face nearly as pale as the white damask tablecloth.

"No Apollo this morning?" I asked as I sat down beside her. I hadn't seen a single servant in the time I'd been here, but food was always ready when we wanted it, baths were waiting and clean clothes laid out every morning, as if the whole household were run by an army of people wearing their own Baseball Caps of Supreme Sneakiness.

"I'm not his keeper," she said, with a touch of her old sassiness.

"No, but you're spending a lot of time with him lately."

"We have something in common," she said, her hand rising to the silver collar before falling back into her lap. She'd barely touched the bacon and eggs on her plate. "He's the only one who understands what it's like."

I slathered butter on a slice of toast that was as crisp and hot as if it had just come out of the toaster, despite apparently having been left on the table some time ago. The invisible army of servants must also have time-altering skills. Or else they were just fiendishly good cooks. "Jake probably understands it. He's worn one before."

"Yes, but his came off." She looked up, and her dark eyes were filled with a terrible fear. "What if we can't find an answer? What if we're stuck like this forever?"

"You won't be," I said immediately. Anything to get that desolate look off her face. "We'll find a way. Hades is going to take us to see Hephaistos this morning."

"Hades isn't back yet." She pushed her plate away in a sudden violent movement. "If only I'd stopped that guy with the key. He was right there! But I just froze up, and he got away."

Bruno had run, with the key that unlocked the collars in his pocket, the minute Cerberus had shown up in that cellar. Now there was no telling where the damn key was. It might even have been destroyed in the collapse of the house. I wasn't crazy; I could see that. Nor was I precisely eager to face the shadow shapers again, but if Hades wanted to throw his weight around and veto my suggestions, he'd better keep his promise to take me to Hephaistos today. I wasn't going to wait forever.

"It doesn't matter," I said to Syl. I couldn't have her blaming herself for the current mess. "We'll come up with something else."

"I hope so." She stared down at the tablecloth, twisting it in her hands without seeming to notice what she was doing. "Sometimes I forget, and I reach for my cat—and there's nothing there, just this terrible emptiness. I don't think I could live like that forever."

I covered her hand with mine, stilling her nervous fingers. "You won't have to."

We'd fix this, whatever it took. I chewed my toast, turning over schemes in my mind. I'd take the Helm and go back to Newport to hunt for that key if I had to. Anything to take that bleak look off Syl's face. My head told me it wasn't truly my fault that she'd lost her cat form—she'd chosen to come with me, knowing how dangerous the human territories were for shifters—but my heart whispered that she'd done it to support me, and that she'd paid a terrible price for our friendship.

Jake came in, his dark hair still damp from the shower, and sat opposite us. "Morning."

"You look tired," I said. The shadows under his eyes

were almost as blue as his irises. Not that they lessened his appeal at all. In fact, his hair being all rumpled like that made me want to run my fingers through it even more than usual.

He helped himself to bacon and eggs, and started shovelling them into his face like a werewolf who hadn't seen food for a week. Guess he was still rebuilding his strength from being shot and beaten up.

"Went topside with Hades last night. I thought it was time to check in with the Council." He shook his head. "Bad idea. I didn't stay long. Berkley's Bay is crawling with provosts."

"Looking for you?"

"Looking for *us*—but mostly me. I don't know how many of the Council Anders had in his pocket, but they've bought whatever lies he told them. There's a warrant out for my arrest, and apparently the Master of the North is in town too, ready to help apprehend the *dangerous criminal*." He sounded disgusted. "I can't believe the whole damn Council's lost their minds like this. I thought at least the Adept would have some faith in me."

"He *was* pretty tight with Anders," I pointed out. This must be hard for Jake, to have his whole organisation turn against him on the word of a man he knew to be a traitor. Frustrating, too, to have them pursuing him instead of the real bad guys. In the meantime, the shadow shapers were still out there killing gods, and if they managed to kill them all, there would *be* no more fireshapers—or watershapers, metalshapers, earthshapers, or airshapers. All the elemental shapers, who'd pretty much ruled this world since the gods had created them, would lose their shaping abilities. The fireshapers couldn't afford to be fighting among themselves.

"I know, but I've known Robert for years—and he knows what I went through to get that damn ring. Why would I want to steal it now? I was the one who gave it to him for safekeeping in the first place."

"People do odd things when they're scared." Particularly if they hadn't had much experience with the emotion. The Ruby Adept was the most powerful fireshaper in the country. He was far more used to causing fear than experiencing it himself. Having someone break into his private quarters and take the ring right off his finger must have been a traumatic experience for him—and now he was reacting with blind panic.

Something else for me to feel guilty about.

"The provosts have taken over a room at the pub, and they're interviewing everyone about Anders' disappearance."

I raised an eyebrow. "His disappearance? Not his death?"

He grinned. "Apparently, they haven't been able to locate a body. They may suspect me of killing him, but they can't prove anything without a corpse." The smile faded.

"Though the theft of the ring is enough to have them baying for my blood."

Hades had disposed of Anders' body, and Mason's, too. That was a handy side benefit of being Lord of the Underworld—corpse removal kind of came with the territory. In fact, Hades was all set up to be the perfect criminal—he'd also used the waters of the River Lethe to wipe the memories of the witnesses to his "crime".

"They can't be having much luck with their investigation," I said, "since no one who saw what happened will remember it."

Jake's smile returned at the thought. "I don't think they are. But Hades sent me back anyway. Neither of us wanted to tempt fate. They have photos of you and me, taken from CCTV footage of the fight in the plaza. Berkley's Bay isn't a safe place for either of us at the moment."

"So where's Hades? Why isn't he back yet?"

"I don't know. As I said, I didn't stay long—just long enough to make a couple of phone calls. Then he showed me how to work the elevator and I came back and went to bed."

"How to work the elevator?" I repeated. They weren't usually complicated. "Don't you just press the button?"

"He wanted to guard against humans accidentally finding their way to the underworld. If you press the button nothing happens. The real button's hidden behind a panel."

"Smart." The Lord of the Underworld's deviousness knew no bounds. I thoroughly approved.

"I thought he'd be back by now, though," Jake added. He glanced at Syl's downturned eyes, then added in a bracing tone: "But I'm sure he won't be long."

I poured myself a coffee from an exquisite silver pot and took a long sip. Heavenly. Or should that be hellish? It was damn good, anyway. "I hope so."

Neither of us voiced the obvious—that someone who was posing as a vampire couldn't be out in daylight. He should be back in his "cellar" down here with us by now. The fact that he wasn't almost certainly meant something had gone wrong.

Hades kept saying that the gods didn't regard the passage of time the same way as we mortals did. Maybe he was just working on god-time but, if so, where could he have gone? Syl fiddled with her serviette, winding it round and round her fingers. I wasn't even sure she was listening to our conversation.

I shared a worried glance with Jake. "Just be patient a little longer," he said.

I didn't do patience. Syl couldn't afford to wait on god-time, so neither could I. If Hades didn't show up soon, I'd have to take matters into my own hands.

❧

I waited all day for Hades to return, hanging around the mansion so I wouldn't miss him. I don't know how many times I walked down the corridor past the walnut-panelled elevator, but every time, the same silence greeted me. The single indicator light above the doors never lit up.

My impatient feet led me at last to the library, where I managed to lose myself for a while in a book. In other circumstances, I would have felt as though I'd died and gone to heaven to find myself in such a place. The ceiling, far above, was painted with representations of the gods gazing down from the clouds. Another family snapshot for Hades. I wondered which one of the stunning goddesses depicted was Persephone, his wife. The walls were a bookaholic's dream. Nothing but books, all the way up. I couldn't even begin to estimate how many there were. A million? More? More than I could ever hope to read in a lifetime, that was for sure.

Galleries ran around the room at two levels, allowing access to the higher shelves, their railings made of wrought-iron and topped with gold. The spiral staircases at each end of the long room were made of wrought iron, too, crafted into designs of flowers and creeping vines. Armchairs were scattered around the room, ready to welcome the reader, or there were desks for the more studiously inclined. I picked an armchair by one of the tall windows and curled my feet up under me.

Unfortunately, the novel I'd chosen, the adventures of a wisecracking earthshaper on the trail of a pack of rogue werewolves, couldn't hold my interest for more than a couple of hours. I closed the book, my thoughts drawn to my own werewolf friends, Holly and Joe, and their newborn baby. Joe was a tough-looking guy with a heart of pure marshmallow. He already doted on Cody, his son from his previous marriage; I could just imagine how besotted he'd be with his tiny werewolf daughter. I'd delivered the baby myself, in the back of a stolen car on that wild ride back from Crosston. I hoped Holly had the sense to keep her head down with the fireshapers in town looking for Jake and me. Her face would be on their CCTV footage from the Plaza of the Sun, too. That bastard Anders had used her as bait to force me to do what he wanted. Fortunately, Hades had been there to finish him off.

I sighed. The light outside the windows was fading, and Hades still wasn't back—I would have heard the chime of the lift from here. Should I go topside myself and find out what was keeping him? But if the town was as full of provosts as Jake had said, I really didn't want to deliver myself on a gold platter to them. Safer to stay here and wait.

I uncurled from my chair, stretching the kinks out of my muscles. The trouble was, waiting wasn't my strong suit, as Syl would probably have said. I walked around the room, trailing my fingers across gold-embossed spines, and stopped at the alcove where the elaborate suit of armour stood. It was hard to believe that tatty old baseball cap was the fabled Helm of Darkness. It had once had some kind of logo on the front, but it was so worn I couldn't tell what it had been. There were sweat stains—at least I hoped it was sweat—on the visor, and the whole thing was such a faded grey it was impossible to tell what colour it had originally been. Blue? Purple? Maybe even dark green.

On the wall behind it—the only part of the walls not covered with shelving—hung a map of the underworld. It was roughly circular in shape, hemmed in by the river Styx, and crisscrossed by branches of the Styx and several other rivers, with Hades' palace towards the centre. Where would Hephaistos be in all that dark realm? Probably not near Tartarus, where the real bad guys were kept, though there was a river of fire near there that might appeal to a blacksmith. Hades had said he'd set up a special area in Elysium for the dead gods, hadn't he? But Elysium was a big place, if the map was drawn to scale.

I eyed the baseball cap again and blew out a sigh. Best to be patient a little longer. It was probably good for my personal growth or something.

By the time the night was half over, Hades still wasn't back and I was done with personal growth. When the great house was quiet, I left my bedroom and ghosted down the stairs to the library again. But this time it wasn't the books that drew me. Bars of silvery light from the long windows stretched across the carpet. I had to hand it to Hades—his underworld had fake moonlight as well as fake sun. It was just as good as the real thing, but without my link to Syl and her feline night vision, it wasn't quite enough for me. I switched on a single reading lamp on one of the desks so I wouldn't bump into the furniture and wake the household.

I stopped in front of the suit of armour in its alcove. For such a priceless object, the lack of obvious security was a little worrying. Nothing had happened to Hades when he removed the cap the other day, but maybe it was magically linked to him, and anyone else who tried to take it would die a horrible death.

That thought did give me pause, but, on the other hand, it was far more likely that Hades was counting on the Helm's camouflage to keep it safe. A thief who made it this far—and how likely was that, considering this was the god's own palace in the middle of the underworld?—would overlook the tatty old cap in favour of the humungous horned helmet, which looked a far more likely prospect to be the famed Helm of Darkness.

Well, here goes nothing. I snatched the cap from its perch, my shoulders tensed against a blow that never came. No electric shocks, no collapsing floor to deposit me into a pit. Maybe I watched too many movies. I breathed out a sigh of relief, then nearly jumped out of my skin when a voice spoke behind me.

"Clearly, I've spent too much time with you lately." I spun around. Jake stood with his arms folded across his chest, close enough to punch. Or kiss. Sometimes it was hard deciding which I most wanted to do. I must be losing my touch—I hadn't even heard him come in. "I knew I'd find you here tonight."

"What do you mean?" I shoved my hands behind my back, keeping the cap out of sight.

"I've been waiting for you." He gestured at a high-backed armchair that faced away from us. No wonder I hadn't heard a door open—he'd been here all the time. Sneaky. My admiration for him went up another notch. "I knew you wouldn't wait for Hades any longer."

He moved closer, looming over me in the dark room. The single lamp glowed behind him, leaving his face lit only by the silver light coming in the windows, but I could see that he was smiling.

"But who knows when he'll be back?" I asked. "And what if he doesn't come back at all? The shadow shapers must have caught him, too—why else would he be gone so long? We could be sitting around here on our arses while the world burns."

"We could," he agreed. "But if you think that I'm going to let you sneak off in the night by yourself, you've got another thing coming."

"We have to do something, Jake."

"We do," he agreed. "But that's *we*. Not just you. I can't have you sneaking around in the dark filching the Helm of Darkness, planning to run off on your own."

I took a step back. He was very ... overwhelming ... up so close. The heat coming off his body summoned an answering heat that speared right through me. His smoky scent was in my nostrils and I swayed toward him without meaning to, my hands itching to roam over the hard muscles of his chest. "I wasn't."

He laughed. "Stop trying to hide the damn thing behind your back. I saw you take it. You may be a great thief, Lexi, but you're a terrible liar."

For answer, I shoved the cap on my head and took three swift, silent steps to one side. Immediately, a large circle of flame sprang up around us. Wow, talk about a blast from the past. He'd pulled the same stunt on me the night he'd caught me snooping in his house. Unfortunately, tonight there were no cats handy to assault him with. I crept closer to the flames, testing them, but they sure felt real. Too hot for anyone but a fireshaper to pass through.

"Hades is going to skin you alive if you damage his library," I said, grumpy at finding myself caught so easily. It seemed like cheating.

He moved toward the sound of my voice, pulling his circle of flame in, forcing me to move closer to him if I didn't want to get burned. Although I noticed it wasn't damaging the carpet at all. But it felt so hot, so real, that I wasn't inclined to test it.

"That's big talk from the woman who just stole his Helm of Darkness. If he's going to skin me for a few old books, what's he going to do to you?" He grinned, knowing that he'd beaten me.

Fine. I snatched the cap off again before he shrunk his circle so tight I was forced right up against the hard planes of his chest. Not that that would necessarily be a bad thing.

Turned out I could have saved myself the trouble, because his arms came around me and gathered me to him anyway. I gulped at the pressure of his body against mine. One muscled thigh thrust itself between my legs, and I forgot all about trying to escape.

"Why didn't you just ask me for help?" he said gently. "You didn't have to go sneaking around in the middle of the night."

"Because there's only one Helm, Jake." I tried to focus on what I was saying, instead of what the insistent pressure of his body was doing to my insides. "I can't take you with me to Newport—they know your face there now. You'd never even make it past the border guards. I have to do this alone."

He groaned and gave me a little shake. "Will you forget Newport? That's never going to work."

"I have to do *something*, Jake. I'll go crazy sitting around here any longer."

"Then let's go see Hephaistos."

Hmm. Hades had been going to take us to Hephaistos, but maybe we could find him on our own. Cerberus probably knew the way. Not that journeying through the underworld without the protection of its master would be any less dangerous than going back to Newport.

"The thing is, I seem to have a habit of getting my friends into hot water." My fingers traced the line of his collarbone and he drew in a sharp breath. "First Holly, then Syl—and you've been shot and beaten up and now there's a warrant out for your arrest. It would probably be safer for everyone else if I handled this one on my own."

He growled, and I felt the vibration in his chest against the palm of my hand. "You won't get rid of me that easily."

I shrugged as if it didn't much matter, resisting the urge to lay my head and my troubles against his broad chest. "I don't want you getting hurt again."

At least he wasn't laughing at me anymore, but the warmth in his eyes was almost more disturbing for my peace of mind. "You should trust people to make their own calls on that," he said. "It's not your job to protect everyone else. That's not how this friendship thing works."

I almost asked him how a fireshaper would know, but I managed to bite my tongue at the last minute. Might be a sore point considering all his fireshaper friends were baying for his blood. See? I could be diplomatic—if I tried really, *really* hard.

"Fine. You can come. Just don't slow me down."

His eyebrows rose. "I can come? How gracious of you. And I won't be slowing anyone down. I think you'll find I can go all night."

Men. They just couldn't help themselves. Abruptly, I shrugged myself out of his arms, before this conversation got totally derailed. Before I found it impossible to keep my hands to myself. "Then let's go."

"Now?"

"Why not?" I glanced up at the map of the underworld on the wall, though I already had it memorised. "If we're quick, we can be there and back before breakfast, and Syl and Apollo will have something to celebrate."

"It's still dark outside."

"So? We're in the underworld. Beyond the palace grounds, it's always dark outside." Besides, I did my best work in the dark. I found it comforting.

"I get the feeling it's not going to be quite as easy as you make it sound."

To be honest, I had that same feeling, but there was a time for honesty and there was a time for putting on a brave face and getting on with the job. I was embarking on a journey through the underworld, with only a fireshaper and a giant three-headed dog for company. What could possibly go wrong?

3

Plenty, as it turned out—but at least our journey started well. We left Hades' mansion, both carrying light packs containing mostly food and water, plus the odd knife in my case. Oh, and the Helm of Darkness. I didn't know what I might use it for, but I could hardly leave a thing like that just lying around, could I? You never knew when a Baseball Cap of Supreme Sneakiness might come in handy, and it wasn't helping anyone just hanging around the library.

I called Cerberus to me, and he came crashing out of the wooded area at the back of the palace, red eyes gleaming with hope, carrying half a small tree in his mouths.

"No. No stick," I said firmly.

His ears drooped as he dropped the "stick", but his manner perked up once he realised we were going for a walk, and he fell in beside us, trotting along jauntily. According to the map in the library, Elysium was to the northeast of the palace, so we struck out in that general direction. Not that I had a compass, or any idea whether concepts like "North" and "South" even applied when you were in the underworld. I was hoping that my canine companion might be a better guide than my memory of the map which, quite frankly, looked more "artist's impression" than "serious piece of cartography".

"Cerberus, can you take us to Hephaistos?"

The nearest head swung to look down at me. Walking next to him made me feel like a midget. He towered over Jake, and was built as solidly as a freight train. I opened a link so I could hear his reply. *HEPHAISTOS?*

His mental voice thundered in my head, as usual. It was a wonder that he could use words at all, I guess, but I wished he had a volume control. There was no recognition in his burning eyes.

"Hephaistos—the god. Hades said he had built a place for him in Elysium."

ELYSIUM. The other two heads turned to regard me, too, and his mental voice developed a weird echo, as if they were speaking in unison. *CHASE HORSES.*

"Uh, sure." Were there horses in Elysium? I supposed there might be, if the place was full of heroes. Horse racing, feasting, and wenching were probably high on the list of most heroes' wish lists for the afterlife. "You can chase the horses when we get there. But it's a big place. Do you know where to find Hephaistos?"

"The smith," Jake added. "The crippled god with the hammer." He glanced at me. "I assume Hades has built him a forge?"

He hadn't given me any details, but it seemed likely. I shrugged.

FIRE HAMMER, Cerberus said. *HAMMER MAN.*

"Yes, Hammer Man. Do you know where he is?"

THIS WAY.

Cerberus veered off in what seemed a more northerly direction. Hades' palace, in its little moonlit bubble, was already fading behind us, and the way ahead was so shrouded in mist it was hard to see where we were going. I stepped up the pace. Following a black dog in a dark place wasn't ideal. It would be too easy to lose track of him.

Don't go too fast, I warned silently. *Our legs aren't as long as yours.*

PUNY HUMANS. I could have sworn there was a haughty sniff in his tone.

"Do we trust him?" Jake asked in an undertone. "He doesn't seem the brightest bulb in the box. He could lead us to anyone."

"I'm not sure we have a choice, if the alternative is finding our way through this." Sure, the Plains of Asphodel had been a little misty, but I hadn't expected visibility to be this bad. Already, I wasn't sure I could find my way back to the palace. Without a compass, I had no hope of reaching Hephaistos without Cerberus's help.

Jake grimaced at the swirling fog that hemmed us in. "We'd better not lose him, then."

"We won't." That, at least, I felt confident of. "I can always call him back."

"What if he gets out of earshot?"

"Then I'll still call, and he'll hear me."

Jake considered this for a moment. "So it wasn't a coincidence, Cerberus turning up in that cellar just in time to save us? You called him?"

"Yes. I called him." I hadn't even been sure myself that it would work, but it did. Just as well, or we would all have become permanent residents in the underworld. And much as I loved stomping around in the mist, I'd much rather be back in Berkley's Bay in the bookshop. That simple life seemed a long way away right now.

"How? What is this power you have? Where did it come from?"

"Good questions. Unfortunately, I don't have any answers for you. When I first met the shadow shapers— before I realised they *were* shadow shapers, and how they'd gotten their powers—I thought I might be one of them. Adrian seemed to be able to control animals, like me." That had been such an exciting moment—to think that, finally,

I'd get some answers to the mystery of my heritage, to feel that I'd found my tribe at last. "But of course, it turned out that he could only control bees because he'd stolen that power from Aristaeus."

"What exactly can you do? And don't give me the brush-off this time." He smiled to take the sting out of his words, but I still bristled. Okay, maybe I'd been evasive with him in the past, but I'd had the lesson drummed into me: never admit to anything. Survival depended on secrecy. The only person I'd ever willingly told was Syl, and even that had been more than half accident.

"I can ... connect to animals. Use their senses. Give them instructions."

"What about this thing you have with Syl?"

He was observant, I'd give him that. "She has a human mind inside her animal form, so when she's a cat, we can communicate mind to mind."

"But not when she's a human?"

"No. My power is only over animals, not humans."

"But you and Cerberus can talk to each other, and he's an animal, not a shifter. He doesn't have a human mind."

I *had* been kind of surprised when the giant dog had responded to my mental overtures. "I don't know, Jake. This thing didn't come with a manual. He doesn't speak the way a human would, but we can make ourselves understood. He's not your average animal, obviously."

Jake glanced at the enormous hindquarters disappearing into the mist in front of us. "I guess not."

The land began to slope downhill and the mist thinned somewhat, enough to show a boggy area ahead. The darkness had faded to more of a twilight grey once we'd left the area immediately around the palace. Spindly trees rose in ones and twos from little clumps of drier land like islands among pools of dank water.

I wrinkled my nose. "Smells bad."

Jake paused. The aroma of rotting vegetation was overpowering. "Do we have to go through there?"

Cerberus stopped on the edge of the swamp to look back at us, clearly impatient with the delay.

"Is there another way, Cerberus?" I asked.

LONG WAY. BLACK WATER. MANY TEETH.

Right. The prospect of wading through a stinking swamp suddenly became a whole lot more appealing. "Looks like this is it, Jake."

"I hope he knows what he's doing," Jake muttered. His feet were already sinking into the marshy ground. "I don't like getting wet."

I did my best to keep to the little tussocks of relatively dry land, following Cerberus's lead, but it wasn't long before I was mud to the knee and both my boots were soaked. Jake kept up a steady stream of curses that got particularly colourful every time he slipped into one of the dark pools. The best you could say was that, after a while, your nose became inured to the stench. I was going to need a serious soaking in a perfumed bubble bath once this was over. Syl had better appreciate what we were going through for her sake.

Cerberus moved with surprising agility through the swamp. *He* wasn't soaked and covered in foul bits of rotting leaf. He leapt easily from tussock to tussock, finding the driest path even when it seemed there was nowhere that wasn't drowned in fetid, stinking water. He had to twist and turn to do it, though. We could be here forever at this rate.

Ahead of me, Jake followed in the dog's footsteps, sticking as closely to his path as he could. I watched where he put his feet and followed suit, sneakily drawing on some of Cerberus's agility to keep me from tumbling into the soup altogether. I was so intent on watching where I put my feet that I hardly had a chance to look up, but every time I did, we seemed to be no closer to finding an end to the swamp. It stretched out on every side of us as far as I could see, which, now the mist had lifted, was depressingly far. I sure hoped Cerberus knew what he was doing. He'd taken such a seemingly random path that now I had no hope of finding my way back again without him.

"Couldn't this be, like, a ghostly swamp?" I muttered as rank brown water splashed up onto my thighs again. My legs ached from the constant battle of pulling my feet out of the sucking mud. "Why does it have to be so real if the only people here are ghosts?"

"The Plains of Asphodel were real enough," Jake pointed out. "Those damn flowers made me sneeze."

"True. I guess it could be worse. At least there are no swarms of biting insects."

I looked back at a splash behind me, but saw nothing. The only other noises were the ones we made ourselves—splashing and squelching, mainly, with the occasional grunt of effort thrown in for variety. Cerberus, of course, moved like a whisper, despite his size. There were definite advantages to being a supernatural creature.

My legs felt leaden from the effort of fighting against the mud. My boots were caked with it. Wherever I could, I used the branches of the spindly trees to help drag myself along. Several times, I'd slipped and landed on hands and knees despite the agility I'd borrowed from Cerberus, and I was mud practically from head to foot. Cold mud had even found its way under the waistband of my jeans. I smelled disgusting.

Jake was an even bigger mess, owing to more frequent slips. He slipped again as he fumbled the landing onto a clump of grass that had managed to take Cerberus's weight, but now seemed unequal to the task of supporting a grumpy fireshaper. He sank straight down into the swamp up to his waist.

"Need a hand?" I balanced on the small clump of grass and reached out a hand to him.

He clasped my hand and I heaved, but he didn't budge. "I think I'm stuck," he said. "I've never wished that I was a watershaper before, but it would be damn handy right now."

He reached out with his other hand and got a grip on a low-hanging branch. We both pulled again, but he didn't move. His eyes widened in fear, and he nearly crushed my hand as he grunted and strained.

"Cerberus!" I called, just as the water rippled behind Jake.

A strange look came over his face, and then he was gone, jerked violently under the dirty water.

"*Cerberus!*" I lunged for Jake's hand, feeling around under the water. I thought I found his head, and pulled hard, but my hand came up full of weeds. "Jake's gone!" I yelled. "Something took him."

Cerberus plunged into the water, sending up a wave that drenched everything in the immediate area, and disappeared into the depths. I hadn't realised quite how deep the water was until both man and giant dog disappeared into it. Wildly, I reached out with my inner sight for whatever had Jake, but all I got was a sense of something big and hungry.

Let go! I screamed at it, frantically scrabbling through my pack for my knife, scanning the dark water for something to throw it at.

The water roiled, and a familiar dark head appeared.

"Jake!"

It had all happened so quickly I'd barely had time to grab my knife. Cerberus surfaced beside him with a pale limp thing in his jaws. It looked like an eel, only I'd never seen an eel with rows of teeth like that. I reached out to Jake, and this time I managed to drag him through the mud to the relatively solid area where I stood. He scrambled away from the edge of the water, coughing and retching, his whole body shaking.

"Are you hurt?"

He shook his head, still on his hands and knees, spitting out water. My gaze roved over his body, checking anyway. Maybe he was in shock? I couldn't see how those teeth could have grabbed him without causing some damage—until I saw the state of his boot. The eel thing must have latched onto his ankle, but fortunately, the hiking boots he wore had protected him. He was lucky; he'd get away with a few bruises instead of potentially losing his foot.

Cerberus dropped the eel monster at my feet, and I stepped back smartly, just in case there was still life in the evil-looking thing. It was huge—the bulk of it was still in the water. That was fine by me; I had no desire to see any more of it, or of any of its family and friends, for that matter. Before, the black pools we picked our way between had seemed mere inconveniences, something that was holding up our journey. Now they loomed far more sinisterly. Who knew what lurked in their depths, ready to pounce on the unwary traveller? I shrank closer to Cerberus's side, well and truly spooked now. So much for coming this way to avoid Cerberus's "black water, many teeth".

Jake shuddered and staggered to his feet, wiping filthy water from his face. He gazed with revulsion at the thing that had almost taken his life. Then he raised shaking hands and blasted it with a bolt of fire. I flinched back, startled, as it burst into flame. It burnt with an unpleasantly fishy smell, and Jake watched it burn, fists clenched.

"Feel better now?" I asked.

"Not yet." Water and mud dripped down his face, and his eyes were wild. He threw both arms out in an extravagant gesture and fire burst from his fingertips, sizzling out in a wide arc. Every tree within reach burst into flames. Every bit of straggling greenery taller than knee-high burned, too, crackling and spitting wetly in an orgy of destruction.

He combed his fingers through his dripping hair, smoothing it back, and wiped his face again. Reflected flames danced in his eyes.

"Now?" I asked.

He turned that fiery gaze on me. "I hate water," he said.

4

We didn't talk much after that. Both of us concentrated hard on putting our feet only where Cerberus did, focusing all our effort on escaping the nightmarish swamp. I kept watch with my mind's eye and turned anything larger than a small fish away from us. I'd have been warier from the beginning but I hadn't expected to find anything living in the swamp. Even so, the occasional rippling sound of movement in the water set my heart to pounding.

At long last, we passed the last pool and the ground beneath our feet stopped squelching at every step. The land rose gently until we found ourselves on a rolling plain, covered in tall grasses that waved shoulder-high. Cerberus turned around three times, trampling the grasses underfoot, then flopped down on his side, tongues lolling from all three mouths. I sat down, too, using him as a backrest.

"How much further do you think we have to go?" Jake

asked. He sat next to me and pulled off his damaged boot. As I'd expected, his ankle was ringed with bruises. The skin was broken in a couple of places, but it was nothing like as bad as it could have been. I offered him a bread roll from my pack. It was a little soggier than when we'd started out, due to a couple of unscheduled dips in the swamp, but still welcome. The Helm was also soaked, and would probably acquire a new stain to add to its collection.

"I don't know," I admitted. "That swamp wasn't even on the map in the library." I actually had no idea where we were, or how long we'd been travelling. My stomach said several hours, so it might be past dawn back at the palace, but here, the unchanging grey twilight made it impossible to judge the passage of time. "Do you think this is Elysium?"

Jake's expression mirrored my own doubt. "The legends tell of palaces of gold and heroes enjoying their reward. It seems a little quiet for Elysium."

I finished my bread roll and took a drink of water. Thank goodness we had real water and didn't have to drink the black muck we'd seen in the swamp—or from any of the rivers here. There were five famous rivers in the underworld, and none of them seemed like a good idea as far as drinking choices went. The Lethe would make you forget—though if you managed to find the pool of Mnemosyne, you might get your memories back—the Cocytus would fill you with despair, the Acheron with pain, and the Phlegethon would burn you to a crisp. And as for the Styx, that was known as the river of hate. Having seen those tormented souls writhing in it down by the ferry wharf, I wouldn't touch that even if I were dying of thirst. Not to mention that I wouldn't trust the nymph Styx as far as I could throw her. I hadn't liked the way she'd eyed Jake as if he were a particularly juicy steak she'd like to sink those pointed teeth of hers into.

If anyone was going to sink their teeth into the handsome fireshaper, it would be me.

He tipped his head back to drink from his own bottle, the muscles of his throat working as he swallowed. When he caught me looking, he rubbed at his cheek. "What? Have I got something on my face?"

"You've got something all over you." I scrambled to my feet and resettled the pack on my shoulders. Covered in mud, he was far from his usual urbane self. "You're going to need a lot of scrubbing when we get back."

"Is that an offer?" He grinned lazily up at me, still sprawled against Cerberus's massive flank. Dammit, even covered in mud he was hot. How did he *do* that? It must be the smile. It was hard to resist that twinkle in his eye. At least he seemed to have recovered from his bad mood.

I kicked him. "Get up, mud monster. We can discuss bath time once we've got what we came for."

He got to his feet with surprisingly good grace. His smile

widened, if anything. A man in his position probably wasn't used to people calling him names and kicking him. But then, he obviously wasn't used to being nearly drowned and eaten, either. Maybe he was just so relieved to still be alive that nothing else would dent his good mood. For someone so used to power and control, it must have been like something out of his worst nightmare to find himself fighting for his life under the water, trapped in the one element where his own power would have no effect. No wonder he'd felt the need to blast a few trees afterwards.

Cerberus heaved himself to his feet and we set off through the waving grasses. I was very glad he was there—with his giant body, he bulldozed a path for us, which made walking easier. In places, the grass stems waved above my head, making me feel as though I were walking through a grey tunnel. I much preferred the areas where it was shorter and I could actually see where I was going.

A light breeze blew, which set the grasses rubbing against each other, a soft whispering that began to get on my nerves after a while. It sounded like people murmuring, and I couldn't shake the feeling that someone—or something—was watching our slow progress across the plain. There could have been anything hiding to either side of the path Cerberus forged for us, and we wouldn't have known. My shoulder blades itched with the constant expectation that something was just about to jump out at us.

"Will we find Hammer Man soon?" I asked Cerberus. The itch between my shoulder blades was getting worse. I was going to go crazy if we didn't find some clearer ground soon.

SOON, he agreed, which didn't help much. His idea of time was probably a whole lot more fluid than mine, living in a world like this.

"What did he say?" Jake asked.

"Soon. I hope he's right. I don't like this place."

"At least there are no monsters lurking."

"Don't say shit like that. You'll jinx us."

Cerberus halted to sniff at something invisible that seemed particularly interesting. I waited, impatient to be on the move again, looking around at the whispering grey grasses under the grey sky. Even Jake looked a little grey in this light.

"You seem very superstitious for someone who didn't believe in the gods until recently," he said.

"That's not superstition, that's just having watched a few horror movies in my time. The minute someone says, 'Well, at least it can't get any worse,' everything goes to hell in a handcart."

"Right. So if we hear a noise, we should run the other way instead of going into the dark to investigate?"

I rolled my eyes. "Exactly. And don't have sex with anyone. That never seems to end well."

"With 'anyone'? I only see two options here, and Cerberus really isn't my type."

"I'm sure he's relieved to hear that." I glanced at the big dog, but he wasn't paying us any attention. One of his heads was still nose to the ground, but the other two were both gazing in the same direction, ears pricked.

"Did you hear that?" Jake cocked his head to one side.

"Ha, ha, very funny." I thought he was making another horror movie joke, but then I heard it, too—a low rumbling, just on the edge of hearing, like a thunderstorm that was still far away. I glanced up at the grey skies, but there were no clouds. Did the underworld even have rain? It seemed unlikely. What would be the point? "What is that? Can you see anything?"

I wasn't short for a woman, but he was nearly a head taller than me. He shook his head. "All I can see is this damn grass."

Cerberus's third head rose from the ground, and his tail began to wag. Maybe I should have asked him—he was way taller than both of us.

"Sounds like horses," Jake said, just as Cerberus began to bark, and then I saw the riders.

Well, I saw their heads above the grass tops, at least. I assumed from the noise of hoof beats that there were horses underneath them. A whole troop was thundering down on us, maybe thirty or more riders, spear points waving above their heads.

HORSES! Cerberus shouted in my head, and then he was off, bounding through the grass, barking his head off.

"Cerberus!" I yelled, but I might as well have been talking to myself.

The riders split into two columns when they saw him coming. One column set off at breakneck speed through the grass, and Cerberus gave joyful chase, his deep bark floating back to us. The other spurred on toward us.

As they grew closer I realised I could see the outlines of grass behind them through their bodies. "Are they ghosts?"

And then they got closer still and I saw with a shock that they weren't riders at all.

"Centaurs," Jake said, summoning fire to his fingertips. I pulled out one of my throwing knives and edged closer to him. Maybe my knife wouldn't be much protection against centaurs I could see through, but I felt better having it in my hand.

Their bare chests were grey, just like everything else on this dismal plain. Through the grass stems I caught flashes of their powerful, stocky horse bodies. They were shaggier than I'd expected from my memories of classical centaurs in books and paintings. Maybe the ancient artists hadn't gotten them quite right. Plus, these ones were clearly dead. Perhaps that made a difference.

For shades, or souls, or whatever they were, they still managed to make a mess of the grass, trampling it down in a wide circle around us. No one was actually pointing a spear at us, but they didn't look all that friendly. I doubted an invitation to afternoon tea was on the cards.

They spread out, surrounding us, which gave me the heebie jeebies. I did *not* like standing with my back to an armed man. Armed centaur. Whatever. I turned slowly on the spot, trying to give them all the death stare at once. Jake merely waited, the orange flames flickering up and down his arms the only spot of colour in this grim place.

"Do you reckon a spear you can see through would still hurt?" I muttered to Jake.

"Let's not find out, shall we?"

One of the centaurs grounded his spear butt and glared at us. He wasn't the biggest, but his beard was the longest, and plaited into intricate braids threaded with beads and little glints of metal that could have been anything but looked silver in the unchanging grey light.

"The living are not welcome in the lands of the dead," he growled.

"We're friends of Hades," I said.

"We're looking for Lord Hephaistos," Jake added. "Do you know where we can find him?"

At a signal from Fancy Beard, the centaurs began to move again, trotting around us in a slow circle. Damn, I'd get dizzy if they kept that up. I felt like a penguin on an ice floe, watching the killer whales closing in.

"Why do you seek Hephaistos the Smith in the lands of the dead? He is a god, foolish mortal."

"You should keep up with the news," I said. "He's now a dead god."

Fancy Beard bared his teeth at me, and the circling horde shook their spears. Jake flashed me a look that said, plain as day, *Please leave the talking to me.* I shrugged. The horse boys looked to be spoiling for a fight. Probably anything was better than trotting through the same boring grey grass for all eternity. Diplomacy didn't stand much of a chance compared to the excitement of battle. I doubted anything I said would change their intentions.

Those teeth were wicked sharp. Maybe Fancy Beard was related to Styx. What was with everyone around here having the same vicious shark teeth? Did they collect their Evil Teeth on arrival at the gates? *Step right up, folks. Free Evil Teeth in every show bag. Start your afterlife in bad-ass style.* I rolled my shoulders, ready for anything. Let's see how evil he felt with my knife buried in his neck.

"Is this Elysium?" Jake asked. You had to give him points for persistence. He stood, apparently relaxed, with his hands on his hips. But the tongues of fire that licked up and down his arms had grown bigger, and his shoulders looked tight. Maybe he was having that same itch between his shoulder blades that I was. "Lord Hades said he had prepared a place in Elysium for Lord Hephaistos."

I reached out with my mind, trying to find a way in. Centaurs were half animal—that gave me a fifty per cent chance of being able to connect with them, right? But I found nothing. Either fifty per cent wasn't enough, or the whole being dead thing caused a problem. It was like trying to grasp the wind.

Fancy Beard scowled, and the stomp of hooves grew louder as the circling centaurs picked up speed. The wind that stirred the grasses around our little circle carried the distant sound of Cerberus's deep bark. "Chase horses", indeed. He hadn't thought to mention that these horses were armed and dangerous.

Cerberus! I called, reaching out with my mind for the deep red spark of his. It wasn't that I didn't have faith in Jake's pyrotechnics, but he'd never tried them before against the dead. Maybe the centaurs would go up in flames, and maybe they'd just plough right on through. I clutched my knife a little tighter. *Stop chasing horses and get back here.*

I felt his reluctance, and pushed harder, forcing my will on him. This was no time for our guardian to get distracted. Another distant bark reached me, and then he headed back our way. *Plenty of horses to chase here,* I told him, which got him moving with more enthusiasm.

The centaurs were moving faster now, too, circling us at a canter, except for Fancy Beard, who continued to scowl menacingly from the same spot. With a wild yell, one of them broke from the circle and feinted at us with his spear. He bared his teeth in a savage grin at my flinch, and several of his companions laughed.

Jake stepped in front of me and flung his arms out wide. Flames shot skyward from his upturned palms. "Try that again and I'll roast your pony butt like a marshmallow."

I doubt the centaur even heard him over the drumming of hoof beats, but he understood a challenge when he saw one. He flung the spear in the space between one heartbeat and the next, so fast that I didn't even have time to scream before Jake scorched it out of the air with a bolt of fire.

As if that was the signal, the dark sky was suddenly raining ghost spears. Jake sent his fire whooshing out in a widening circle as I felt something strike my leg. A few centaurs disintegrated into writhing smoke, but most of them fell back from the flames, unhurt.

I couldn't say the same. A cold numbness was spreading up my leg. A spear had gone straight through it and now lay smoking on the ground within our circle. There was no blood, not even a tear in my jeans, but I could no longer feel my left leg below mid-thigh.

"Jake, I'm hit," I said as the leg buckled beneath me and I sagged awkwardly against his back.

More spears arched through the wall of flame around us, and Jake zapped them all into smoke and ruin. Then he made a pushing motion with his hands, and the wall of flame sprung outwards, herding the centaurs before it, crackling and snapping through the dry grasses.

"This whole place is going to go up," I protested.

He caught me and hoisted me into his arms. "And I should care why, exactly?" Soot had joined the mud on his face, and both mixed with sweat from the heat of the flames. Little fires danced in his eyes as his gaze swept over me. "They can all burn. Where are you hurt?"

"My leg. It's gone completely numb."

Centaurs still roved beyond the wall of fire, but no more spears passed through the flames. Jake stared out anxiously. "Where is that damn dog?"

I'd forgotten him in the excitement, but I didn't have to cast my mind out to find him. He appeared on the other side of the flames, snapping at centaurs the way a lesser dog lunges at flies. The teeth of one great head closed around the torso of a centaur, lifting him off his feet, but the creature dissolved into mist a moment later. Each one that he caught dissipated like smoke on the wind. As Jake strode through the flames with me in his arms, the rest of the band took to their heels. I stopped Cerberus with a word when he would have chased after them.

"We need to get you to help," Jake said, anxiety replacing the flames in his eyes, and his arms tightened around me.

I coughed; the air was thick with smoke. I couldn't tell how far the centaurs had gone—or when they might come back. The spreading numbness had reached my hip now and I knew Jake was right. Clearly, I needed help, but it was just as obvious that I couldn't walk in this state.

Which only left one option.

"Cerberus, could you carry us?" I asked.

Three big heads turned to stare at me. I wouldn't have thought a dog could look affronted, but he did. *NOT HORSE.*

I know, I know, and I'm sorry, I said, switching to inner speech. *I wouldn't ask, but ...* I swallowed hard, letting him see my fear. *I'm scared. We need help. Fast.*

A giant, pink tongue licked me gently. *HORSE FOR BOSSY GIRL.*

Bossy Girl? In other circumstances, I might have taken exception to that, but I was too grateful for the ride to quibble about it now. He could call me whatever he liked.

It was a little difficult to manage, but Cerberus laid down and eventually we got ourselves arranged on his back, me at the front, with Jake's arms encircling me from behind. Giant dog-back riding proved to be every bit as uncomfortable as I'd imagined, and if it hadn't been for Jake, I probably would have slipped off at the first bump, but Cerberus soon settled into a ground-eating stride.

"Take us to Hammer Man," I whispered. One huge black ear flicked toward the sound of my voice. "Hurry."

I didn't want to think about what might happen when the creeping numbness reached my heart.

5

After a while, I began to shiver, even with my back pressed up against the warmth of Jake's chest. The cold had spread its creeping fingers across my belly, and little tendrils of icy numbness lanced into my right leg, too. It was like standing in a freezing river up to the waist—the whole lower half of my body was so cold it burned.

Jake's arms tightened around me. "Hang on. I'm sure we'll be there soon. Let me warm you."

His arms glowed orange where they touched my body, and tiny tongues of flame crept from him to me. I'd seen him do this once before, when we'd found two lost boys soaking wet in the cold night bush. I hadn't realised, then, how much it tickled. The little flames didn't hurt at all, but they felt like ants marching across my skin. Very warm ants. Gradually, my shivering subsided, though the warmth didn't reach down into my legs. It felt as though I'd just snuggled into a thick woollen jumper, and I sighed with pleasure.

We'd finally left the grassy plains. Cerberus was loping through fields of tumbled rocks towards a range of stony mountains that rose forbiddingly over the blasted landscape. A strong smell of sulphur hung in the air. Cerberus picked his way through the rocks with ease, never slowing. Our weight on his back seemed to make no difference to him.

The path began to climb, winding its way past ever-larger boulders up towards a cleft between two peaks. Jake cursed as we slipped backwards. He had his legs clenched tight against Cerberus's sides, but he had to hold on for both of us. My legs didn't even feel like they were attached to me anymore, so I was a dead weight in his arms.

"Lean forward," Jake said, as the angle of the incline grew steeper. "See if you can get your arms around his neck."

I pitched forward, laying my chest against the great dog's warm back, and got my arms as far as I could around his middle neck. Jake huddled protectively over the top of me, his breath stirring my hair. Between his warmth and Cerberus's, my top half felt deliciously cosy. I couldn't feel my bottom half at all.

Black rocks rolled away down the slope behind us as Cerberus climbed, dislodged by his massive paws. I didn't want to choke him, but I had to hang on pretty tight. It wasn't exactly a smooth ride. Jake's breath was warm in my ear as he curled around me, helping me to hold on. We must have looked ridiculous, like a couple of baby monkeys clinging to their three-headed mother.

Up ahead, light glowed in the cleft between the two peaks, like a beacon amongst all the grey. "What do you think that is?"

"Hopefully our destination." Jake's voice showed the strain of keeping us both on our precarious mount. Cerberus's back was much wider than a horse's, which made me almost glad my legs were numb. It was a very unnatural sitting position. Would Jake even be able to walk once we reached Hephaistos?

Finally, Cerberus crested the rise, and I realised we were in a pass between the peaks. Below us, a soft, green land spread out, lit with a golden light that was richer than daylight. Sunlight on steroids. Houses nestled on the sides of gentle slopes, some grouped together, others on their own, all scattered across the green fields. Gracefully drooping willows marked the position of several small streams that crisscrossed the wide-open land. It was like a pastoral dream, only apparently without the backbreaking labour and the animals stinking the place up. At least, I couldn't *see* any cultivated fields or animals grazing. It looked too good to be true.

"Elysium?" I guessed. It certainly looked like a pleasant place to spend the afterlife, though I couldn't help wondering if the average hero might find it just a teensy bit quiet after a while. Smoke rose from the chimneys of the nearest cottages, though nothing else moved. Maybe there were drinking halls, too, and places to joust or whatever heroes did for fun. Whacked each other with swords, probably, or took bets on mud-wrestling matches.

On this side of the range, an easy path, bordered by tiny white flowers like stars, switched back and forth in a gentle incline down the mountainside. At the bottom, Cerberus turned left and loped along beside the foothills. His every step released a scent like jasmine and, behind us, the grass sprang back as if he'd never passed through.

Jake's flames, which still flickered and tickled across my skin, seemed to have halted the advance of the creeping coldness. Now that we were back on the flat, I released my death grip around Cerberus's neck and Jake helped me sit up, though he continued to cradle me in his arms as if I were more precious than gold. I could get used to this kind of solicitousness—it was just a shame I had to get shot by a dead centaur's freaky arrow to bring it out. Losing the feeling in the bottom half of my body was a steep price to pay for a cuddle, however nice it was to relax into his strong arms and feel taken care of for once.

Cerberus followed a small stream that chattered over

smooth pebbles away from the mountain's flank until we arrived at a stone cottage. No smoke rose from this one's chimney, but the big dog stopped as if we'd reached our destination.

"Is this it?" I asked. "Is this where Hammer Man lives?"

HAMMER MAN, Cerberus agreed.

"We're here," I said to Jake.

He slid down from Cerberus's back, staggering a bit as he landed. Ouch. Just as I'd thought, he was going to be stiff after that ride. Maybe I should offer to rub the affected parts for him. I had to grab my right leg and haul it over Cerberus's back before I could slide down to join him. He caught me when I would have collapsed in a heap and swung me into his arms. I nestled my head against his shoulder with a sigh. I could get used to this.

"Lord Hephaistos!" Jake strode toward the cottage. "Are you home?"

No one answered, so Jake kicked the door open and carried me inside.

"Shouldn't we have knocked?" I protested. I mean, what was the point of being all polite and calling him *Lord* if he was just going to kick the door in?

Jake rolled his eyes. "You're a thief. Do you usually knock on the doors of the houses you break into?"

"The difference being that I'm not robbing this house," I pointed out.

"Do you argue this much with everyone, or is it just me?" he asked.

I opened my mouth to say, "Just you," and then paused. I did argue with Syl a lot, after all. "Maybe you're too used to your underlings saying 'yes, sir, no, sir, three bags full, sir'. Think of it as a public service to keep your ego in check."

The cottage was just as small as it had looked from outside. The main room had a large fireplace, in which a fire was neatly laid, ready to be lit, with a lounge and two armchairs placed invitingly in front of it. To one side was a rudimentary kitchen, not much more than a sink and a couple of cupboards along the wall.

"Remind me to thank you one day," Jake said.

"No problem. Happy to help."

Through an open door was a bedroom featuring a bed covered in animal skins. Clearly, Hephaistos was into the minimalist lifestyle. Deathstyle? Whatever this was called. There didn't seem to be a bathroom, even though there was a kitchen. Did that mean that being dead meant you could eat without ever having to go to the toilet? Or that you didn't sweat and need a shower? Maybe I'd ask Hades one day. It didn't seem like the kind of conversation I could have with Hephaistos, when we hadn't even met yet. First impressions were so important, particularly when you were trying to get a grumpy dead god to help you.

Jake deposited me gently on the lounge, which was

brown leather and simply enormous, like something you'd find in a hunting lodge—or a swish hotel that was pretending to be one. I was glad he didn't put me on the god's bed—that seemed too presumptuous.

"How do you feel?" he asked, stroking a stray lock of hair back from my face with more gentleness than his testy tone indicated.

"I feel fine," I said, trying to sound calm and fearless. "The parts of me I can still feel, anyway. Everything from the waist down is numb with cold. It's like someone's just chopped the bottom half of me off."

I laid my hand on my own leg, and I couldn't even feel it. It was as if my legs belonged to someone else. There was nothing to see where the arrow had pierced me—not a drop of blood, not even a tear in my jeans. How could it have done such damage?

Jake perched on the lounge next to me and ran his hands over my legs, all the way down to my feet. Little flames followed the path of his fingers.

"Can you feel that?"

"No." What a waste. I'd imagined him running his hands over my body before, but somehow, I'd never pictured the scene quite like this. I leaned back against the cushions and shut my eyes. So far, the quest to find Hephaistos was an epic failure. I'd come all this way, got injured in the process, and the god wasn't even here. Maybe

I should have stayed put and waited for Hades after all. "What are we going to do now?"

"I'll go out and look for Hephaistos," he said, rising from the lounge.

"No, wait!" I caught at his hand. "Don't leave me here."

I wouldn't admit it, but I was afraid. What if the bitter cold continued its march up my body while he was gone? Without his warmth, I might be cold and dead by the time he got back. And what a shitty way to go that would be, lying here, waiting for the cold to snuff me out, knowing what was coming but being unable to move or do anything to stop it.

"I need to find Hephaistos," he said. He bit at his lip, an action that, in other circumstances, I might have found impossibly sexy, but right now tugged at my heart with its unexpected vulnerability. "I don't know what to do."

Well, that was an admission and a half from the all-powerful Master of the South-East. I tightened my grip on his hand in response, tugging him closer. "I'm scared, Jake." If he could admit his failings, I could, too. "Please don't leave me."

He sat back down, raising my hand to his lips. They were warm on my cool skin. At least I could still feel that. He sent another wave of tiny flames washing over me, warming those parts that still had sensation. Fire had always seemed such a destructive force in the hands of shapers like

Erik Anders. I'd never seen it as something beautiful until I'd met Jake. "All right. I'll stay here and keep you warm. I'm sure Hephaistos won't be long."

Stupid man. I shut my eyes again, smiling. He had no idea where Hephaistos was. For all we knew, he could be off on an undead road trip. Jake's confident act wasn't fooling me, but it was sweet all the same.

"Maybe the effects of the arrow will just wear off," I said. See? I could be overly optimistic, too.

"Maybe. Can you feel that?"

Feel what? I opened my eyes to find him running his hands down my legs again. "No." Dammit.

Those flames sure were pretty, though—orange at the base, flickering with yellow in the centre, and disappearing at their peaks into a clearness like dancing glass. I'd seen what Jake's flames could do when he used them in anger, yet now they caressed me, warming me with their gentle touch.

Maybe this was why Prometheus had wanted mankind to have fire in the first place. It did have a few important non-destructive uses, after all. Heat, light, warmth. Cooking and protection.

"Do you think Prometheus is still down here somewhere?" I asked, watching the flames through half-closed lids.

"Probably. Most likely all the Titans are still in Tartarus."

"That's the pit where all the monsters are kept, right?"

"It's the lowest level of the underworld, where the evil are sent to suffer. Some monsters, like the cyclopes, ended up there, too, for one reason or another—usually because they'd managed to get on Zeus's bad side."

Well, well. That was the most critical thing I'd ever heard him say about the gods. On the whole, he seemed a pretty devout follower. He'd driven Hades mad with his deference, until the god had insisted he call him just "Hades" and drop the "Lord". "I'm not Zeus," he'd said on the second day of our stay. "I don't need people bowing and scraping twenty-four-seven to remind me I'm a god."

Jake stood up and moved closer to the cold fireplace, leaning one elbow on the mantel and holding his other hand out to the stacked logs. They burst into flame, and the fire leapt towards him as if in welcome, a stream of orange and gold playing across his fingers. He didn't react, other than to turn his hand over, watching the play of light and colour across his flesh, so I guess it didn't hurt. It seemed astonishing to me, but then, I'd never spent much time with fireshapers before, so I had no idea what they were capable of, or what they got up to in their spare time.

Outside, Cerberus barked, and a deep voice answered. Then the door of the cottage opened, and a large man stood framed in the doorway. My first impression was of hairiness: he had a curly beard, and his thick eyebrows met in the middle to form one giant hairy caterpillar above his eyes. Wiry chest hair poked out the opening of his linen shirt, and the sleeves were rolled to the elbows, showing more hair on the arms that cradled a pile of logs.

He stopped short at finding strangers in his house, and those crazy eyebrows rose at the sight of the flames playing over Jake's hand. Hastily, Jake let them fall back into the fireplace, and he straightened like a little kid caught with his hand in the cookie jar.

"Who are you, and what are you doing in my house?" Hephaistos growled. At least, I assumed it was Hephaistos. He was certainly built like a smith, with massive shoulders and muscles bulging in those bare arms. His legs were not as well muscled, and he limped as he moved away from the door. Hephaistos was meant to be lame, wasn't he?

"Forgive us, Lord Hephaistos," Jake said. Clearly, he had no doubts about the new arrival's identity. "I'm Jake Steele, and this is my friend, Lexi Jardine. We didn't mean to intrude, but Lexi has been wounded by the centaurs."

Hephaistos crossed to the fireplace and stacked his wood in a neat pile next to it. Unlike the see-through centaurs, his body seemed as solid as Jake's or mine. Jake stepped out of the way, looking a little horrified to be standing there uselessly as the god replenished his own woodpile. The smell of fresh sawdust filled the cottage.

Hephaistos brushed himself off. "And what's that to me? I have no interest in the affairs of the living."

"My lord!" Jake looked shocked. "You are my god."

"You're a fireshaper, boy. You're all too busy bowing down to the sun god to remember an old smith."

"I'm a metalshaper, too. I've made offerings at your temple in Crosston all my life."

Hephaistos considered him with new interest, a hint of gratification on his weathered face. "You'd be one of the few, then." He turned to me. "How long since they hit you, girl?"

I glanced at Jake. "An hour? Maybe two?"

He nodded, though he didn't look much more certain than I felt. It was hard to measure the passage of time in the underworld, without the usual cues of changes in the light and the sun's movement to judge by. I'd been wearing a watch when I arrived, but I'd left it back at Hades' palace, since the damn thing had frozen at the time we'd entered Hades' realm and had refused to tick a single tock since then.

Hephaistos looked surprised. "Then it's a wonder you're still alive."

"Can you help us, my lord?" Jake asked. I was too busy trying not to hyperventilate at Hephaistos's words to speak.

"Me? I'm no healer. Steel I can work with. Bodies, no."

"But you're a god." A note of desperation entered Jake's voice.

"A dead god, son. Don't look to me for miracles. You'll have to make one yourself."

6

"Tell me what to do," Jake begged.

I clenched my fists to stop them shaking. Did I feel a little colder? Dread ran through me, colder even than the chills from the centaur's arrow. Was I going to die in this strange place, with all these unanswered questions weighing on me? Without being able to free Syl and Apollo from their collars? I'd never find out what had happened to my mother and all the people I'd known in Newport, or where my odd power had come from. I'd never see my friends again, or get to watch Holly and Joe's baby grow up. I didn't even know what they'd named her.

"The Phlegethon is not far away. You could try that."

"The River of Fire? She's human—it would kill her."

"But you're a fireshaper. Perhaps you could use it to drive the cold of the grave from her bones."

Hephaistos needed to work on his bedside manner. I

glanced at Jake, whose face reflected the same worry that gnawed at me. "Perhaps isn't good enough," he said.

"Well, what did you do to keep her alive this long?" Hephaistos asked. "Keep doing that."

"I warmed her with fireshaping." Tiny flames still flickered on my legs, though I couldn't feel them. "It stopped the advance of the cold, but—"

Hephaistos eyed me thoughtfully. "But it's not enough to reverse it? Those centaurs have been here a long time. They're barely more than wraiths now. In a couple more centuries, they will have faded completely—but, in the meantime, their arrows remember the poison that made them so deadly in real life. Not to the dead, of course. But to the living ..."

To the living, their poisoned arrows were just as dangerous as they'd ever been. Gosh, lucky me.

I met Jake's gaze, and I must have looked as scared as I felt, because he crouched down beside the couch and took my hand.

"I'll fix this," he said. He squeezed my hand, his grip warm and reassuring. "I promise. I'm not letting anything happen to you."

Well, something already *had* happened to me—that was the problem. But I bit my lip and managed to stop myself from pointing this out. He would only say I was arguing again, and I knew it was just my brain's way of diverting me from the very real fear that he wouldn't, in fact, be able to save me. I hated having to depend on him, to literally have my life in his hands. Not that I didn't trust him. I did. In Hades' absence, there was probably no one else I'd rather have at my side in a situation like this. I just hated feeling so helpless, like some princess draped on the couch waiting for a prince to save her. I'd much rather tackle the dragon myself, but unfortunately, I was way out of my depth here. Surveillance, I could do. There was no one better at sneaking in and out of other people's houses. But fighting the dead? Curing the effects of their phantom weapons? Not high on my skills list.

Not that those things were high on Jake's, either. They weren't the kind of things that came up often on most people's schedules. I realised I was starting to pant, and forced myself to take a couple of long, slow breaths. Panicking wasn't going to help.

I clutched at Jake's hand like a drowning woman. "I'm holding you to that promise. If you let me die, I'm going to come back and haunt you."

"No one is going to die," he said, almost glaring at me, as if daring me to defy him.

"Then what are you going to do?"

He perched on the edge of the lounge next to me, though I couldn't feel him against my numb hip. "I need to get more fire into you. Applying heat externally isn't enough."

He glanced at Hephaistos, and I did, too. Did that sound safe? Not that I really had much choice at this point.

Hephaistos shrugged. "That could work."

"How exactly are you going to do that?" I asked.

"Well …" Jake just looked at me, apparently unable to finish the sentence, and my imagination went into overdrive. I had a sudden horrifying vision of the two of us having sex right there on the couch, with Hephaistos standing beside us, watching. My cheeks flamed, and suddenly I felt much hotter. I was no prude, but I drew the line at onlookers to my private moments. Sex was *not* a spectator sport.

While I was still imagining Hephaistos giving Jake pointers on his technique, Jake leaned closer. "I thought I might kiss you," he whispered.

Seriously? This was his big plan—tongue hockey?

I was doomed.

"Do you really think this is a good idea?" I hissed, casting a panicked glance at Hephaistos. Okay, so he was dead, but I still felt as though I'd be making out in front of the headmaster.

Perhaps he realised from my expression that I wasn't too keen on an audience, because he scowled and said: "I'll go chop some more wood."

The door slammed behind the god and Jake grinned down at me. "Anyone would think you didn't *want* to kiss me. You're breaking my heart."

77

"I wasn't aware you had one," I shot back reflexively. Of course I didn't want to kiss him! Well, I did, but not with him sounding so smug about it, as if every woman within a ten-mile radius should be lining up to kiss him. Who did he think he was? But before I could think of a proper put-down, his lips somehow landed on mine, and he breathed into my mouth.

It was the weirdest kiss I'd ever had, and I'd had some doozies in my time. As if someone had poured a shot of pure alcohol down my throat, I felt the burn all the way down as his breath entered my body. I swear I could feel heat spreading through my chest and seeping down into the cold numbness of my lower half.

I pulled back and stared at him. "What the hell was that? That wasn't a kiss."

"That was the essence of fire," he said. "From my heart to yours."

"I've never felt anything like it." The sensation of warmth was still spreading, bringing feeling back to my right leg. I sneaked a peek at my leg, wondering if the glow of warmth would be visible.

"I've never *done* anything like it. Did it work?" He looked at me with anxious eyes, and I realised his previous banter was an act to distract me. It was a horrible responsibility that Hephaistos had dumped on him, to figure out a new way to use his power in order to save my life. No pressure.

"Yes? I think? I still can't feel my left leg, but the sensation's coming back everywhere else." I twined my hands behind his neck and pulled him down. It was remarkable how much better I felt with the threat of imminent death receding. "Maybe you should do it again."

He grinned again and, this time, it was no act. "I bet you say that to all the guys."

He took a deep breath, and I opened my mouth to receive it. His lips found mine and I felt his warmth flood me, filling me with his fiery essence. His tongue slid smoothly into my mouth as I breathed him in, sending a jolt of electricity through me. I wriggled, pressing myself closer, wanting more of his warmth, more of *him*. His hands slid over my body, spreading heat in a smoking hot caress that sizzled over my hips and down my legs.

"Can you feel that?" he murmured against my mouth, and I nodded distractedly. Hoo boy, could I feel that. Why was he still talking?

He pulled away so he could see my face, and I stared up at him, hungry for more. Beside us, the fire crackled merrily in the fireplace, but that was nothing to the fire that was roiling inside me. It didn't hurt. On the contrary, I felt alive in a way I hadn't in years. "Is this how fireshapers feel all the time?" For the first time ever, I kind of regretted not being a shaper.

"Is what how fireshapers feel? Tell me what you're feeling."

"All warm and sort of tingly, as if my blood is superheated." Tingly in some very specific places, too. I tried to pull him back down, but he resisted me, his eyes still shadowed with worry.

"What about your leg?" He trailed kisses down my neck. "Can you feel it now?"

I wriggled my toes. Well, that was progress—I could feel my whole leg, though it tingled as if I had pins and needles. "Sure. It feels great."

"No more cold?" He nipped lightly at my neck, just where it joined my shoulder, and I shuddered against him.

"It's fine, Jake." Was it cold? I couldn't even tell anymore. Who cared when he was kissing me like that? "Maybe you should kiss me some more, just in case."

He groaned against my throat, then his lips returned to my mouth, kissing me with an urgency that stole my breath. My fingers tangled in his hair, dragging him closer still, my body on fire with need.

Abruptly, he got up and walked to the fireplace, dragging in deep breaths as if he'd just run a marathon. What the hell? I felt bereft without his warmth. "I'm not kissing you."

"Really?" I sat up and swung my legs to the floor, relieved to find that I could. My lips felt bruised. So did my ego. I'd thought we were both enjoying that. How could he just walk away? "I beg to differ. Maybe not that first one, but the rest of it sure felt like kissing."

"That was a mistake."

Way to make a girl feel good, Jake. "A mistake?"

He gestured around the tiny cottage. "This is not how I want to do this, with a dead god lurking outside, and everything still hanging in the balance. Since I met you, I've spent as much time wanting to kill you or at least kick your infuriating arse as I have wanting to kiss you, and I know I haven't always treated you right. You deserve better." His eyes lingered on my lips, and he swallowed hard. "You deserve so much more."

I moved closer to him. The hungry look in his eyes made me want to kiss him even more. There was something so appealing about this new, more vulnerable Jake. Was he actually apologising? A fireshaper? Out of all the marvels I'd experienced lately, this could be the most astonishing.

"So make it up to me." I tilted my face up to him encouragingly.

"I plan on it. I was serious about that date. I want to wine and dine you, and do this properly. Not just squeeze in a few kisses in the odd moments when people aren't actively trying to kill us."

"I don't mind a bit of squeezing."

He laughed, his hands caressing my shoulders. "Lexi, I'm not looking for a quick fling. I can get those any day of the week in Crosston. I want to get to know you."

"Oh." Well, that could be tricky. My face must have reflected the sudden dampening of my mood.

"What's wrong?"

I flung away from him, all urge to kiss him drowned by the flood of bitter confusion rushing back in. I could forget for a little while—particularly if people were trying to kill me—but it was never far away. "How can anyone get to know me when I don't even know myself? If I'm remembering my life history wrong, or—" I swallowed hard, then forced myself to say it: "Or if what I think I remember isn't actually real, then who am I? If our experiences shape us into the people we become, and my experiences are a lie, who am I really? Maybe I'm not the person I think I am at all. Maybe I really am a shadow shaper."

An amnesiac shadow shaper. That would be truly ironic. I couldn't find it in my heart to believe that—it just felt so wrong—but honestly, how would I know? What made me, me?

Jake considered me thoughtfully, the firelight playing on his handsome face. "You're right—our experiences do shape us to some extent. It's the old nature versus nurture argument: are our personalities set at birth, or are we the product of our upbringing? I think the answer lies somewhere in the middle. But does it really matter?" He followed me across the room, until he again stood close enough to touch. He reached out and tucked a lock of hair that had escaped my ponytail behind my ear. For someone who said he didn't want to kiss me, he seemed to have a lot of trouble keeping his distance. "I judge people by their actions."

I pulled a face. "That hasn't always worked out in my favour."

He grimaced. "I admit, I thought you were a shadow shaper when we first met, and that coloured my opinion of you. But I was wrong. I see the real you now, and I like what I see. You could never be one of them."

"I stole the ring from you," I reminded him.

"You also risked your life to save Holly, when it would have been easier to run and abandon her. You even risked your life to save me, when you didn't even like me." That wasn't quite true—I'd definitely moved into the liking stage by then, even if he hadn't realised it—but I let that one slide. If he thought I was so great, who was I to disabuse him of the notion? "I see a woman who's brave, resourceful, and loyal to her friends. A woman who does what's right, no matter what it costs her. That's the woman I'd like to know better. I really don't care about her past."

Well, that made one of us. I cared, but at the moment, there was nothing I could do about it. I sighed and stepped into the circle of his arms, resting my head against his chest. His heartbeat was firm and strong under my ear. Was this enough? Maybe it could be.

Maybe it would have to be.

We sat outside under the cool silvery light that had replaced the golden "sunlight" of Elysium's false day. I missed the moon—the light kept making me think there should be a full moon in the sky, but there weren't even any stars. There were no small animals rustling in the woods around us either, nor any mosquitos buzzing around. They were only small differences, but they were enough to keep me constantly on edge, subconsciously aware that things were not quite as they should be. The underworld could be frightening or it could be serene, but it was never quite the same as the real world.

Hephaistos sat on a log, a chunk of wood and a knife in his big hands. He was whittling something that looked more and more like a centaur as it took shape. Maybe I could stick pins in it. I flexed my calf surreptitiously; it still didn't feel quite right. There was a glass of wine at the god's elbow, perched on another stump, but he didn't stop to drink from it often. His hands were always moving, as if he couldn't stand to be idle. Warm light spilled from the open back door of his cottage, but it didn't reach quite to where we sat. Red eyes blinked from the shadows where Cerberus lay stretched out.

Jake and I had eaten some of our dwindling rations, and now he was sprawled on the lush, cool grass, his head pillowed in my lap. I had my back against a small apple tree whose fruit hung low enough to reach out and pluck, even from my sitting position, but I resisted the temptation. If even a goddess could be trapped in the underworld for eating its food, I wasn't taking any chances.

Hephaistos and Jake had spoken for a long time of metalshaping and other aspects of their craft. I admit, I hadn't paid much attention, letting the words wash over me, watching as Hephaistos lost his surly aspect and became more animated. Jake had made no mention yet of our reason for visiting, and I was chafing to get on with it, though I could see that he was worming his way into the god's good graces. Probably a smart move, considering Hades had warned us that he could be difficult.

Hephaistos emptied his glass and regarded the bottom of it morosely. "It still tastes as good as I remember, even if it's not real."

"It's not?" Jake asked.

"Of course not." The god barked a sharp, bitter laugh. "I'm dead—why would I need food or drink? But it passes the time."

"How did you die?" Jake asked. I sat up a little straighter. This would be more interesting than discussions of how to get the most heat out of your furnace.

"Why do you care? Are you going to avenge me, boy?"

"Yes, I am. Though I need a little help from you first."

"Ha! You're as bad as everyone else. They look down their noses at poor old Hephaistos until they need me, and then suddenly they're my best friends. Zeus used to do it all the time."

"Do you know where he is now?" I asked, seeing an opportunity.

He snorted. "I didn't even know where he was *before* I died. I haven't seen him in years. He only showed up when he wanted something, and in this modern age, he obviously had little need for the work of a smith."

There was a bitter note in his voice. It must have been tough, being the greatest living master of a craft, and having your only skill outpaced by technology. Zeus had managed to adapt, transforming his command of lightning into an all-purpose mastery of electricity. Perhaps Hephaistos should have gone into IT. Or weapons manufacture.

Jake sat up. "But we do, my lord. Your great skill could help us in the fight against your killers."

Hephaistos's craggy brows came together into a suspicious frown, and his hands stilled. "How do you know who killed me? Were you there?"

I suddenly felt vulnerable sitting there at his feet while he held that knife. The blade glinted in the fake moonlight.

"Of course not, my lord," Jake hurried to assure him, his eyes on the knife. "We're working with Lord Hades to destroy the group responsible. You aren't the only god they've attacked. We need your help to stop them before they kill again."

"How do I know you're telling the truth? You could just be a pair of adventurers, come to steal my secrets."

Jake paused, at a loss. I wondered if Hephaistos had always been so suspicious, or if being killed had made him that way.

"Would Cerberus be with us if that were the case?" I asked.

Hephaistos stared at me for a long moment. "I suppose not." He bent his head and returned to his whittling. I breathed a sigh of relief as the tiny chips of wood began to fly again. "You had better tell me all about it."

Quickly, Jake explained the situation with the collars, and outlined the things that he and Hades had already tried, without success.

Hephaistos's shaggy eyebrows rose higher and higher as the story went on, until he cut Jake off mid-sentence. "Describe these collars to me."

"They're made of a metal I've never seen before, that looks like pewter, with a dull silver sheen. Patterns are inscribed on them—"

"Like runes," I said.

"—like runes," Jake agreed, "but no one can read them, not even Lord Hades."

"I know these collars," Hephaistos said.

"You've seen them before?" Jake asked eagerly.

"I made them."

There was a shocked silence before Jake found his voice. "*You* made them? Why?"

Why would Hephaistos make such things, that could hold a fellow god captive, unable to use his or her powers? Evil things, that could allow the gods to be slaughtered by humans? Jake barely managed to keep the accusation out of his voice, but I knew he was thinking it. Hell, I was thinking it myself.

Hephaistos frowned. "I think somebody asked me to."

"You think? Who? Who asked you?"

The knife moved again, and a tiny chip of wood flew off into the grass. Hephaistos frowned down at the centaur emerging from the wood. "I don't remember."

Jake glanced at me, one eyebrow raised. There seemed to be an awful lot of people with memory problems around all of a sudden. Apollo and me, and now Hephaistos. And Hades had said that none of the gods who'd turned up dead in the underworld could remember how they'd been captured. What the hell was going on?

"Even so," said Jake. "If you made them, you should be able to get them off."

But Hephaistos was already shaking his shaggy head. "I cannot leave this place."

"We could bring them to you." Jake was practically bursting with eagerness.

"Even if you did, I could do nothing." He held up the

piece of wood he was carving. Definitely a centaur: the barrel chest and equine rump with its swishy tail were clearly delineated now. The little bastard was even holding one of those cursed spears. "This is of the underworld, like me. I can work it into any shape I please, just as I did in life. I could create a sword fit for a king in my smithy here, but only a king of the dead could wield it. I can no longer affect things of the overworld, including its metals. I am a smith of the dead now. These strange collars of yours would not answer to me any longer."

Damn. That was disappointing. But Jake wasn't giving up so easily. "There must be something we can do. Is there no way to cut them? Some tool we could retrieve from your earthly smithy that would help?"

"You cannot cut them. You need either a spell of unmaking or a key."

"We don't know where the original key is," Jake said. "If it's not lost forever, our enemies have it. I've tried making another, but none of the keys I shape will open the collars."

"That's because the collars require a key made of the same star-metal."

"Star-metal? You mean the ore came from an asteroid?"

"Originally, yes, though it's had many charms worked into it since."

"Is there any left? Enough to make a new key?"

Hephaistos paused. "You would have to go to my smithy to get it."

"We can do that," Jake said.

I sat up straighter. Finally, progress. Cerberus raised one head to watch me, but let it sag back to the grass when I made no further move.

"I've always kept its location a secret." Hephaistos sighed. "I suppose it doesn't matter now. I'll never use it again." He gave Jake a fierce frown. "But I don't want you messing around in there. There are things inside that are not meant for mortal eyes."

"Only tell me how to find the star-metal, my lord. I won't touch another thing."

"Hmm. Perhaps I should have you destroy the place, before some other mortal fool gets into it."

"Anything you like," Jake said. He would have promised the moon if it would help persuade the blacksmith god. "You will have Lord Apollo's eternal gratitude."

Hephaistos spat into the grass. "As if I care for that pup's gratitude. He cost me the best assistants I ever had— Brontes and his brothers, all thrown into Tartarus by his demand. The other Olympians had no time for the cyclopes, but they were good men. They deserved better. No, boy, you will make an offering in my temple when this is over. Even a dead god may help his worshippers."

Thank goodness. I felt my whole body relax as I sagged

back against the apple tree. The light glinted off huge canines as one of Cerberus's heads yawned. It had been a busy day for all of us. I rubbed absently at my left leg. The bone still ached, and my toes prickled with pins and needles, despite Jake's best efforts. Hephaistos caught the movement.

"Does your leg still pain you?"

"A little," I admitted. "Hopefully it will pass."

"Perhaps it will," he agreed, though his tone implied that the alternative was just as possible. Well, we'd deal with that if we had to. No point borrowing trouble—we had plenty on our plates already. He considered Jake, as if sizing him up. "The Phlegethon is the hottest fire known to man, in this world or any other. It's what I use to power my forge here. If you channelled that into her, you could burn out the last of the centaur's poison."

Jake frowned, as if he wasn't sure he could handle that kind of firepower. I can't say that the prospect thrilled me either. I almost preferred Hephaistos when he was too grumpy and suspicious to talk to us. This chattier version was simply bursting with bad news. The Phlegethon was one of the five rivers in the underworld—the River of Fire. Having that channelled into me didn't sound exactly comfortable, even supposing Jake could manage it. Could Hades do it? He wasn't a fireshaper, but he *was* the Lord of the Underworld.

"I hope it doesn't come to that," Jake said. *Yeah, me too, buddy.* "Is it getting worse?"

"No. About the same."

"Good. Tell me if there's any change."

"Or if you could find a fireshaping god who's still alive and not collared …" Hephaistos added. "Hestia, perhaps."

The frown cleared from Jake's face. That was more like it. Apollo would be perfect, just as soon as we managed to get that collar off him. Because we were definitely getting that collar off him, and Syl too. Failure was not an option.

7

"Are you sure you won't come with us, my lord?" Jake asked, but Hephaistos was shaking his head before he'd even finished speaking.

"I have a project at a delicate stage in the forge. Besides, a few minutes in Apollo's company makes me want to punch him back into the sun he came from. I don't need his false sympathy or his scorn that I managed to get myself killed." He laid a massive hand on Jake's shoulder. "You'll be fine. Remember what I said—don't touch anything in the smithy except the star-metal. Oh, and you'll need this."

Hephaistos offered him a small golden horn, engraved with hunting scenes. He sighed as he handed it across, as if reluctant to let it go.

"This is beautiful." Jake turned the horn over, examining the work reverently. "Did you make it, my lord?"

"A long time ago. It's the key to the smithy. Wherever I

was in the world, blowing the horn would open a path directly to it." He smiled. "Saved me a lot of travel time, I can tell you."

"Can we blow it now?" I asked, envisaging a much swifter end to our quest than I'd expected.

"You'll have to wait until you leave the underworld. Hades is the only person who can open gates at whim between the underworld and the upper realms. The horn will only work for you in the real world." He sighed again, a gusty whoosh of air that stirred the long hairs of his beard. "Hades let me bring it with me when I died, even though it won't work for me anymore, to stop anyone from stumbling on the smithy. Without the horn, only gods could find it—it lives in the between places, not in any physical reality."

"The between places?" That was a new one on me.

"Like the underworld, and Olympus itself. Places that can't be reached by normal means—at least not by normal people. There are a few around. Once you've found the star-metal, blow the horn again and it will return you to where you started."

Though it would no longer work for him, he still looked a little sad as he watched Jake tuck it safely in his pack. I guess when you'd been alive for millennia it took longer than a year to get used to being dead.

"Good luck." Hephaistos gave us both a nod, then turned and went back inside his cottage.

"Not much for goodbyes, is he?" I settled my pack more comfortably on my shoulders. It was lighter than before, since we'd eaten most of the food we'd brought with us. Hephaistos said the water from his well was safe for us to drink, so we'd refilled our bottles. A good thing, since we faced a full day of travel. But we'd got what we'd come for—kind of. We were on the right track, at least. The horn would open a gate to the hidden smithy, and then we'd be on the home stretch.

"He's never been the social type. He probably spoke more in the last few hours than he has in the last year. Even his own priests call him the Silent One."

We fell into step together, following Cerberus's black butt back across the fields towards the low range of hills that separated Elysium from the centaurs' plain.

"Shame we can't blow that horn here and save ourselves a walk." I wasn't looking forward to meeting up with the centaurs again. My left foot still tingled with pins and needles as a reminder of our last encounter. The sooner we got back to Apollo with a key for his collar, the happier I'd be.

"Yes." His expression was calm as he gazed at the hills, but he had to be feeling some kind of apprehension, surely? He was the one who'd been nearly drowned by that eel thing. At least this time I'd be prepared, though I still couldn't do anything about those damn centaurs. I'd have to rely on him and Cerberus to get us through that. "If

Hades were here he could open a gate from anywhere in the underworld, but since he's not, we'll have to get ourselves to one of the official gates."

"If Hades were here, a lot of things would be easier," I said. "I hope he's okay."

"Maybe he's back by now."

"Maybe." I sure hoped so. His unexpected absence made me nervous. There were too many things going wrong lately—I couldn't help feeling that something bad had happened. Had the shadow shapers managed to find him somehow?

"If he is, you'd better hope he hasn't noticed that his Helm of Darkness is missing."

"Why? He wasn't using it."

I'd nearly forgotten about the Helm, still tucked away in my backpack. Could I use that to evade the centaurs? I considered the problem as I followed Jake through an orchard bearing pink fruits of a kind I'd never seen before. I had no objection to getting up close and personal with Jake—far from it!—but even so, there didn't seem to be any way for both of us to wear the Helm at the same time. I had a vision of trying to balance a baseball cap between our two heads and couldn't help smiling.

Jake chose that moment to look back at me. "What?"

I shooed him on with a wave of my hand. "Nothing. Just thinking."

Hades had said that wouldn't work anyway—there were no "two for one" deals. The cap could only be worn by one person at a time. If we couldn't both be invisible, there didn't seem much point. For a brief moment, I considered trying to rip the Helm in half somehow. I could almost hear Syl yelling at me at the very thought. Maybe that was a little risky even for me. It was far more likely to destroy the magic of the Helm than to double it, even supposing I could do it. Just because it currently looked like a baseball cap didn't mean it really was. Magic artefacts wouldn't be much good if they were that easy to destroy.

We left the orchard of the tasty-looking pink fruit and began to climb the first of the low hills, my stomach rumbling in regret. Breakfast had been an apple and half a stale bread roll. Really, I'd have to talk to Hades about that map in the library when I saw him again. It had honestly looked like a couple of hours' walk to get to Elysium. I hadn't expected to be gone this long. Syl might be worried—or perhaps she hadn't even noticed, given her current mood. Apollo probably didn't care. A little warning about Eel Swamp and the spear-toting pony boys wouldn't have gone astray either. A notation on the map would have done, even if "Here be Centaurs" didn't have quite the same ring as "Here be Dragons".

"Where do you think Hades went?" I asked.

Jake shortened his stride to fall into step beside me. The

path was wide enough for two. "Maybe he got another message from Zeus and he's gone off to investigate."

"Maybe." Zeus's messages so far hadn't been exactly coherent, so it didn't seem all that likely that he would suddenly be broadcasting anything useful. "It would be nice to get Zeus back. He might know who's behind this whole thing. But Hades doesn't seem the type to go haring off on his own without even telling us. He's too cautious."

I didn't want to say "cowardly" because, hey, who was I to judge? But he *had* been keeping his head down in Berkley's Bay for years, as if he didn't want to be involved in whatever games the other gods were playing. It seemed an odd time to pick to suddenly launch himself into the action.

"For all we know, he could be back in the palace by now, ready to chew our arses out for heading off like this without him." Jake grinned down at me. "If that's the case, I'll make sure he knows it was all your idea. I only came along to keep you out of trouble."

"Thanks for the support."

"Any time."

Cerberus was a fair way ahead of us on the track, sniffing around a group of boulders as though he expected to flush out a rabbit or two. Did they have rabbits in the underworld? Dead or alive? He looked up, long pink tongues lolling out of his mouths, then bounded ahead again.

"At least Cerberus seems to be enjoying himself," I said.

"He's probably just excited about chasing centaurs again."

"That makes one of us."

He glanced down at me, his expression serious again. "I won't let them hurt you. I'll be ready for them this time."

I nodded, reassured in spite of myself. "Hopefully they'll all go galloping the other way when they see us coming, after our last meeting."

"If they don't, they'll soon wish they had," he promised.

After that, we saved our breath for the climb. At the top of the pass, I paused, looking back the way we'd come. Elysium spread out behind us like a patchwork quilt, stitched together from greens of many different hues. Lit by a warm golden glow, it lay dreaming in the soft light like a pastoral paradise. All it needed was a few fluffy sheep grazing on the gentle slopes to complete the look.

By contrast, the way before us was bleak. I sighed as I turned to face the path down onto the grey plain. No soft golden light on this side of the hills, only grey, grey, and more grey. Nothing but mists and darkness and stony ground until the hills met the waving grey grasses of the plain. Beyond that, I knew, stretched the even less appealing swamp, where the eels lurked beneath the murky water.

At least this time I'd be prepared for the slimy bastards.

"What do you think that orange light over there is?" I pointed to our right. Way off in the distance, the unrelenting grey gave way to an orange glow, very faint. It was only because we were so high up that we could see it at all. I hadn't noticed it on the way through the first time, but I'd been too busy holding onto Cerberus and trying not to die to pay attention to the landscape then. I tried to remember what the map had shown in that area, but came up blank.

"The pits of Tartarus, maybe?" Jake squinted into the distance. "Or it could be the Phlegethon. That should be over there somewhere."

The River of Fire. It would be kind of cool to see that, but I was glad our path led in a different direction. The underworld had proven a little hazardous for sightseeing. Maybe one day, I'd get Hades to give me the grand tour. For now, I'd be happy just to make it back to Hades' palace in one piece. Thank goodness we had Cerberus with us. I rested one hand on the dog's big black shoulder. The nearest head turned to me and gave me an enthusiastic slurp of its tongue.

"Good boy," I said, rubbing his thick fur.

FIND STICK? he asked hopefully.

I laughed. "Maybe when we get back."

"Come on," Jake said. "It's not going to get any easier standing on this mountain. Let's get this over with."

I cast a last wistful glance back at the green fields of Elysium before turning to face the path into Grey McGreyland. "It looks so crap down there."

"It probably looks like heaven if you're a centaur," he said.

"Let's not stop to ask any of them."

"Fine by me. I was thinking we should ride Cerberus again, if he'll let us, to get through there as fast as possible. I can keep them at bay with fire if I have to, but it would be better to fly through without seeing any of them."

"They're probably watching us right now," I said, nerves making me grumpy.

"You're a real ray of sunshine today, aren't you?" He grinned. "It reminds me of when we first met. You used to look at me as though I was something nasty you'd stepped in, and call me 'Steele' all the time. Was that because you liked spitting the 's' sound at me?"

"That was because I didn't like you enough to be on a first-name basis."

"So when did you decide you did like me?"

"Who says I like you?" But I remembered the first time I'd called him Jake. We'd been outside the pub, after that dramatic car chase with Holly in the back seat giving birth. Jake had been covered in blood and I'd thought Anders was about to kill him. Such things have a way of making you assess your priorities. It had seemed childish, and worse, in that moment, to continue to pretend that I didn't care for him.

Not that I'd thought about it in that kind of detail while I was living it. I'd opened my mouth to scream a warning, and, "Jake!" had come out. I'd been calling him Jake ever since.

"What's your middle name?" I asked.

He gave me a suspicious look. "Why?"

"In case I get really pissed at you."

His blue eyes danced with laughter. "Then you'd sound like my mother, telling me off."

"That's the idea. So what is it?"

"Harlan."

"Jake Harlan Steele?" Interesting. "*Harlan steel* sounds like a brand of knife."

"Harlan is a family name. Do you have a middle name?"

Did I? The usual fog greeted me and I sighed. I was almost used to this by now. "If I do, I can't remember what it is."

"Oh. Sorry."

I shrugged. "It's no big deal."

"Yes, it is." His face was serious now, all traces of laughter gone. "It *is* a big deal, and I promise you we'll get to the bottom of it."

"After we get through the current disaster."

"After we get through the current disaster," he agreed. He held out a hand to me. "Are you ready?"

I took his hand. As always, he was warm to the touch. "Ready as I'll ever be."

He pulled me after him down the rocky path. "Chin up. It's just a short gallop through the grass and then we'll be knee-deep in mud again."

"Now there's an enticing prospect." I let him lead me, glad to let someone else take charge for a change. My left foot was tingling again, and felt heavy and clumsy. I stumbled a couple of times, tripping on nothing. He looked at me sharply but said nothing.

At the bottom of the hill, I called Cerberus over and explained our wish to avoid the centaurs and the need for speed. He grumbled a little at having to make like a horse again, but allowed Jake to boost me up onto his back, then scramble up behind me. I leaned forward and took a handful of fur in each hand. Before us, a sea of grasses waved in the grey light. Nothing but grass and mist in any direction but the one we'd come.

"I'm surprised there's any grass left after the firestorm you started on the way through." The grey plain looked unchanged from when we'd first seen it, with no sign of the destruction Jake had wrought.

"Maybe it regenerated. There's no reason for the rules of the real world to apply here."

Good point. I took a deep breath. Best get this over with.

"Let's move," I told the big dog. "No chasing horses this time."

He whined, but set off at a fast trot. If anything, it was even more uncomfortable than last time, because I had more feeling in my body. My legs were stretched so wide over Cerberus's broad back that my jeans were in imminent danger of splitting at the seams. I was jostled and bounced as the giant dog lengthened his stride, and the grass swooshed past in a grey blur, whipping at my face and body as we went. I vowed never to take up horse riding.

I wanted to shut my eyes and just endure, but every time I did, I had to jerk my head up again, convinced that the centaurs were only a blink away. Why couldn't Cerberus be stealthier? He was making enough noise for a whole herd of giant dogs. Surely the centaurs would be on us at any minute?

Do you smell any horses? I asked him, when I was so tense with dread I was almost ready to scream. My left foot throbbed in time with my heartbeat.

YES, he responded, sounding way too pleased about the fact. *CHASE HORSES?*

No! No chasing. Let's stay as far away from them as we can.

One head turned to regard me, its dark eyes pleading. *SMALL CHASING?*

Not even a little bit! You can come back and chase them all you like later, but I don't want to see them again. They hurt me last time.

He growled, a thunder that vibrated all through my body. *BAD HORSES. EAT THEM.*

Sure. Eat them all you want—later. For now, just keep running, okay?

He put on a burst of speed and Jake grabbed at my waist in alarm, nearly sliding off the back.

"Problems?" he asked.

"The centaurs are nearby." I spoke quietly, straining to hear anything over the thud of Cerberus's giant feet hitting the ground and the swishing of the grasses as he mowed a path through them. There was no thunder of hooves approaching.

Flames sprang to life on Jake's arms. He was ready for anything. I crouched lower against Cerberus's neck, trying to present the smallest possible target. I was more than ready for the grasses to thin and the stinking swamp to appear. I'd jump in and hug the nearest eel if we could just make it through without seeing a single centaur.

Suddenly, Cerberus swerved violently, and Jake went flying, tumbling through the long grasses trailing fire like a blazing comet falling to earth. I barely managed to keep my own grip, perilously close to sliding off Cerberus's broad back.

"Stop!" I shouted. "We've lost Jake!"

We had bigger problems than that. Cerberus swerved again, dodging the centaurs that had popped up from the ground like some kind of infernal gophers. Either Cerberus had managed to disturb a nest of them sleeping or the bastards had been lying in wait for us. My money was on option two.

I clung to Cerberus, my fists knotted in his fur, as his heads snapped left and right at centaurs. Behind us, Jake staggered to his feet, summoning the fire that had been snuffed out by his unexpected landing. He roared, and flame rushed out from him in a great wave of heat and light. Cerberus danced to the side, as did several of the centaurs, but a whole clump of them disintegrated like dust on the wind, caught in the fire.

The survivors stood their ground. A few of them launched spears at Cerberus, which bounced off him as if he were made of rock. One of them struck perilously close to my injured leg, and I jerked it away with a squeak of horror. Unfortunately, that put me terminally off balance, and I slid gracelessly from Cerberus's back and landed in a heap on the ground, scrambling to avoid being stepped on by those giant feet.

Jake threw a fireball and a whole swathe of grassland went up with a rush. More centaurs disintegrated. Next thing I knew, Jake's hand, still trailing fire, reached down and hauled me to my feet.

"Are you hurt?" he rasped, not taking his eyes from the centaurs that circled like sharks. At least there were a lot fewer of them than there had been mere moments ago.

"I'm fine."

Cerberus lunged at a foolhardy pair who'd come closer than was safe to those snapping jaws. I shrank closer to Jake, feeling exposed without the hellhound at my side. Instantly, Jake encircled us with a wall of fire twice as high as the burning grasses. He crouched, hands ready to shoot flames at anything that made it through. Several centaurs decided discretion was the better part of valour and took off at a gallop. With a joyful bark, Cerberus gave chase.

"Cerberus! Come back!" I shouted.

Jake forced his circle of fire wider. The flames licked hungrily at the dry grasses. Little sparks danced in whirling eddies amid the smoke. It was harder to see our enemies through the smoke and flames, but they were still there. I caught glimpses of them now and then, and Jake was kept busy searing spears out of the air.

Then Cerberus reappeared through the flames, and the last of the centaurs gave it up as a bad job. They scattered through the burning grasslands and I heaved a sigh of relief as the sound of their hoof beats receded. The air was thick with smoke, and I coughed.

"Nice work," I said to Jake when I'd caught my breath again.

He nodded, but didn't release his flames. I admit, I found the sight of them flickering up and down his arms reassuring. And that was something that I never thought I'd say—but I'd come to appreciate fireshaping in a way I never had before. I was all for its destructive energies being used in the cause of keeping me alive.

"Let's keep moving," he said, "in case they come back with a few more friends in tow."

"Good idea." I'd seen enough centaurs to last me a lifetime. "How about a ride, Cerberus?"

But the big dog paid me no attention. All his heads were turned away, ears pricked, as if listening to a sound I couldn't hear.

"Cerberus? What's up?"

For answer he took off like a bolt of black lightning. I'd never seen him move so fast—never even knew that he could.

"What's wrong?" I shouted. This was more than his playful chasing of centaurs. "Where are you going?"

HELP MASTER! he thundered into my head.

Wait! We'll come with you. Don't leave us here!

But he didn't stop, or even break stride. In a moment, he'd disappeared into a swirl of mist and smoke. Shit.

Jake raised an eyebrow. "What's got into him?"

"Hades must be in trouble. He said he was going to help him."

Jake looked around at the burning grass, wreathed in smoke, and sighed. "Looks like we're walking from here."

8

By the time the grasses thinned and we stumbled out onto the barer land that sloped down toward the swamp, Jake's fires had died to the barest flicker and he was stumbling almost as much as I was. Without discussing it, we both dropped to the ground at the edge of the swamp, far enough from the grasslands to be out of spear range, and dug through our packs for the last of our food.

"Are you all right?" I asked, watching him lie back with a sigh once he'd finished chewing.

"Just tired. It takes a lot of effort to draw on that much fire." Cerberus had left us over an hour ago, as far as I could tell with no watch, and the whole time we'd been on tenterhooks, waiting for the centaurs to jump us again. "Modern shapers have gotten soft. Our ancestors in the human-shaper wars could shape for hours without raising a sweat. They'd run rings around me."

"These are hardly optimal conditions," I protested, taking offence on his behalf at the implied criticism, even though he was the one making it. "I bet none of your ancestors had to face dead bloody centaurs waving spears in their faces."

"True. I'm still glad I live in modern times. Mostly, we don't even have to use our shaping unless we want to."

I laid back next to him, staring up at the grey "sky" above us, hands clasped behind my head. "That's because you've terrorised the population into bowing down before you, so demonstrations of power aren't necessary anymore."

"Really?" He turned his head to regard me. "And here I was thinking that it was because, in these enlightened times, diplomacy rules rather than brute strength."

"Ha. Only a shaper would say a thing like that."

"Do you still hate us that much?"

About to give him another flippant reply, I paused at the wistful note in his voice. "Some more than others. At the moment, you're top of my list of favourite shapers."

"Good to know. Who else is on it?"

"Actually, you're the only one, but I'm open to persuasion."

I half-expected him to make some risqué comment about "persuading" me, but he must have been truly tired, because he only smiled and let the opportunity slide. I sat up and took a drink from my dwindling water supply, then offered him the bottle. He shook his head and levered himself into a sitting position with a groan that made him sound like an octogenarian. Falling from Cerberus's back hadn't done him any favours—even his bruises had bruises now.

He looked out across the misty swamp and sighed. "What are we going to do now? Got any bright ideas?"

"I can keep the eels away from us," I said. "We'll still get wet, but we won't get eaten."

"I was more thinking about the problem of finding our way through without drowning or getting caught in the mud. Cerberus took such a twisty way I couldn't find it again if you paid me. We could wander for days in there without finding our way out."

Shit. I hadn't considered that, too focused on the danger of the eels to consider more mundane things like directions. There were stretches of deep water and sucking mud that made it impossible to take a straight path through. But the swamp was wide, with poor visibility and no landmarks. Every tussock and miserable dwarf tree looked much the same as the next one. He was right. With no sun or compass to mark direction, we might walk around in circles forever, unable to find the right path. And our water was nearly gone already. We needed a guide and, with Cerberus gone, we didn't have one.

I stared at him, aghast. "What are we going to do?"

We couldn't go back the way we'd come, not with Jake so exhausted. Only his fire would keep the centaurs at bay, and I wasn't facing them without it. Maybe if he slept? But that still left the problem of our dwindling water supply— and even if we made it back to Elysium, what then? Hephaistos had already given us all the help he could.

"It's a shame that horn Hephaistos gave us can't open a gate right here."

"Yes." We could already have been to the smithy and back again if we could have blown the horn in Elysium, where Hephaistos had given it to us. But he'd said it could only open the way to the smithy once we were out of the underworld, so we needed a gate first.

I cast my mind back to the map—that oh-so-unreliable map—on the wall of Hades' library. It had shown four gates to the underworld. They even had poetic names, like the Dawn Gate, or the Gates of Horn and Ivory. There was also one within Hades' palace—the elevator that he rode up to the cellar of the pub in Berkley's Bay—though that hadn't been marked on the map. It probably didn't have a cool name, either. The Gate of Beer and Spirits? The Gate of Inebriation?

"We could try for a different gate," Jake said, "rather than going back the way we came."

"Just what I was thinking," I said. "I'm trying to remember which one is closest."

"Probably the Gates of Horn and Ivory," he said, "but we'd have to go back past the centaurs and all the way through Elysium."

"Not an ideal option." I squinted my eyes shut, picturing the map. "What about the Dusk Gate? That was near the Phlegethon, wasn't it?"

I made vague gesturing motions in the general direction of the orange glow we'd sighted from the top of the pass— or at least, the direction I thought it was. We couldn't see it anymore from this elevation.

"Closer to Tartarus, I think, but in that direction."

I wasn't thrilled about getting too close to Tartarus, but we weren't in a position to be picky. I mean, it wasn't as if we had to go *into* Tartarus, after all. We'd just be passing by. And all of the inmates were trapped in the pits. We wouldn't be waylaid by angry Titans or cyclopes.

I got to my feet. The sooner we got going, the sooner this would be over, and Syl and Apollo freed from their collars. "Let's do that, then."

And then we could find out what had happened to Hades, and why Cerberus had gone haring off in a panic like that. I had that filed under "Problems for Later", because just thinking about it started little panicked butterflies in my stomach. Hades had been our staunchest ally through this madness. How would we cope without him? Surely the shadow shapers couldn't have caught him.

They didn't know he was living as the vampire Alberto Alinari in sleepy Berkley's Bay.

"All right." Jake clambered wearily to his feet. "Let's hope we don't find any more of the locals who want to kill us."

I shouldered my pack, though all it contained now was a spare knife, a length of light rope, the Helm of Darkness, and half a bottle of water. Oh, and Jake's little explosive gizmo that he'd given me to crack the Ruby Adept's safe. That seemed like years ago now, but I kept it with me because it seemed like it should come in handy for *something,* eventually.

"Hey, it wouldn't be an adventure if people weren't trying to kill us."

He rolled his eyes. "I wanted a date, not an adventure."

"Should have asked somebody else then."

That forced a laugh out of him. "True."

We kept the swamp on our left as we walked, and a healthy distance between us and the beginning of the grasslands. Fortunately, they were at the top of a long slope on our right, and started off with low grasses for a while before growing to full, centaur-concealing height. I was reasonably sure we were safely out of spear range.

Even better, after a couple of hours' walk, the grasslands receded further until eventually they petered out altogether, replaced by patches of low grass and widening areas of bare, rocky ground. Everything was still grey, but now it was grey desert rather than grey plain. As we continued through the arid landscape the hills, which had been on the far side of the plains, crept closer, and the land began to be marked by dry creek beds and clumps of boulders, as if a band of giants had been playing marbles here. Ahead of us, an orange glow lit the horizon, telling us that we were on the right track to find the Phlegethon, at least.

We stopped to drink on the banks of another creek, though this one had some dark, still water in the bottom of its bed.

Jake eyed the black water as he drank from his water bottle. "How much water do you have left?"

I shook my bottle, judging the splashing sounds. "Maybe a quarter of a bottle. But I'm not filling it up from there."

"No. I'm not suggesting you do. But I hope we get there soon. It's starting to warm up."

He was right. It did seem warmer here. I wiped my sweaty face, wishing for a bucket of ice water, though I couldn't decide if I'd rather drink it or pour it over my head. "I thought you fireshapers thrived on heat."

"Actually, we carry so much heat of our own that we're quite sensitive to high temperatures. You never find any fireshapers living in the tropics."

"Is that going to be a problem, then?" I gestured at the orange glow ahead.

"I'm not planning on setting up a home there," he said. "Let's hope the gate isn't much further, though. I'm sick of eating dust."

It *was* pretty dry out here. We passed bigger and bigger boulders, until they couldn't really be called boulders anymore but small hills, with steep canyons in between. The orange glow grew stronger, burning away the grey until everything carried a faint rosy hue. It would have been pretty if I hadn't been so sick of the barren landscape. There were only so many rocks and boulders a girl could take in a day. Both my feet were complaining about all the walking, my left one even more than the right. It was still tingling, marring my usual agility with stumbles on the uneven ground, and I could feel a familiar numbness returning to my lower leg. I bit my lip, and said nothing. Jake had already done all he could; there was no point worrying him further. Best to just get this journey over with.

The dry creek beds, with their puddles of dark water in the bottom, had grown more frequent as we walked. We rounded a rocky outcrop to find the latest one growing wider and deeper as it joined a river with actual water in it that cut straight across our path. Sheer rock walls rose on either side of us. The only way forward was across the river.

Fortunately, there was a bridge, but we both stopped at the sight of it. It seemed such a strange thing to find in this desolate place. It wasn't wide, but it was built of stone and looked sturdy enough.

"Do you think that's the Styx?" I gazed down at the dark water. There was no telling how deep it was, and I had no intention of finding out if I could possibly avoid it. But there was just something so odd about that bridge. Who would build one way out in the middle of nowhere like this?

"Could be. It has many tributaries." He watched the black water as if he expected something to leap out of it at him. "But the underworld is full of rivers and waterways."

"Not that it matters, I guess. We just walk across the bridge, right?" So why did I feel like an extra in a horror movie?

"Right." Jake seemed to share my hesitancy, but eventually he moved. "Stay close."

"Bet you say that to all the girls," I muttered, but he wasn't listening, too focused on our bleak surroundings and trying not to fall victim to the usual fate of extras in horror movies.

I fell in behind him, trying to ignore the nerves that were churning in my stomach. *It's just a bridge. How else are you going to get where you need to go? Swim?* I glanced down at the inky water as I stepped onto the bridge. I couldn't see into it, not even an inch. There could have been anything lurking right below the surface. Watching us. I shuddered. No, swimming was definitely not an option.

I reached out with my mind, probing. What the hell was *that*? I stopped in the middle of the bridge and grabbed at Jake's arm. "Jake! There's something down there!"

A dark mind beneath our feet. Not human or I couldn't have seen it, but not like any animal I'd ever felt—and definitely not friendly.

"Where? Oh, *shit.*" The question answered itself as something enormous heaved itself onto the opposite end of the bridge, blocking our way. "What in the name of the gods is that?"

At first, I thought it was a spider, though a spider as big as Cerberus, covered in black hair like thick ropes. Then I saw the spiked tail that reared up behind its bloated abdomen. Awesome. A giant spider-scorpion cross.

I drew a knife as flames appeared on Jake's arms. The spider thing hissed. *Hissed?*

"Are those *snakes*?" Jake asked in disbelief.

Half a dozen snakes writhed among the thick hair on the monster's back, apparently a part of it. Delightful.

"All the best monsters have them these days," I said, uneasily aware of how low Jake's flames flickered. They were barely visible. "Let me take care of this."

He gave me a sharp glance and his flames burned a little brighter. "I can handle it. I don't want you sullying your mind by joining with that thing's consciousness."

My spine stiffened at a hissing from behind us. Now I really felt like I was living a B-grade horror movie. I turned, already knowing what I would see. It was that kind of movie.

"Yeah, but can you handle all of those?"

Behind us, the canyon walls had come alive with all of the monster's friends and relatives, climbing all over each other as they fought to be first to the bridge. There were so many of them I couldn't see the rock beneath them anymore, just a heaving mass of black hairy spider things, skittering down the canyon walls, their scorpion tails dripping poison. Not all were as big as the horror on the bridge with us, but that was no consolation in our present predicament.

"Shit." Jake threw fire at the one blocking our way across the bridge. His fireball wasn't enough to kill it, but it shrieked in pain and hurled itself over the parapet and into the dark water below. Then he turned to face the oncoming horde, trying to push me behind him though his flames were almost out and he was leaning against the parapet, trying not to look as though he were so exhausted he could barely stand up on his own.

"Quit trying to protect me," I said, refusing to budge. "If it's a choice between sullying my mind with these monsters or becoming monster snacks, it's sullying all the way, baby."

I reached out to the dark minds bearing down on us. They were animal enough for me to work with, though there was something so wrong-feeling about them that I couldn't help a small shudder as I sank into as many as I could manage.

That wasn't nearly as many as there were, unfortunately.

I pushed my will into those cold, dark minds, forcing their owners to stop their single-minded pursuit. But so many still rolled toward us in a black, hairy wave. The ones I had stopped clung to the walls or to the ground, like stones in a stream, and the wave simply rolled around and over them, ready to break on the bridge and sweep us away.

Okay, maybe that wasn't going to work. "Get off the bridge!"

I backed up, shoving Jake along when he didn't move fast enough. Then I focused my attention on the creatures closest to the bridge, turning them around and massaging them into a living wall of monster, giant stingers waving menacingly over their heads at the oncoming crowd. I was counting on the fact that these things had no fellow-feelings for each other. It was a monster-eat-monster world out here.

Some of the oncoming spider things wavered when they were confronted with the dark menace blocking their way. Others rolled on regardless, pushing and shoving to get across the bridge and make a meal of the intruders. Stingers flashed and snakes hissed, and a high squealing sound erupted as monster met monster.

Sweat rolled down my face as I held my spider wall firm. It took a lot of effort, since their natural inclination was to turn and join the rush to destroy us. I groped behind me with one hand and found Jake's. "Let's back it up," I murmured.

I didn't dare look away, lest one of them break free of my control while I was distracted. Jake held my shoulders and guided me as I backed off the bridge and up the rock-strewn slope beyond it.

"Now what?" he asked as we paused in the shadow of a huge boulder. If we'd really been in a horror movie, a monster would have leapt on us from the top of it, but fortunately, this encounter wasn't following the script.

I pushed harder on the minds under my control, planting the suggestion that these others must be destroyed before they could enjoy the reward of eating the soft squishy creatures on the far side of the bridge. Fangs slashed and stingers darted out in renewed frenzy. Some of the spiders at the back of the group pushing to get onto the bridge drifted away, deciding to give up the fight.

Yes, there's easier prey elsewhere, I suggested, pushing the idea into as many minds as I could. Heaven only knew what all these creatures usually ate. Jake and I hadn't seen another soul since we'd left the centaurs' grasslands. Maybe they didn't need to eat. Maybe their only purpose here was to make life literally hell for whoever was unfortunate enough to pass this way. They could have been some hero's test, or even his punishment. The underworld was strange like that. It didn't have to make sense like the real world did.

I shut my eyes so I could concentrate better and took a firm grip on Jake's hand. To my mind's sight, the spiders' life forces glowed a sickly green. At least they were alive, otherwise I wouldn't have been able to do anything with them. "Now we keep going. Slowly. Gently. Let's put some room between us and them."

And so, I walked through Hell, eyes tight shut, battling monsters in my mind. The only real thing in my world was the feel of Jake's hand in mine, and the sound of his breath at my side. He said nothing, just lent me his strength when I stumbled, guiding me past obstacles and leading me safely over the rough ground. Behind us, more of the green splotches that marked the spiders broke away from the heaving mass at the bridge, heading back to whatever monster business had occupied them before we arrived. It seemed that out of sight was out of mind, and now that we'd disappeared, they couldn't remember what had been so urgent about getting onto the bridge.

A few of my troops who'd defended the bridge also lost interest. The ones that crossed to our side I gently turned away into the dark recesses beneath the bridge or halted them on the river bank. My head was spinning with the effort by the time I judged we were safely away and I could open my eyes again.

I stopped short at the sight that greeted me. In the distance, a volcano belched smoke into the dark sky. Lava flowed down its side like a bright orange ribbon and wound across a blasted plain toward us. We had arrived at the River of Fire.

9

"Whoa. Is it just me, or is it getting hot around here?"

Jake rolled his eyes. "Funny. So what happened to the spiders?"

"They've gone back to doing whatever giant spider monsters do in their spare time."

"Excellent."

The river of lava snaked across the plain in our general direction, before dipping into a gully off to our right and out of sight. Way off to our left a wide black river that could only be the Styx also wound its way across the uneven rocky plain. The two rivers appeared to meet at the base of the mountain, though the area where they met was so wreathed in steam that most of the mountain's foot was hidden. From our vantage point, it was as though we were standing on the base of a wide triangle, with the junction of the rivers and the mountain at its apex.

"Is that where we're going?"

Jake nodded. "The entry to Tartarus should be around the base of that mountain somewhere. The Dusk Gate will be nearby."

I regarded the great triangle of land before us doubtfully. The steam hid our destination from us. "I hope we don't fry before we get there. Is that the Phlegethon?"

"Yes. We shouldn't have to get too close, if I remember correctly. Tartarus should be quite some distance from the Phlegethon."

Except if the River Phlegethon was actually a lava flow, it might move around, depending on eruptions, mightn't it? But this was the underworld. I reminded myself that the normal laws of geology didn't apply. The Phlegethon could probably fall straight down out of the sky if it wanted to.

"Not that we want to get too close to Tartarus, either," I said.

"Nothing down there can hurt us," he said. "It's a prison— the inmates are all securely locked away. They won't be forming a welcoming committee on the doorstep. Relax."

"I'm relaxed." I rolled my head on my shoulders and swung my arms to loosen muscles taut from the tension of navigating us safely away from the spiders. "Look at me relaxing! This is better than a weekend at a health spa."

He grinned, though there were shadows of exhaustion under his eyes. "Are you ready for your massage, madam?"

"I was thinking more of a drink by the pool."

He took out his water bottle and offered it to me with a bow. "I'm afraid I can't recommend the pool today. We'll have to sack the pool boy—the water's gone black. But I have some lovely natural spring water here, if madam approves?"

I shook his bottle, smiling at his unexpected silliness. It felt even lighter than mine, so I pushed it back at him and took out my own. "Madam thinks you should drink your own natural spring water. You're probably going to need it. It looks hot out there." I remembered what he'd told me about fireshapers' sensitivity to high temperatures. It didn't come much hotter than molten lava. I sure hoped he was right that we could give the Phlegethon a wide berth.

Still, there was no point worrying about what trouble we might get into. Trouble had proven more than capable of coming and finding us.

"Do you need a rest?" he asked.

I felt as though I could sleep for a week, but this was hardly the place. I shoved my now nearly empty bottle back in my pack. "Let's just keep moving. The sooner we get this over with, the better."

He led the way out onto the plain. Well, I say *plain* because it was more-or-less flat, but it wasn't some smooth, unbroken surface. Slabs of rock were tilted at all angles, as if some giant had smashed the whole area with his hammer in a fit of rage. Fissures ran everywhere, many of them emitting steam or a stench of sulphur. Jake picked a path through, avoiding the biggest steam vents, but the path wasn't straight, and it required a lot of scrambling up and down over boulders and leaping from one slab to another. I saw black water at the bottom of one fissure I jumped across; another blasted super-heated steam way above our heads just after I'd crossed it. If I'd been a little slower that would have cooked me.

"Be careful," Jake said, watching steam fountain into the lowering sky.

"You're the guide," I pointed out. "I'm just following where you're leading."

He nodded and shut his eyes.

"What are you doing?" I asked after long moments of watching his steady, deep breaths.

"Feeling for the fire." When he opened his eyes, there was guilt in them. "That was too close."

After that, we moved slower, but there were no more near misses. Every so often Jake stopped to "feel for the fire" again. It occurred to me during one of these pauses that if we had to run, things were going to get very awkward. I kept a watch behind us, with my inner and outer sight, in case any of the spider monsters decided to chase us after all, but the only thing moving anywhere in sight was us.

I plodded after Jake, trying to ignore the odd tingling in

my left leg. My foot felt almost as if it belonged to someone else, heavy and awkward. Now would be the perfect time to link to a cat or two, to up my agility. I tripped more than once. Part of that was because of the rough, unpredictable surface—Jake stumbled a couple of times, too—but not all of it.

Even more reason to keep soldiering on. This leg wasn't going to fix itself. I needed a god with fireshaping powers, according to Hephaistos, to burn the last of the centaur's poison from my body. The sooner we got that collar off Apollo's neck, the sooner he could fix me.

I reached out, searching for Cerberus, as I'd done several times already. He'd managed to cover a lot of ground—he was a long way away, perhaps already back at the palace—but he steadfastly refused to respond, however much I tried to force him. He was single-mindedly focused on something else. Had he found Hades? What had happened to the Lord of the Underworld that had put his hellhound into such a panic? Had he been captured by the shadow shapers, or gone off on some other mission of his own? I placed one tired foot after another, watching the uneven ground for anything that might trip me up.

Cerberus's departure had been particularly bad timing. If he'd stayed only a few hours more, we would have been back at Hades' palace—or at least through the swamp and able to find our way alone. If someone had been trying to find a way to doom our little quest, they could hardly have done better. Why had Hades picked precisely that moment to get himself into trouble? The joke would really be on us if it turned out Hades was behind the whole attack on the gods, and all the time that he'd been hiding out in Berkley's Bay, he'd really been masterminding the whole shadow shaper assault on the gods' power. I hadn't forgotten that odd guilty look on his face the night I'd been talking to him and Jake about my memory issues.

I sighed and stopped on top of a pile of ash and rock to get my breath back. I wasn't normally so paranoid. Maybe the fumes were getting to me, or maybe I was just exhausted. Hades was one of the good guys. It was too late now to go doubting everything and second-guessing my judgement. That was the trouble with memory—once you started doubting your recall of events, everything became suspect. But some things remained true. Syl was my best friend, and I was doing all this for her. Jake was—what? A friend, too, I guess. Hopefully more than a friend. If we ever got to go on that date of his I might find out. At any rate, I was glad he was here now.

He stopped and looked back at me. "Everything all right?"

"Just peachy." There was no point mentioning the growing numbness of my leg. He had enough on his plate already. "How's the fire-feeling going?"

"Getting warm." He drained the last of his water, then wiped his sweaty forehead onto his sleeve. "Shame we can't drink that." He jerked his head in the direction of the Styx, which was still a good distance away but getting closer as the land between the rivers narrowed toward a point.

The mountain loomed ever higher as we approached, but only its head reared above the great steam cloud that enveloped its base where the two rivers met. Its top was laced with lava, as if the mountain wore a fiery crown. High above, dark birds circled in the smoke from the volcano's crater.

Wait ...

"Do those look like birds to you?"

Jake's head whipped around at my tone. His eyes narrowed as he followed the direction of my gaze. Most of the time, the distant figures were shrouded in smoke, but now and then one became more clearly visible for a moment. They had wings, but the outline wasn't right for birds. "Zeus's balls! Harpies."

I squinted at the distant figures in the smoke. He was right. They were harpies—the famed monsters of Greek legend. They had women's heads, but their bodies were birdlike. I scrambled to remember what I could of harpies. Legend said they had a fearsome smell and a temper to match, plus a taste for meat and a dislike of humans. Maybe that was a taste for human meat. Not good news for us. I guess that was no surprise. Not much had gone right since we started this adventure. My leg twinged at the thought. It was probably too much to hope that the harpies would fly off and leave us in peace.

As if summoned by my thoughts, three of the harpies wheeled away from the group circling above the volcano and headed in our direction. How I wished I still had my bow and arrow. There would be three harpy pincushions coming right up.

"Incoming." At least I still had my knife. Two, in fact, counting the one in my backpack. Shame there were three harpies. It didn't take a mathematician to realise that sum didn't work out in my favour.

Jake noted my warlike preparations, but his attention was on the sky and the approaching menace. "Stay there. I'm going to try something."

Obediently, I stayed put, watching as he backtracked to a particularly treacherous stretch that we had just navigated. It was full of small fissures that belched sulphurous smoke from their glowing red depths, lending an appropriately hellish aspect to the scene, and a stench to rival even the harpies'. He chose a spot in the middle of the field and closed his eyes. Was he "feeling the fire" again?

Without opening his eyes, he said: "Don't come any closer."

"You worry about yourself. I've got my knives. Don't

meditate too long or the fun will be over and you'll be harpy snacks."

He snorted and clenched his fists. He looked like he was concentrating hard on something, or maybe just straining to cough up a hairball. I watched the approaching harpies, the first knife balanced loosely between my fingertips, ready to throw as soon as they came within range.

The leading harpy screeched as she came closer. Her sisters were close behind, long hair streaming back in the wind of their passage, their faces screwed into identical expressions of rage. Their wings were the only beautiful thing about them, feathered in black, tipped with silver.

Almost. Just a little closer. I drew my arm back in a smooth arc, ready to release the knife—and then the ground behind me erupted. Jake was done with standing still. He raised his arms, bringing the fire with them. Smoke and superheated steam burst into the air, engulfing the leading harpy. Her sisters tried to pull up, but only the third harpy, trailing a little behind, managed to evade her doom. The second fell to earth to join the first in a scorched heap without so much as a shriek.

I released my knife. It was a long shot, and my aim was a little off, but I caught the remaining harpy right where the huge tendon of the wing joined the body. She screamed as she circled above us, raining down curses on our heads.

"Nice shot," I said approvingly to Jake.

"How about this one?" Jake wound back his arm as if preparing to pitch a baseball and released a stream of fire into the air. The harpy fell back with a squawk of fright and fled toward the volcano.

"Pretty good," I said, "for someone who was supposed to be out of juice."

Jake checked his hands as if seeing them for the first time, a look of surprise on his face. "I feel great."

He looked pretty great, too. Gone were the sagging shoulders, the exhausted bags under the eyes. He looked like a man who'd just had the best sleep of his life and woken fully rested.

"What did you do?"

"I don't know," he said. "I just reached into the fire because I knew I had nothing left in the tank." With speculation in his eyes, he stretched out a hand in a commanding gesture. Fire leapt from the nearest fissure and crawled up his arm, winding around it like a caress. He dipped his hand this way and that, watching the fire move. When he looked up his eyes were shining. "It's everywhere. I can feel it."

"You mean the lava?" He seemed skittish, like a child hyped up on too much sugar. I kept one eye on the distant harpies as we spoke. They were massing over the peak of the volcano. We could be in for some serious trouble. "The lava is giving you energy?"

He shrugged. "The lava, the fire, the river. It's everywhere.

I've never felt anything like it. So much energy. So much power."

"That's good timing." Harpies were boiling out of the crater of the volcano like a mini eruption. Where had they all come from? And how the hell could we handle that many? I nodded at the approaching storm. "Do you reckon you have enough for all those?"

Jake's enthusiasm dimmed at the sight. "Balls." His hands clenched into fists as the sky darkened with a swarm of harpies.

Half-heartedly, I reached out with my mind but, as I suspected, the harpies' minds were closed to me. Only their bodies were birds; the thinking half was all woman. And now I was down to one knife. Shit on a stick.

Jake called fire to his hands. Even I could see the difference from his usual firepower—the fire burned a deep red that reminded me of Cerberus's eyes. And there was plenty of it, wreathing him in flame from head to toe. He could have been a god himself, or a hero from ancient legend. He coaxed steam and foul-smelling smoke from the fissures in the ground, billowing all around us. I coughed. It felt like being trapped in the world's hottest sauna.

"What are you trying to do? Kill me with the stench?"

"I was thinking more of camouflage," he said. "I don't think I can fight off that many harpies even with the boost from the River of Fire, and if we can hide instead, so much the better. I'm not as bloodthirsty as you. I just want to get to the damned gate."

"Works for me." Bloodthirsty? Who was he calling bloodthirsty? I wasn't the one torching people left, right, and centre. Not that I was complaining, mind you. It was kind of handy having a human blowtorch along.

"Stay close," he said. "And keep quiet. They have excellent hearing."

I rolled my eyes. Keeping quiet would be a lot easier if both my legs were working properly. Still, that wasn't his fault, so I did my best to keep up and not kick too many rocks as he strode through the steam and smoke. "You know, all that fire is going to stand out like a beacon. Maybe you should tone it down."

"Shhh," he said, making a broad gesture with his right hand. A geyser of steam blasted into the hidden sky, and a screech sounded from above, closely followed by the thud of a body hitting the ground. "I hope Hades will forgive me."

"For what?" With the amount of steam he was pulling from underground, we were walking nearly blind, and it was unnerving, knowing that the harpies were lurking somewhere above us. I felt that familiar itch between the shoulder blades, as if at any minute the hidden watchers would strike.

"For killing his harpies."

"There are a lot of monsters down here—do you really think he cares about every last one?"

"But the harpies are his particular messengers, carrying messages between the living and the dead."

"Nice. I think I'd prefer an email, personally." The harpies gave me the horrors. Besides, they were trying to kill me, which made it hard to feel bad about wiping them out. "If they're his messengers, what are they doing hanging round the Gate of Dusk?"

"I assume that part of their job is guarding Tartarus, and the proximity of the gate is coincidental."

"Shame they have to take the job so seriously," I grumbled. "We don't even want to go near Tartarus." Not that they'd believe that, as their initial attack showed. So much for *halt! Who goes there?*

I tripped yet again and nearly went sprawling on my face but Jake caught my elbow just in time.

"What's the matter? Are you all right?"

"Just tired."

This was not the time to go into detail, not with harpies circling above us. He couldn't afford to be distracted. I could hear the flapping of mighty wings gradually coming closer, although the smoke and steam Jake had produced kept us hidden.

A crash sounded off to our right and Jake flinched. "What was that?"

We were both on edge. Another one sounded, closer this time. Close enough to see what caused it. Through the steam and smoke I saw a boulder the size of a basketball hit the stony ground with such force that shards broke off, flying away like shrapnel. The harpies were bombing us.

Jake realised it, too, and shot another blast of steam into the sky. Above us, a harpy cackled.

"There you are, pet," she called, and I dragged Jake to the side only just in time to avoid another boulder.

"You're giving away our position," I hissed.

He nodded, face grim, and wiped blood from a cut on his cheek. We were lucky it wasn't worse. The last boulder had stayed mostly intact, with only a little shrapnel flying off on impact.

"Move," he said. "That way."

I headed in the direction he indicated, hoping that he knew where he was going. With all the steam and smoke obscuring our surroundings, I wasn't sure anymore where the volcano was. He stayed at my side, helping me over the rough ground, his hand sure at my elbow. Both of us kept a wary eye on the sky, though there was nothing to see. The smoke blanketed everything, so I strained my ears, listening for the sound of flapping wings over the hissing of steam.

Another boulder crashed to earth not far away, but this time, Jake didn't retaliate. He'd learned his lesson and wasn't about to give the harpies any clue where to aim their ammunition.

The next one fell further away, though it slammed down between us and our goal. Were they just bombing at random now? And how many harpies were up there?

Jake was working the whole time, sending geysers of steam spraying into the air all around us and replenishing our smokescreen. Though he stayed close, at times I could hardly see him, moving through the steam like a ghost in the mist, appearing and disappearing from view. It was like walking through the world's hottest fountain. My whole body was streaming with sweat.

"How much further?" I asked, as quietly as I could. I'd heard no sound of flapping for some time, though the occasional rock still crashed to earth in the distance. Had the harpies given up, or were they massing somewhere to ambush us?

"Don't know," Jake muttered, barely glancing at me. He was fully occupied with keeping up our smokescreen, though it didn't seem to be taxing him the way fireshaping had when we'd struggled our way across the centaurs' grasslands. The energy of the River of Fire was obviously still working its magic on him. At least something was finally going our way, although I couldn't help wondering when the other shoe would drop. Call me suspicious, but I was getting used to things going from bad to worse.

We scrambled up a slight rise in the uneven ground, and Jake stopped so abruptly that I nearly ran into his broad back. No wonder it had seemed to be getting hotter—the River of Fire lay right in front of us. The air was so hot I didn't know how we could be standing here and not evaporate or shrivel up. Maybe Jake was doing something with his power to protect us. I couldn't imagine being able to stand this close to molten lava in the real world and still live. It was beautiful in a horrifying kind of way, so bright it almost hurt my eyes to look at the orange glow of it.

"Did we get turned around somewhere?" I asked, trying to see through Jake's smokescreen.

"I don't think so," Jake said, his face full of uneasiness. He glanced around then gave an exasperated sigh. "I can't see a damn thing through all this smoke."

He waved an impatient arm, and the smoke cleared as if by magic. Well, I guess it *was* magic. I'd never get used to hanging around with shapers.

"Are you sure this is a good idea?" I gazed uneasily at the sky above us.

Sure enough, a harpy's shriek of triumph split the air. In a moment, a band of them were wheeling our way, great black wings sweeping through the air with a sound like thunder.

"Ah, Jake … harpies at three o'clock." What was he doing? Couldn't he see them coming?

"Shit," he said. "Look at that."

I dragged my eyes from the oncoming harpies and

looked. Shit was right. For a moment, I forgot the harpies as my heart sank into my leaden feet. We hadn't got turned around after all. The great triangle of land that we'd been following towards the mountain had come to its point, and that point didn't reach all the way to the mountain's foot after all. Instead, we had arrived at an unholy confluence of the rivers—the black waters of the Styx on the left and the living lava river on the right. How was this possible? It certainly wouldn't have been in the real world, but somehow the Styx didn't evaporate in the heat, or the lava spread into it. The dark water boiled and hissed where the two rivers met and then it just seemed to stop. Perhaps it dived underground; I couldn't tell. All I knew was that our way forward was blocked.

10

"Jake," I said urgently. "We can't stay here like this. We're sitting ducks." The band of harpies was close enough to see that most of them carried rocks clutched in their claws, ready to unleash on our heads. I wasn't keen on being harpy target practice. "Which way? What do we do now?"

We needed to reach the foot of the mountain. The Gate of Dusk, our way out of the underworld, was over there. We couldn't go back, but now we couldn't go forward either. Not unless we wanted to swim the Styx, and that was *waaay* down on my list of things I'd like to attempt in this lifetime. I'd seen the souls of the dead writhing in that water back near the wharf where Charon's ferry docked. It hadn't looked like a pleasant experience, and I had no desire to see what happened to the living who ventured in.

Jake raised his arms and lava arced up from the River of

Fire, crashing down into the black water of the Styx, causing an explosion of steam to boil up into the sky. Under its cover, we backed away, putting some distance between us and where the harpies had last seen us. But we both knew it was only a temporary measure. Where could we go? How long before the harpies managed to score a lucky hit?

Jake stood still, his head tipped to one side, listening. His eyes were on the sky, though nothing could be seen through the clouds of smoke and steam above us. I could hear the harpies calling to each other, their voices coming closer, and I braced for a rain of rocks. Sweat ran down my face, and not just from the heat. I hated feeling so helpless. All I could do was wait, hoping that the harpies' aim would be off.

"If they fly low enough I might be able to hit a few with fire from the river," Jake said. He quirked an eyebrow at me. "Ready? I'll let the smoke clear enough to lure them down."

"Yeah, but what if they decide to just drop their rocks from a distance?"

He shook his head. "I guess we have to risk it. It's the best I can do."

And then what? We'd still be stuck here, with no way forward, the rivers blocking us from our goal. "We don't even know how many harpies are up there." There'd been perhaps a dozen in the band I'd seen swooping towards us when the smoke cleared, but there'd been others behind them, and still more in the skies above the volcano. This was starting to look like a fight we couldn't win. "Can't you, like, move the River of Fire to one side, or make a gap through the middle of it, or something?"

He snorted. "I'm not a god, Lexi."

"My, you *have* got yourself into a pickle," a voice said behind us.

I jumped like a scalded cat and spun around, expecting to see one of the harpies stalking towards us on clawed feet through the smoke. As it turned out, the voice didn't belong to a harpy, but its owner was almost as unwelcome.

Styx rested her forearms on a rock on the riverbank like a drinker leaning on the bar back home in Berkley's Bay. Her chin was propped on one cupped hand and her dark hair flowed down over her naked shoulders until it merged with the black water. The proximity of the River of Fire didn't seem to bother her at all. I suppose I should have expected to see her here. After all, the Styx was her river. But somehow, I'd imagined, if I'd thought about it at all, that she lived closer to where I'd first seen her near the ferry wharf. Why would she be all the way out here in the back of beyond?

"Don't suppose you'd like to help, would you?" I asked, one eye on the sky. Talk about being caught between a rock and a hard place. I didn't like to turn my back on the pointy-toothed horror, but right now, the harpies were the more pressing concern. There was only one of Styx and, for the moment at least, she didn't seem inclined to kill us.

"I'm afraid I'm not much use in a pitched battle," she said. "You do seem to have a habit of making enemies wherever you go."

A heavy flapping sounded overhead and Jake hurled a bolt of molten lava into the sky, dragging it from the fiery river. He must have missed, because there was no screaming, only a swooshing sound as another boulder smashed to the ground.

We changed position, scurrying through the smoke. That one had been too close. Styx moved with us, lazily propelling herself through the dark water, watching as if this was a fine entertainment. I half expected her to hold up scorecards.

"Is there a way across the river?" Jake asked, sparing her a quick glance. The battle was taking most of his attention, as he continually had to replenish the steam that kept us hidden. I felt completely useless, and longed for my bow.

"For you, handsome, one could certainly be arranged," the nymph said, with a coquettish smile whose effect was completely ruined by the sharp teeth it displayed.

He gave her a hard look. "For both of us."

She pouted. "Couldn't we ditch the girl? It's not as if she's doing anything for you."

"Come out of that river and I'll do something all right," I said. "You won't be able to walk for a week."

Jake gave me that look again, the one that said *leave the talking to me*. "Play nice, Lexi. We're a little short of allies, in case you hadn't noticed."

"She's no ally," I muttered, but I could see the wisdom of letting him do the negotiating. He was used to getting what he wanted, particularly from women, I imagined, looking the way he did. It remained to be seen if he could work his charm on Styx.

"Is there a bridge?"

Another boulder crashed to the earth nearby, swiftly followed by another and another. I couldn't help cringing with each impact. It looked like the harpies were stepping up their campaign against us. Jake increased the level of steam and smoke hiding us, but didn't retaliate. Maybe he was still hoping they'd come close enough for him to hit a whole bunch, or perhaps he'd decided not to risk letting them pinpoint our location while he bargained with Styx. I nearly went cross-eyed, trying to watch every direction at once and still keep an eye on the sharp-toothed goddess.

"Why would there be a bridge? Who around here is going to use one? The harpies? Or maybe you think the Titans will come out of Tartarus for a stroll."

If you'd asked me, I would have said it wasn't possible to dislike Styx any more than I already did, but obviously, I'd been wrong. I spared a moment from my close watch on the smoky skies to give her a dirty look.

"Well, I need a bridge," Jake said. I could see his politeness was costing him an effort. Asking nicely wasn't his strong suit. Good to see he could make an effort when circumstances required it. "Or some way across."

"Sorry, sweetheart. I'm all out of bridges." She studied her nails as if she had all the time in the world for this conversation, and wasn't particularly interested in the outcome. I suppose she did, unlike us. *She* wasn't the one caught out in a storm of boulders, all perfectly sized to turn a mere mortal into a smear of pink jelly. Some of those rocks were hitting pretty close now. I wondered uneasily if the harpies were trying to herd us even closer to the rivers so we would have no way out. Was Styx part of the plan? Was she supposed to be distracting us?

Jake growled in frustration. "Let me say it clearer, then. Can you help us? I'm sure Hades would be grateful."

"I'm not interested in Hades' gratitude," she said. She'd stopped pretending to be engrossed in the state of her nails and there was a gleam in her eye I didn't care for. "*Your* gratitude, on the other hand ..."

"I have nothing to give you," he said, "other than my thanks."

She laughed. "Oh, I'm sure we can do better than that. A handsome man like you? I could think of any number of things you could supply."

Oh, please. And here I'd been thinking that my day

couldn't possibly get any worse. Now I had to watch this creepy nymph trying to crack on to Jake?

Three more boulders crashed to earth, way too close for comfort. Jake sent a bolt of fire lancing into the sky in retaliation, bringing a screech of pain and another boulder even closer than before. He caught my hand and dragged me further along the riverbank. Our position was becoming untenable. How many boulders did those damn harpies have, anyway? Their supplies seemed to be limitless. Sooner or later, one of them was going to score a lucky hit, despite all Jake's attempts at camouflage.

Jake seem to have arrived at the same conclusion. "Let's speak plainly, then. What do you want?"

She gave him what was meant to be another of those coquettish smiles, but it came out looking a lot more like a smirk. "Nothing much. Just a little ... quality time."

"In there? You want me to go swimming with you?"

"Swimming?" She laughed, a full-throated sound. "Is that what they're calling it these days in the land of the living?" I swear Jake blushed, although I suppose it might have been the heat. "No, darling, I don't want to go swimming with you. I'm sure I can think of better ways to spend a day or two."

"I can't spare a day or two," he said. "We're on a very important mission. Every moment counts."

"It doesn't have to be straight away," she said. "I'm a reasonable woman. As long as you give me your word that you'll return, you can go off and save the world and we'll catch up when you're done."

I didn't like the triumphant grin that spread across her face, as if she was putting one over on us. Where was the catch? "And in return, you'll carry us both safely across this river?" I asked. I wanted her to say it straight out.

"Your little friend sounds so hostile," she said to Jake with a wounded look. "I am a woman of my word. Ask any of the gods—they always come to me when they want a solemn oath witnessed. They know I'm all about keeping promises."

That was great, but exactly what were we signing ourselves up for? "How long is Jake supposed to spend with you in return for this help? A day? A week?" Heaven forbid. Jake looked horrified at the thought.

She shrugged. "From sunset to sunrise. That should be plenty … and not too exhausting for our young stud here."

"I don't like this," I whispered to Jake, not really caring if Styx heard me or not. "I don't trust her."

"I don't see what other options we have," he whispered back. "These harpies aren't going to let up. If it's a choice between dallying with the scary nymph or dying on this riverbank, it's dallying all the way, baby." His smile was surprisingly sweet as he gave my own words back to me.

"Smart arse."

He turned back to Styx. "One night only, when we finish our quest?"

"From sunset until sunrise," she confirmed. "But I'm not going to wait forever. I'll give you twelve hours to complete your business, and then I expect to see you back here, ready and willing."

"Agreed," Jake said.

Twelve hours should be enough time. All we had to do was get to that damn gate, open the way to Hephaistos's forge, find the star-metal and have Jake make it into a key, then get it back to the underworld. If you said it fast enough, it all sounded totally doable. "But what if it takes us longer than that?" I asked.

Styx gave me a look of frank dislike. "I'm offering twelve hours, starting now. Take it or leave it. You're not really in a position to negotiate." That was true, dammit, but did she have to rub our noses in it? She fixed Jake with a challenging stare. "Is it yes or no, mortal?"

"Yes," Jake said. A boulder splashed into the dark water behind Styx, punctuating his agreement.

"Excellent! Come closer, pretty boy." Obligingly, Jake stepped up to the riverbank. Styx waved him down impatiently. "Do I look like a giraffe? I can't reach you all the way up there."

Jake knelt on the pebbled shore and the nymph surged up out of the water, catching him around the neck and dragging him down. She planted a long, slow kiss on his lips. "Consider the bargain sealed."

❦

Jake pulled away, an odd look on his face. Was that disgust? It had certainly turned *my* stomach, watching the nymph play tonsil hockey with him. Memories of my own recent activities with Jake resurfaced, and I felt a twinge of something sharp and nasty. Was that jealousy? I'd sure like to stick *her* with something sharp and nasty.

Jake brought his fingers to his lips. Maybe it wasn't disgust. I could always stick *him* with something sharp, too, if it came to that. The force of my feelings caught me by surprise—I wasn't normally a jealous person. Well, I thought I wasn't, anyway, but what did I know? Maybe I'd killed my last three ex-lovers in a fit of jealous rage. But this churning feeling in my gut seemed new, and entirely unpleasant. *He's doing it for us*, I reminded myself, but apparently, logic had little to do with feelings, because knowing that didn't improve my mood any.

"What did you do to me?" Jake stared at his fingers as if expecting to see something on them. They looked fine to me, but his tone of voice was off, raspy with a fear he hadn't shown under fire from harpies or chased by giant spiders. In fact, not since the eel monster had pulled him underwater.

Styx looked entirely too pleased with herself. "Just a little insurance. I've put my mark on you. If you keep your oath and come back as you said you would, there won't be a problem."

"And if I don't?"

"I wouldn't advise that," she said. "Oathbreakers die. In agony."

The bitch! A torrent of abuse threatened to burst from my mouth, but I held it back with a supreme effort of will. There would be time to tell her exactly what I thought of her *after* she'd transported us across the river. The harpies hadn't let up their aerial bombardment, and every minute we spent on this side of the broad, dark river was another minute in danger.

Not to mention another minute closer to an agonising death for Jake, if we were late getting back. I drew a deep, shuddering breath of the sulphurous air. Time was truly not on our side.

Jake pressed his lips together in a thin white line and said nothing, though I could see it cost him an effort.

"Let's begin, shall we?" Styx smiled, a bright, fake smile. "You don't have time to be standing around chatting to me, after all."

The urge to punch her smirking face was almost overwhelming, but I clenched my fists and fought it down. Jake's hand sought mine, his fingers gently prying mine open. I relaxed my furious fist and took his hand, finding comfort in the familiar warmth of his skin. Our clasped hands didn't escape Styx's notice, and now it was her turn to press her lips together, looking as though she'd just sucked a lemon. I have to admit the expression on her face gave me a considerable amount of pleasure. I moved closer to Jake, until our shoulders were touching, forming a united front against the nymph.

With a swirl of dark water, she turned and lifted her dripping arms into the air. Something rose to the surface in response to her silent call, though I couldn't say exactly what. It changed before my eyes, twisting and reshaping itself, refusing to hold a single form. I saw pieces of bodies, glimpses of arms, hands, and torsos; here a curving shoulder blade, there the long sweep of a backbone. And everywhere the screaming, contorted faces, just as I had first seen them in the river down at the ferry wharf. I shuddered; I couldn't help it. Were these the souls of the damned, the ones who hadn't been able to afford Charon's price for passage across the river? And yet, they seemed more than souls as they surged toward the surface of the dark water, as real as Jake or I, as real as the hands clasped firmly between us. Pieces of bodies coalesced into a thin but solid-looking band that stretched from the riverbank at our feet across the water, disappearing into the smoke.

"Your bridge awaits," Styx said, oozing self-satisfaction.

"Thank you," said Jake, with a politeness that I certainly couldn't have mustered. The bridge turned my stomach; I could hardly imagine actually setting foot on it. It was like a serial killer's wet dream. I focused on the part immediately in front of us. An eye stared up at me and fingers writhed as if straining to reach something lost long ago. I tightened my grip on Jake's hand and wrenched my gaze away from the ghastly bridge.

Jake looked down at me and gave my hand a gentle squeeze. "All right?" he asked.

"Never better," I lied, with more determination than truth. "Ready when you are."

He nodded. "Let's go."

We moved together, as if we were part of a marching band. The bridge gave slightly beneath my foot, and bile rose in my throat, but I swallowed hard and took another step.

"That's it," Jake said. "One foot after another. Good girl."

I trod on a hand, and shuddered at the sound of knuckles cracking beneath my foot. Styx moved through the water beside us, watching our progress with a smile, enjoying every minute of my discomfort. "Remember, twelve hours," she said. "Don't be late."

Jake didn't look at her, keeping his eyes fixed on the smoke-filled way ahead. "I won't forget."

If it weren't for his hand pulling me on, I don't know if I could have made it all the way across. I was walking on people, and that's exactly what it felt like, as the bridge gave beneath my every step. Soft moans accompanied us, forming a counterpoint against the crash of rocks smashing against the hard ground behind us. At least we were leaving the danger zone behind.

They say that all good things must come to an end. Fortunately, so must the bad things. After what felt like an eternity of horror, we finally stepped ashore on the other side of the river. I've never been happier to set foot on dry land in my life.

"Hurry back," crooned that hated voice behind us, but neither of us looked back. "See you soon!"

We hurried away from the river and its revolting bridge of bodies. It was still smoky on this side, and the air smelled just as bad, but I felt a new lightness in my step. We were getting closer to our destination, and soon, this ordeal would be over.

The terrain on the other side of the bridge was just the same, and shrouded in smoke which Jake augmented to keep us hidden from the harpies. He still held my hand in his and I didn't object. Behind us, the sound of smashing rocks grew fainter. It was punctuated by the occasional shriek of frustration from high above, as if the harpies were aware we had somehow slipped their net. Apparently, it hadn't occurred to them that we might be able to cross the river.

"Is it just me or is it getting darker?" I asked. My eyes were burning from the smoke, but now there was more than just smoke swirling around us. Darkness crept out of the cracks, oozing across the land, swallowing rocks and bushes. Shadows stretched their inky fingers toward us on every side. I could hardly see where I was putting my feet anymore.

Jake gave my hand a reassuring squeeze. "That's a good sign. It means we're getting closer to Tartarus."

Yay, Tartarus. Thank goodness our path didn't actually lead us there. I didn't know much about it, but what I'd heard sounded pretty uninviting. Imprisoned giants, tortured souls, eternal punishments of the particularly gruesome kind—fun times. And to top it off, the place was guarded by harpies. I'd had quite enough of those to last me a lifetime.

"How far from Tartarus to the gate?"

Jake shrugged. "Your guess is as good as mine. The map wasn't exactly accurate, was it? But legends say it's not far."

"Does it seem weird to you to have a gate so close to the entrance to your biggest, most important prison? I mean, if these guys broke out of Tartarus, they'd be out of here and back on Earth faster than you could say 'destruction time'."

"No one has ever broken out of Tartarus. There have been a few rescues, but no one ever gets out under their own steam. It's a prison for gods and monsters. It would hardly be effective if a smuggled nail file was all it took to escape."

"Hercules got in there, didn't he?" I thought I remembered reading something about that. "Wasn't that one of his trials to become a god?"

Jake snorted. "No. Zeus wouldn't have rewarded him with divinity for doing something like that. Hades mightn't have been too happy either. When Zeus wants you in prison, you stay in prison. I don't know of any mortal who has managed to break someone out of Tartarus. Hermes managed it once, and I bet even he wouldn't try again. Zeus was not a happy chappy."

"Zeus sounds like a hard ass. Doesn't he ever forgive anyone?"

"Don't ask me. That kind of stuff is way above my pay grade."

The darkness was definitely deepening now. I could barely see where we were going anymore. "Is it night time?"

Jake looked doubtful. "I don't think this part of the underworld experiences night and day. Only Elysium and the area around Hades' Palace. We must be getting close."

I liked darkness as much as the next person—probably more, in fact. I did a lot of my best work in the dark. You could say it was my workplace. But there was something about this darkness that set my teeth on edge, as though something was stalking me under cover of night. The occasional harpy screech still floated on the still air, though they seemed to have abandoned their game of rock dropping. Apart from that, there was very little noise other than the sound of our own breathing and the odd pebble being kicked away as we stumbled on the uneven ground.

Somewhere off to our right, a geyser vented, and I jumped at the hissing sound, my imagination leaping to large cats or even snakes before I realised what it was. Cautiously, I sent my awareness out, just in case, but I found no animal life nearby. Shame. I could have done with a boost to my night vision.

I glanced back the way we had come. The River of Fire glowed orange, forming a bright thread against the black, but that was the only thing I could see. Ahead, a small red circle appeared out of the gloom. As we came closer, the circle grew until I could see it was the opening to a cave or tunnel. Red light spilled from it, painting the ground in front of the cave in blood-red tones.

"There it is," Jake said.

"The Gate of Dusk?" I wasn't too keen on going through there if so. It looked like the mouth of Hell.

"No. The entrance to Tartarus."

A winged shadow fell into the ruby light—a harpy returning to the cave.

"Let's keep moving," Jake whispered, drawing me away.

Good plan. I didn't want to come to the harpies' attention again. Besides, the place gave me the creeps. There was a moaning sound coming from the cave that might just possibly have been the wind. At least, that's what I told myself.

"Who's down there?" I whispered as we left the hellish

glow behind. My imagination was supplying all kinds of monsters, complete with clanking chains.

"Most of the old gods," Jake said. "Only a few, like Styx, managed to hang on to their freedom once the Olympians took over. Chronos is there, Chaos, most of the Titans. Various cyclopes. Probably a few other monsters, too. I don't know what happened to that dragon that used to guard the golden apples, for instance."

"I thought Jason killed it?"

There was enough light to see the flash of white teeth as Jake grinned. "You can't believe everything you read in books, you know."

I glanced back at the fast receding cave mouth. Shadows moved against the ruddy light, but no one came in or out. "Brontes is there, isn't he? The cyclops Hephaistos mentioned?"

Jake nodded.

"What did he ever do? Hephaistos said he was the best assistant he ever had, almost as good as himself."

"Same as the rest of them, probably. Pissed off Zeus."

Note to self: don't piss off Zeus. Sounded like the guy had a short fuse.

Another glow appeared ahead of us, but this one wasn't the red of Tartarus's mouth or the orange of the River of Fire. It reminded me of the grey light just before dawn, just a slight break in the unrelenting blackness. My stride lengthened as I sensed an end to our journey.

"There it is," Jake said. "The Gate of Dusk."

An archway appeared out of the gloom. Made of rough stone, it looked as though it might tumble down any moment. "I'm guessing this doesn't get used much anymore."

Jake's face was awed as he traced a hand over the large blocks of the gate. "Don't let looks deceive you. This has been here since the dawn of time, and it will probably still be here after the world ends." He shook his head. "I never thought I would see this. My life has gone completely crazy since I met you."

"Mine hasn't exactly been a picnic either." Conscious that I was still holding his hand, I tried to pull away.

His grip on my fingers tightened, and he smiled a slow, sweet smile. "I didn't say it was a problem."

Right. I could feel my cheeks heating and looked away. Beyond the gate mist swirled, hiding whatever awaited us on the other side. "You ready to blow that horn?" Another time, I could probably have come up with some cute pun on 'horny', but I felt unaccountably flustered by our conversation.

Thankfully, Jake at last let my hand go. He reached into his backpack and pulled out the horn that Hephaistos had given him. "Ready?"

Ready to leave this place? You bet I was. "Let's go."

Together we stepped through the gate. Jake lifted the horn to his lips and blew.

11

Damn, but that thing was loud. The echoes of the horn were still ringing in my ears when reality kind of glitched, throwing me completely off balance. It was like when you're watching TV and the picture suddenly goes on the fritz—all jagged, wavy lines. I staggered as reality twisted around me, feeling as though I was about to throw up.

I swallowed hard and managed to hold it all together. We stood high on a rocky mountainside, a warm breeze ruffling our hair. Moonlight showed a few wisps of cloud scudding across the sky, and a dark sea stretching to the horizon on every side. A jungle rioted at the mountain's foot, filled with the cries of night birds and the cough of some nocturnal predator. The heavy perfume of night-blooming flowers drifted up on the breeze.

We were on an island, and it was hot, hot, hot. I tilted

my face to the dark sky and enjoyed the cooling breeze on my face.

In front of us, a golden door set into the mountain's face glittered in the moonlight, looking very out of place in its craggy surroundings.

"Seems kind of ostentatious," I said. "Surely anyone who happened upon this place would realise there was something important here."

"No one is going to just stumble upon this," Jake said. "I know it all looks real enough, but this isn't really Earth, but a little pocket between worlds." He pushed hesitantly on the door and it swung open.

I tried to crane over his shoulder, but he was way too tall and his bulk filled the doorway. "What are you waiting for? We're on a tight deadline here, remember?"

"I know." He stepped inside and I followed him in, eager to see the fabled forge of the god of metalshaping. "It's just so unbelievable to be here. The actual forge of Hephaistos. How did my life ever turn out this way?"

He looked around like a small child in a toy shop, his face alive with wonder. It wasn't as impressive as I'd been expecting, considering the flashy door. It all looked pretty workmanlike to me. We stood in a large, natural cave. Two tunnels led deeper into the mountain's heart, both dark. But there was plenty of light in this large space, mostly supplied by the torches that had sprung to life as soon as we entered. A giant furnace took up most of the wall between the two tunnels, and the wall to our left was covered with tools whose purpose I could only begin to imagine, all hanging in neat, orderly rows. A large anvil stood near the furnace, and there were two heavy tables in the middle of the room, whose scarred surfaces showed their years of use.

I turned slowly, taking in the whole room. To our right, on the wall opposite the tools, the wall was covered in shelving, which displayed all manner of things, some beautiful and some more utilitarian. Golden cups sat beside iron chests, jewel-encrusted swords shared space with things that looked more like farm implements, and there were many other things whose purposes I could only guess at. Beside the door through which we had entered stood two full suits of armour, one on each side, the torchlight glinting off the intricate engravings on the breastplate of one and the hundreds of tiny interlocking rings of the other. It was a big place, and between the tools and all Hephaistos's creations, I could see us being here for a while, searching for the one piece of star-metal that we needed.

"Where do you think the star-metal is?" I asked. I could practically hear a ticking clock in the back of my mind, filling me with a sense of urgency.

"It should be in one of those chests," Jake said.

He moved toward the wall of shelving. So many shinies

that winked and sparkled in the torchlight! It was truly a cave of wonders.

"Remember not to touch anything," I cautioned him. Hephaistos hadn't said exactly what would happen if we did, but I had no wish to find out. I'd had enough nasty surprises to last me for quite some time.

"I hadn't forgotten," Jake said, shooting me a rather exasperated glance. "I'm actually quite good at remembering basic instructions."

"Just checking that Hephaistos made it basic enough for you." I had to force myself to stand still, or I might have been the one to trigger whatever disaster befell those who couldn't keep their hands to themselves. All those pretty things called to me in a professional capacity. It wasn't every day you got to share space with so much treasure. The urge to sample something was hard to resist.

I hugged my arms around myself and drifted closer as Jake opened the first chest. The lid creaked as he lifted it, revealing a chess set, cast in gold and silver. Jake's hand reached out automatically before he remembered. He closed the lid with a bang and gave me a sheepish grin.

"Next," he said.

I hovered at his elbow as he opened the next chest. There were a lot to get through. "Did he say it was in this room? It could be somewhere back there." I jerked my head in the direction of the two dark tunnel mouths.

"Let's hope not. This could take longer than I thought."

I wandered over towards the massive forge. It was hot here; almost as hot as it had been near the River of Fire in the underworld. "Does he keep a fire going here all the time?" I asked. "That seems a little wasteful."

"How so?" Jake didn't look at me, too intent on his search. "The fires are powered by the volcano itself."

"Really?" I inspected the forge with renewed interest, though I kept a careful distance. "Do you think it ever erupts?"

"It probably does exactly what Hephaistos wants it to," Jake said. "Aha!"

"What? Have you found it?" I left the forge and hurried back to his side. He was staring into a chest full of bars of metal. Most of them appeared to be gold, shiny, and glorious, though a few were a darker, dull grey. "Is that the star-metal?"

"It looks like ordinary iron." He frowned, catching his lower lip between his teeth. "But I'd have to touch it to be sure."

"Oh." We stared at each other. "Well, you've been touching all these chests and nothing's happened."

"True. And Hephaistos told me to look inside the chests. He couldn't have meant not to touch anything in them. That wouldn't make sense."

I gazed up at the wall of shining beauty, at all the

goblets, knives, swords, and other pretties. "There can't be any harm in touching a few bits of metal. He must have meant to keep our hands off all these treasures."

"You're right." But Jake still let out a deep breath before picking up one of the grey bars. As soon as he touched it, he shook his head. "Just iron."

He put the bar back in the chest and closed the lid. The next one also contained iron bars.

"We must be getting closer," he said.

I agreed, but several more chests came and went without revealing the star-metal. I moved closer to the shelving, my eye caught by a particularly beautiful dagger. I'd lost one of mine, throwing it at that harpy. Not that I would be stupid enough to take one from Hephaistos's forge. I just wanted to look.

A long, ominous metallic scraping sounded behind me. I whirled around to find Jake standing with a small bar of metal in his hand.

"Jake Harlan Steele! What did you do? Did you touch something?"

"It wasn't me," he said, shoving the metal bar into his pocket.

I looked around; what had made that noise? There was no one here but Jake and me.

The suit of armour to the left of the golden door caught my eye, and adrenaline jolted through me. "Jake, wasn't that sword sheathed when we came in?"

The sword was now clutched in a mailed fist, held in the ready position. As we watched, the suit of armour on the other side of the door stiffly drew its own sword with a long hiss of metal. I backed up towards Jake.

"Zeus's balls," he breathed.

In unison, the two suits of armour took a step away from the door, swords at the ready. I eyed the wall of weapons. It probably didn't matter now what we touched. I mentally discarded the swords; I was no swordswoman. But there were a couple of spears that looked pretty inviting.

As I eyed the closest one, the suits of armour moved again, turning to face the door. Jake and I exchanged confused looks—why were they turning their backs on us?

A moment later the golden door opened with such force it smashed back against the rock wall, and we had our answer. Fire surged into the room as three newcomers leapt through the door, and the armoured figures opposing them disappeared into a maelstrom of flame. That was all I saw as Jake shoved me down behind a table. I landed hard on my back, my backpack crushed beneath me. Catching my breath, I twisted around and scrambled up into a crouch, my heart pounding from the shock. Jake brought up a wall of his own flame as figures surged through the inferno towards us.

"Stay down," he ordered, before striding forward to meet the threat, a shield of flame held in front of him.

What the hell was going on? Who were these people, and how had they found us? Because there was no doubt in my mind that they had come here to find us. How much of a coincidence would it have to be for a bunch of fireshapers to turn up at exactly the same moment that we did? A bunch of hostile fireshapers. I hadn't forgotten the warrant the Ruby Council had out for Jake's arrest. The only question was how they had managed to track us, when even *we* didn't know where we were.

No, scratch that. There was another question, too. Hephaistos had given us his horn to open the way to his forge, and said that only a god would have been able to find this place without it. So where had these fireshapers found a god to aid them?

All this tumbled through my brain in a flash while I groped in my backpack for my spare knife. I didn't dare go for one of the weapons on the wall now—I would be seen as soon as I stood up. At least we'd had a moment's warning, courtesy of the animated suits of armour. They had to be the guardians of this place, since they'd activated the minute the fireshapers had reached the golden door.

My hand closed on an unfamiliar object. Holy shit. I'd forgotten all about the Baseball Cap of Supreme Sneakiness. I shoved it onto my head, cowering behind the table as flame roared across the room towards Jake. The noise was unbelievable and the air crackled with heat. From where I crouched, I could see Jake, his arms outstretched. They trembled with the effort of supporting his shield of flame. A maelstrom writhed between the two parties where the flames met. Flames licked at the roof of the cavern far overhead, spinning and turning. The stone beneath my feet began to warm. Now I knew what it felt like to be a turkey roasting in an oven. I didn't know how long I could last in this environment.

Jake threw a glance over his shoulder, desperately searching. "Lexi!"

Of course he couldn't see me. I couldn't even see myself. The minute I touched my backpack, it disappeared, too. I shouldered it and, crouching low, ran to Jake's side, taking shelter behind his wall of flame. Immediately, I felt relief from the heat of the firestorm. I drew a breath that didn't sear my lungs and wiped my sweaty face with my shirt.

"I'm here," I said, leaning close to Jake's ear to be heard above the noise of battle. "I'm wearing the Helm."

"Stay close," Jake said, "so I can protect you."

Three fireshapers stood arrayed against Jake, lined up shoulder to shoulder just inside the golden door. Between them and Jake, a furnace roared, in which I caught occasional glimpses of the half-melted suits of armour lying on the floor. Whatever magic had animated them obviously wasn't proof against the fireshapers' power. Hephaistos had probably only been expecting mortal thieves.

"Friends of yours?" I asked.

"I would have said so once," Jake ground out between clenched teeth. His face showed the effort he was putting into his barrier of flame. "The one in the middle is a fellow councillor, and the other two are the Ruby Adept's nephews."

Shit. This was worse than I thought. It seemed the Ruby Council was taking its usual "strike first and ask questions later" approach. You would think that there might have been some leeway given to a fellow councillor, but apparently not. It was a dog-eat-dog world out there in fireshaper-land.

I cast a longing look back at the wall of weapons. I didn't dare risk leaving Jake's protective bubble to grab one now, though. But I still had my knife.

"Which one do you want me to skewer?" This would be like shooting fish in a barrel. They wouldn't even see the knife until it left my hand, and with all this fire between us, chances were good they wouldn't notice it until it speared them right through the eye.

"Wait a second," Jake said. "Let's try negotiating first."

I had a feeling negotiating wouldn't work with these guys. I gripped my knife, ready to let it fly as soon as he gave the word.

"What do you want, Owen?" Jake shouted above the roar of flame.

"Your head on a stick, if it were up to me," the guy in the middle replied. "But the Ruby Adept wants you alive, unfortunately."

"Is there no one left on the Council who isn't in league with the shadow shapers?" Jake roared. His face glistened with sweat. He was a powerful fireshaper—one of the most powerful on the Council—but three against one wasn't a fair fight. "I thought Anders was the only rotten apple in the barrel, but it seems I was mistaken."

"Shadow shapers! You think you can scare us with your children's fairy tales?" I couldn't see his face clearly through the flame, but I could picture the sneer on Owen's face from the venom dripping from his tone. "You killed a fellow councillor, and now you think you can excuse it by sending us on a wild goose chase for something that doesn't even exist. Justice isn't that easy to escape."

I bristled at the shaper's easy use of the word "justice". What did any of them know about the subject? This guy had probably just been waiting for a chance to take Jake down. It seemed that climbing over the bodies of their fellows was the only way they knew to get ahead.

"You're a fool if you don't believe me," Jake snarled. "Let me talk to the Ruby Adept. I can't believe you have his blessing to attack me like this. What happened to due process? What happened to the judgement of my peers?"

"*You* happened to it," said a new voice. Beyond the wall of flame, the golden door had opened, admitting a new figure. He strode forward, right through the flames, until he stood just the other side of Jake's fiery shield. My heart sank. I knew this guy. Last time I'd seen him, he'd been lying naked on the carpet at my feet, but I still recognised that balding head, that fleshy face. He was wearing more clothes now, but it was the Ruby Adept himself.

"Robert," Jake said, and his shield of flame faltered a little. "You too?"

"You said you wanted to speak to me, Jacob," the Ruby Adept said in a conversational tone. "Here I am. Talk to me." He folded his hands over his sagging belly, and assumed an expectant expression.

"Remember, he was wearing the ring," I whispered in Jake's ear.

Jake nodded, the smallest of motions. When I'd stolen Apollo's ring from the Ruby Adept, we'd both expected it to be hidden away in a safe. But it turned out the guy was wearing it, which, at best, suggested a lack of respect for the god of his order. At worst, it made him a shadow shaper.

"What's the point, if you're in league with them, too?" Jake's voice was heavy with bitterness. Perhaps, in spite of the irregularity with the ring, he had believed the Ruby Adept was still on the side of righteousness.

"In league with whom, Jacob?" The Ruby Adept assumed the patient expression of a man speaking to a small child. "There are no such things as shadow shapers. Not outside your imagination, anyway."

One of the fireshapers behind him sniggered. They'd

dropped their flames for this conversation, although they stood ready to renew the battle at a moment's notice. Jake, I was pleased to see, wasn't so trusting. His fiery shield was still in place, separating us from the Ruby Adept.

"But there is the small matter of the murder of Erik Anders," the Ruby Adept continued, his voice hardening. "I'm afraid you can't explain that away. Cameras all around the Plaza of the Sun caught your attack on him—and then he disappears, and you expect us to believe you had nothing to do with it? You were also in the company of a woman believed to have stolen something very precious from me, though I see you have abandoned her just as easily as you abandoned your fellow councillors."

I bristled on Jake's behalf, even though the accusations were untrue. Sure, Jake and Anders had fought in the plaza—very publicly—but it had been Hades who'd later killed him, in Berkley's Bay. And gotten rid of the body. Without that, how were they so sure he was dead? Maybe I'd send my knife whizzing into the Ruby Adept's eye, the crooked bastard, instead of Owen's. And how could he know that I was the one who'd stolen the ring, unless Erik Anders had told him? All he had seen of me were my boots. If he had been in league with Anders, he wasn't one of the good guys.

Clearly, Jake had come to this conclusion as well. "How do you manage to sleep at night?" he marvelled. "You had the avatar of Apollo himself in your possession, and all you could think of was your own power. You didn't spare a thought for the god you professed to worship, did you? I suppose you knew what he was enduring and you just didn't care."

The Ruby Adept gave up all pretence of politeness. "Where is that ring now?" he snarled.

"On Apollo's finger, where it should be," Jake said.

The Ruby Adept laughed. "Oh, really? You selflessly returned the avatar to Lord Apollo, did you? One wonders why he has not returned in all his glory, then. You're lying, Jacob. I know you still have it." He lowered his voice to a menacing growl. "And I want it back."

Jake laughed. "And what's in it for me? I give you the ring, you kill me. Hardly an incentive, is it?"

The Ruby Adept beamed. "Well, I'm glad to see you haven't completely lost your mind. Let's talk about that, shall we? If you return the ring, I'm sure we could come to some arrangement about those murder charges." His eyes gleamed demonically, reflecting the flames from Jake's wall of fire. I wouldn't trust him as far as I could kick his flabby arse.

"I don't have the ring on me," Jake said.

"I didn't expect you to." The Ruby Adept sounded almost approving. "I imagine you have it hidden somewhere safe. Why don't you drop those shield flames, and we can talk about this like reasonable men."

"Give me a moment. I'll pray to Lord Apollo for guidance."

The Ruby Adept eyed him thoughtfully for a moment, then shrugged. "Go right ahead."

Jake turned slightly away from the man and bowed his head.

"What the hell are you doing?" I whispered, fear strangling my voice. "You can't trust this guy. He's going to stab you in the back the minute he gets the chance."

"Not until he gets that ring," Jake muttered, head still down, doing a good impression of a man communing with his god. "I can stall them for a while. He'll expect me to try to cut some kind of deal now, in the hope of doublecrossing him later."

"Let me kill him. That will even up the odds a little."

"Not enough. I can't beat those other three. I don't even know how much longer I can keep this shield up for. And the minute I drop it, they'll be on me like a pack of starving wolves, unless I make them think I'll play their game."

"Then what do we do?" All I had was my knife. "Maybe I can sneak around behind them, knock them out or something."

"No, don't do that. It's too risky. The important thing is to free Apollo. Take the metal from my pocket and get it back to the underworld."

"But Hephaistos—"

"—can't work the star-metal anymore now he's dead.

Yes, I know. But Apollo is a smith, too. Give it to him. He can make the key, probably better than I can."

"Even with the collar on?"

"Smithing doesn't require magic, only muscles."

"But what about you? If you don't get back to Styx in time, you'll die." He couldn't afford to spend an extended period behind bars. Or any period, actually. His life was measured in hours unless he fulfilled his side of the bargain with the nymph of the black river. I was so afraid for him I could barely think.

"Don't worry about me. I'll figure something out. Free Apollo."

"There's got to be a better way." I hated the thought of leaving him, but in my panic, I couldn't come up with an alternative. Four fireshapers on one side versus one fireshaper on the other, and no prospect of any help finding us here, tucked away from reality. We were out of options, and my heart beat a panicked tattoo against my ribs.

"Just do it. Take the star-metal now. Go."

I reached into his back pocket and withdrew the small bar of precious metal. Was it really worth this kind of sacrifice? Jake placed himself in danger so calmly, but I was a long way from calm. The ticking of the clock in my head grew louder, adding to my fear. We'd already used a couple of those precious hours searching for the star-metal. What if Apollo couldn't make the key in time?

I threw my arms around him for a moment and pressed my lips to his, inhaling his familiar smoky scent. "I'll come back for you. I swear it."

Jake finished his "prayers" and dropped his shield. The Ruby Adept smiled as the flames winked out, and my desire to put a knife through him increased tenfold, but I clenched the star-metal in my fist and held back. If I could have thought of any other way out of the situation, I wouldn't have let Jake do it. His devotion to Apollo was unprecedented, and I felt sure it was leading him to a terrible mistake. I suppose I shouldn't have been surprised; I already knew how much he'd been through for the sake of his god. I'd seen the vicious scars of the whip on his back. How would it feel to be the object of such complete devotion? I felt a twinge of jealousy—I'd probably never know. Apollo had better bloody be worth it.

"Excellent choice," the Ruby Adept said, still wearing that infuriating smirk. "I'm sure we can work out something to everyone's satisfaction."

Oh, yeah? The only way *I* was getting any satisfaction out of this arrangement would be when I got to watch Apollo smite this guy. Until then, I had to be content imagining all kinds of painful deaths for the Ruby Adept and his minions.

But Apollo was waiting—the undeserving swine—and Syl, too. Vengeance would have to be delayed a little longer. Quietly, I moved away, towards the golden door.

"It will take me some time to retrieve the ring," Jake said as the Ruby Adept beckoned his minions forward.

"Owen and the boys will be happy to take care of that for you," the Ruby Adept said. "All we need is a location."

The other fireshapers surrounded Jake. He made no attempt to defend himself as they closed on him. Something glinted in Owen's fist, and I whipped my knife up again. Plan be damned; I wasn't standing by while he stabbed Jake in the back.

But it wasn't a knife, only a hypodermic, as it turned out and, in the split second I hesitated, he'd plunged it into Jake's neck.

They're not going to kill him, I told myself. *They want that ring.*

Standing by and letting him do it was one of the hardest things I'd ever done. *Grow a set, Lexi. If Jake can handle it, so can you.*

Jake's eyes rolled back in his head and he sagged against a waiting fireshaper. Two of them ducked under his arms in a well-rehearsed movement and took his weight, while Owen diverted to pick up the backpack Jake had left on the floor next to the heavy wooden chests.

Oh, shit. The backpack.

Inside it was the horn I needed to get back to the underworld.

12

God, how could I have been so stupid? My own pack was firmly on my back—much good that did me. Admittedly, the last few moments had been kind of busy with life-and-death decisions and avoiding being fried, but how could I forget the horn? Here I was, all ready to take the star-metal back to the underworld, and my way back was heading for the door, surrounded by fireshapers. *You had one job, Lexi.*

I hurried after them, fuelled by the fear that slammed into me as I realised that if I couldn't follow them back to wherever they'd come from, I had no other way of leaving this place. I'd be stuck here forever.

Owen had the door open and was out in a flash. I hung back as his two companions manhandled Jake's dead weight through the door, frantic to get my hands on that backpack. The Ruby Adept followed them and I slipped through on his heels, anxious to get out before they slammed the door and trapped me in the forge. It was a delicate dance, making sure that no one bumped against me, and for a moment, I was oblivious of the world we had stepped into.

When I realised where I was, my mouth fell open. I spun to look back at the golden door, but it was no longer there. From all appearances, we had just stepped out of a solicitor's office, and now I was standing on the pavement in downtown Crosston. This was insane. Where was the tropical island that we'd seen when we first arrived from the underworld? How had they managed to open the way to Hephaistos's forge from here?

A long black limousine idled at the curb, and the fireshapers bundled Jake into it with ruthless efficiency. I leapt forward, my heart beating a panicked staccato against my ribs, but there was no way to get into the car with them without being discovered. I was forced to stand there and watch it pull away. There was nothing I could do.

I guess I knew where they were taking him anyway. The Ruby Palace in the centre of town was the heart of the fireshapers' empire. I knew it well, and my feet instinctively turned in its direction as the car rounded a corner and disappeared from view.

But I had other responsibilities. The bar of star-metal was still clenched in my invisible fist. It was heavy, but not as heavy as the weight on my heart. My instinct was to run after them and do everything in my power to free Jake, but if I did, we risked losing everything. The tension between my desire and my duty thrummed in every part of my body. I didn't even know what time it was, much less which day. Night had fallen and the street lights were on. How much time did Jake have left?

And how the hell was I going to get to the underworld now?

When the street was clear, I took off the Helm and stowed it and the star-metal safely in my backpack, then set off in the opposite direction to the one which the car had taken. I felt an almost physical pain at turning my back on Jake, but he had sacrificed a lot for this chance and it was up to me to make it work. I had no phone, no wallet, no money, and no friends. I needed a miracle, and I had only one faint hope of finding one.

My path took me through the famous Plaza of the Sun. The great bronze statue of Apollo was back on its plinth, and someone must have found an earthshaper to rebuild the wall around it. No one had bothered to fix the facade of the building that Apollo's spear had plunged into, though. The sight of that jagged hole made me smile in spite of our dire situation. I hurried through the Plaza and up the hill of Jackson Avenue. Popular restaurants lined the road on either side, boasting cuisines from all over the world. Most of them had tables and chairs out on the pavement, and inviting smells wafted from their open doors—garlic and steak and the sharp tang of rosemary, cinnamon, and fennel, plus other herbs I couldn't identify. Many of the tables were full already, and the sounds of clinking cutlery and laughter followed me up the road. My empty stomach rumbled as I marched determinedly on.

Away from the bright lights of the restaurant strip, I came to a less affluent area, where apartment buildings huddled together, all squashed in cheek by jowl. This close to the centre of town, they'd be worth a pretty penny, and they were certainly better than the building where Syl and I had lived so briefly, but I much preferred my little apartment over the bookshop in Berkley's Bay. It was small, but nothing beat the view of the ocean and the sound of the waves lulling me to sleep at night. I could hardly wait to get back there.

My shoes tapped on the hard concrete, echoing in the empty street. The air smelled of rain, though the ground was dry. Must be a storm on the way. I cast my mind out, just because I could, for the joy of touching those little sparks of animal life that lurked everywhere in a big shaper city the size of Crosston. I hadn't realised how much I had missed my ability to do this until it was taken away from me. I sharpened my eyesight with a link to a cat prowling the rooftops above me. It felt so natural. The scarcity of animal life in the underworld had made me feel as if I had lost one of my senses.

Most of the people I had known when I lived in Crosston before had died in the fire that destroyed our apartment block. The ones who hadn't probably wouldn't welcome me. That left me with only one person to turn to, although I had never met him. I wasn't precisely sure where I was going, but in one of those conversations where Joe was always singing his brother's praises, he'd said that Lucas worked as a bouncer at a nightclub on Dixon Street. I knew that Dixon ran off Park Avenue, and I was nearly there. There probably wouldn't be more than one nightclub in the street.

It was called Roxy's, as it turned out, and it was set back from the street with a large single-level car park laid out in front of it. The car park was only half full at the moment— either Roxy's wasn't that popular or it was too early in the evening for the cool clubbers to be out. Every now and then, as I approached, the automatic doors would slide open as someone entered, emitting a blast of sound into the car park, dominated by a deep bass beat. Two big, hulking guys stood at the door, one on each side, like sphinxes guarding the entrance to some pharaoh's tomb. I threaded my way through the cars, checking them both out. The guy on the left had almost no neck. His head just seemed to float on top of his massive shoulders, which bulged under his tight shirt. The other guy was only slightly smaller, with a three-day growth on his face and dark rings under his eyes. If one of these was Lucas, I was putting my money on the stubbly guy. Werewolves always had trouble with excessive facial hair.

They both watched me approach across the car park. No-neck frowned. Guess I didn't look like one of the usual clientele. I certainly hadn't dressed for clubbing. I was wearing the same dark T-shirt and jeans I'd left Hades' palace in—yesterday morning?—and they had seen a lot of dirt and swamp water since then. He moved forward, half blocking the door as I stopped in front of them.

"Is one of you lovely gentlemen Lucas Kincaid?" I asked.

"That's me," the stubbly guy said warily. "Who's asking?"

"Hi." Relief surged through me. Finding him hadn't been too challenging. With a bit of luck, convincing him to help me would be just as easy. I gave him my best smile, wishing I had brushed my hair sometime in the last twenty-four hours, or even cleaned my teeth. "My name is Lexi Jardine. I'm a friend of Joe and Holly's."

A welcoming smile replaced the suspicious look. He was cute when he smiled, if a little young for me. There was definitely a family resemblance to his big brother, particularly around the eyes. "Lexi! It's a pleasure to meet you. Joe told me all about what you did." He seized my hand and shook it with such enthusiasm that the bones of my hand ground together. Damn werewolves never knew their own strength. "Thank you for saving Holly! Let me buy you a drink when my shift is over. What are you doing in town?"

"Long story. Can I talk to you privately for a minute?"

Lucas looked inquiringly at the other bouncer. "Cover for me, buddy?"

No-neck grunted and shrugged one massive shoulder, which seemed to indicate assent. Lucas draped a friendly arm around my shoulders and led me a little way away. I'd forgotten how touchy-feely werewolves could be. He politely ignored the stench of swamp and sulphur that clung to me, though it must have smelled even worse to his werewolf nose than it did to me.

"I get the feeling this long story may not be a happy one," he said. "Do you need a place to stay?"

I shook my head. "No, I need a ride. I have to get back to Berkley's Bay. I know it's a big ask when you've only just met me, but could I borrow your car?"

"Sorry," he said. "I don't own one."

My heart sank. I'd ask for money for a train ticket, but there'd be no train running until the morning, and that was too late. I had to make every minute count.

"But I do have a motorbike," he added.

I sighed. "Unfortunately, I don't know how to ride one."

"That's no problem. Joe's been nagging me to come

down and see the baby. I'll give you a ride there when my shift's over."

"When is that?"

He glanced at his watch. "Another four hours."

Dammit. Jake couldn't afford a four-hour delay. I gave him a pleading look. "Not to sound like a drama queen or anything, but it really is a matter of life and death. I need to go *right now*." I laid a hand on his arm. "Please."

He glanced back at No-neck, who was watching the car park, his face completely expressionless. "I don't know … My boss won't be happy if I skip out early and leave Dylan on his own."

"Please, Lucas. This is really important."

His face softened as he gazed down at me. My puppy dog eyes must have been working. "Hell, I can't say no to the woman who saved my baby niece. Let me just grab my stuff and tell the boss I'm going."

He headed inside, stopping to speak to No-neck on the way past. The other bouncer scowled at me, but I ignored him. He looked big enough and ugly enough to handle any trouble that might arise at Roxy's on his own. I turned my back on him and pretended to find the car park immensely interesting as I waited for Lucas to return.

He wasn't long. He came out juggling two motorbike helmets from arm to arm as he shrugged into a black leather jacket.

"I hope it didn't cause any trouble with your boss," I said. In fact, I really didn't care. A hundred people could lose their jobs, and I would still think Jake's life was more important, but it seemed polite to at least pretend to be concerned.

"It'll be cool," he said. "He wasn't exactly thrilled, but he owes me a favour or two. I've done a lot of overtime in the last few weeks."

That probably explained the tired shadows under his eyes. We headed across the car park to where a gutsy-looking motorbike was parked against the fence.

"Lucky I brought the spare helmet tonight," he said. "I don't always carry it, but I was planning on hitting the town after work. You never know when you might need another helmet."

He didn't exactly wink, but I got his drift. Joe's little brother sounded like a bit of a party animal. No wonder Joe was always trying to match him up with someone. Having found happiness in his second marriage, Joe was like a reformed smoker, full of evangelical zeal. He was so happily married that he wanted everyone else to get married, too. Watching his brother flit from girl to girl must have driven him nuts.

"You might want to braid your hair back out of the way before you put it on—your ponytail will be one big knot by the time we get there otherwise."

Hastily, I plaited my hair, then Lucas helped me get the helmet settled comfortably on my head and adjusted the strap. The bike gave a throaty growl as Lucas kicked it into life, and I threw my leg over the back of it. My seat felt a little precarious, but at least it was more comfortable than sitting astride Cerberus's broad back. Lucas had better know what he was doing. I didn't fancy getting acquainted with the road surface on this trip.

He turned to grin at me. "You all comfy back there?"

I nodded.

"Good. Hang on tight. I wouldn't want to lose you on the way."

I took a firm grip on his leather-clad waist. I wouldn't want to lose me either. It was a three-hour drive to Berkley's Bay, and I couldn't afford any hiccups.

Lucas revved the engine, and we roared out of the car park as if the hounds of hell were on our tail. I couldn't help a squeak of surprise as we leaned into the first curve, and I took a much tighter grip on Lucas's waist, practically plastering myself against his back. I felt him chuckle, though I couldn't hear anything over the noise of the bike and the wind rushing past us.

Maybe it wouldn't take three hours to get to Berkley's Bay after all.

13

Lucas pulled into the curb right outside the bookshop. It felt good to be home again, even if we weren't staying long. The door up to my apartment was right in front of us. If only I had time to stop for a shower. With a groan, I released my death grip on Lucas's waist as he cut the engine. I eased my helmet off as its throaty roar died away. It was going to take a bit longer to unclench my thigh muscles, though.

"Home sweet home," Lucas said, removing his own helmet. "So, what was the rush? What was so important that you needed to get to Berkley's Bay at—" he glanced at his watch "—ten minutes after midnight? You going to tell me that long story now?"

I handed him the helmet and stared across the street at the pub. Someone came out as I watched, followed by the faintest wisp of music and just a hint of light. Looked like the door protocol was fully functioning again. This pub was famous in the area for being owned by a vampire, and there was a second set of doors just inside the first to make sure that no daylight entered to put its owner at risk. Nor were there any windows.

"Let's go in." I started across the street and Lucas laughed.

"I told you," he said. "I would have bought you a drink back at Roxy's. You didn't have to drag me all the way down here just to go to the pub."

I smiled at him over my shoulder. "I'd tell you what's going on, but then I'd have to kill you."

"Ah. Just as I suspected—you're a secret agent. I always wanted to meet one of those." He really was very good-natured. He must be tired after the long ride, but he didn't complain at being kept in the dark.

"Maybe we'll see your brother inside." I pushed open the outer door and motioned him in.

Lucas laughed. "In the pub at this hour, with a newborn baby at home? I reckon Holly would have his balls."

I hadn't considered that, but he was probably right. Holly was small but fierce. He made to open the inner door and I stopped him. "Make sure the outside door's shut properly first."

"What's with the two doors?" he asked.

"The publican's a vampire. He's got all the regulars

trained—only one set of doors to be open at a time. Keeps the light out and the vampire happy."

"Keeping vampires happy is always a good option," he said.

"You can say that again." Alberto was the only vampire I had ever known, which I guess wasn't really a fair sampling of the vampire population, since he wasn't, in fact, a vampire at all. Not that I could explain all that to Lucas.

Inside, the pub was more than half deserted. Only a few of the diehard regulars still clustered at the tables underneath the big wall-mounted TV, which was playing some football game. There was always a game of football somewhere in the world, and a great many of them were followed by the residents of Berkley's Bay. Shifters got surprisingly excited about human sporting competitions. Maybe all that running appealed to the predator in them. Needless to say, they weren't allowed to participate, due to their superior strength and speed, though there was at least one all-shifter comp that I knew of. Joe watched it religiously.

Lucas's gaze drifted in the direction of the TV. "We going to be here long?" he asked, his attention more than half on the game already.

"Not sure," I said. "I need to ask some questions. Why don't you sit down and I'll grab you a drink while you wait? You want a beer, or something stronger?"

"Beer's fine, thanks."

"Coming right up."

I headed over to the bar. Jeremy was behind it tonight, though he didn't have much to do. Most of the regulars were engrossed in the game, and he was stacking a tray of clean glasses from the kitchen back into the racks.

"A beer for my friend." I nodded in Lucas's direction. "And one for me."

"Sure thing. Haven't seen you around for a while. You been on holidays?"

"Kind of. I didn't expect to see you here—don't you normally work the day shift? Where's Alberto?" It would have been too easy to find Alberto here, polishing glasses on the other side of the bar, but I'd still hoped for a miracle. It was surprising how quickly I'd come to depend on the fake vampire. Having the Lord of the Underworld at your back was a good feeling.

Jeremy called Lisa, who was sweeping at the other end of the bar, to deliver Lucas's beer to him, then began pouring one for me. He didn't answer until he had pushed the foaming glass across the bar toward me.

He leaned closer and dropped his voice confidentially. "I wish I knew. I've been pulling double shifts—came in tonight to give Lisa a hand. Frankly, I'm worried. No one's seen him in days."

I took an appreciative sip of my beer. God, but that felt

good. I hadn't realised how thirsty I was. The whole world might be going to shit, but a girl still had to eat and drink, right? I drained the whole thing and set it back on the bar with a sigh of relief. "Have you checked the cellar?"

He looked horrified. "You can't be serious. Me—go down there?" His gaze slid toward the door marked *Private* and he shuddered. "Not a chance."

"But if something's happened to him—"

He started shaking his head before I'd even finished speaking. "If something's happened to him, it didn't happen in the cellar. He told Lisa on Tuesday night that he had to meet someone, but he never came back."

"Maybe he sneaked in." There were all sorts of rumours about vampires' abilities to pass undetected, and even more about Alberto than any other vampires. Hades hadn't always been careful enough in his roleplaying. "He could be hurt. Someone should go down there to check."

He snorted. "You volunteering?"

"Sure." That gave me a plausible reason for trespassing on the vampire's private domain.

"Well, you're braver than I am, that's for sure. Wild horses wouldn't get me down there. But I can't let you do it. Mr Alinari's instructions are very clear: no one but him is to pass through that door."

Damn. Why did Jeremy have to be so law-abiding? Harry would have let me do it for sure. In fact, he would have been right beside me, egging me on. But Harry wasn't working tonight, and I couldn't afford to wait until the morning.

"But he might need help."

Jeremy looked unconvinced. "He's a vampire. What could possibly hurt him? No, I'm afraid he's either stayed out too late and got fried by the sun, or someone's staked him, though I don't know anyone around here who'd do a thing like that."

I contemplated the door. It was solid timber, not one of those hollow jobs that were usually used for interior doors. I'd heard it slam shut enough times to tell. As far as I knew, there was only one key, and Alberto usually wore that on a chain around his neck. Even if I could persuade Jeremy to let me, getting through would be a challenge.

"You want another drink?" Jeremy asked.

"Not right now, thanks." I wandered over and sat down next to Lucas instead.

He smiled at me. "Secret agent business all done?"

I sighed. "Sadly, no. Do you reckon Joe's got an axe?"

He blinked in surprise. "I doubt it. But Dad would, for sure." Lucas and Joe's father was the alpha of the local werewolf pack. He lived just down the road from Jake's magnificent clifftop mansion. "What do you need an axe for? You're not planning to murder someone, are you?"

I slumped down in the chair, tapping my fingers on the

table top. "Not right now." What I needed was a diversion. Something to keep Jeremy occupied long enough for me to get through that door. Explanations could come later. It was always easier to ask forgiveness than permission. "Could we go get that axe now?"

"Seriously?" He frowned, looking more like Joe than ever. "I'm always happy to help a friend of Joe's, but I have to ask—what's the axe for? Am I going to spend the rest of the night in jail?"

I blew out a sigh. The urge to be up, to be moving, was making me twitchy. As close as I could figure it, it was nearly five hours since Jake had made his bargain with Styx, which meant he only had seven hours left. I clasped my hands in my lap to stop my fingers from fidgeting. "Are you a religious man, Lucas?"

He looked surprised by the turn in the conversation. "Depends what you mean by religious, I suppose. I observe the festivals, make an offering at the shrine a couple of times a year, but I'm not much for praying to the gods about every little thing, so if that's what you mean by religious, I guess I'm not." He shrugged his broad shoulders. "I think you'll find that most shifters are the same."

I nodded. Someone could probably write a book on the reasons for that, but it tied in with what I knew of shifters. Most of them seemed too self-reliant to lean much on a belief in higher powers. "What would you say if I told you the gods were real?"

"Define 'real'."

"As in, flesh and blood, walking around here on Earth just like you and me."

He sipped at his beer, dark eyes watching me over the rim of his glass. "I'd probably wonder what you were trying to sell me."

I snorted. "Not so long ago, I would have had the same reaction as you. But it turns out they're as real as we are, and I've managed to get mixed up in their affairs. Quite frankly, I'm in way over my head and people are depending on me." People like Syl and Apollo, whose dilemma had started this whole quest, and Jake, of course, whose very life depended on me getting him back to the underworld before time ran out. And there was still so much to do before then. And even Hades was in some kind of trouble. Where had he gone, and why hadn't he returned?

"Suppose I believed you," Lucas said. "That still doesn't explain why we need an axe. And don't tell me again that it's a long story."

"Well, it is," I said, trying not to sound too defensive, "but the relevant part is that I need to get through that door." I jerked my head at the door marked *Private*. "My friend's life depends on it and I don't have time to mess around."

Lucas eyed the door, sizing it up. "Shouldn't need an axe. A couple of good kicks, maybe a shoulder charge if it's really solid, and *bang*—you're in business."

"Maybe you missed it, but I'm not built like one of those guys." I indicated the front row forwards currently mowing down everything in their path on the TV.

He smiled, showing the wolf below the surface. "Maybe not, but I am."

I returned his rather feral grin with one of my own. "Are you volunteering?"

He shrugged, rolling those massive shoulders. "Just tell me I don't have to do it in front of all these guys." It was possible they wouldn't even notice, too engrossed in the football game, but it seemed a poor thank you for his help to get him into trouble the moment he arrived in town.

I looked around the room. Eleven guys watching the football. Jeremy behind the bar. Lisa somewhere in the kitchen. From the clattering, it sounded like she was unpacking the dishwasher.

"How's your night vision?"

"Do you really have to ask? I'm a werewolf."

I rose from my seat. "I'll be back in a minute. Hit the door as soon as the lights go out."

He shook his head, but it was a *I can't believe I'm doing this* kind of shake, not a refusal. He was still smiling as I headed out into the night, searching the darkness with my mind's eye.

A narrow alley ran behind the pub. My boots rang on the concrete pavement as I headed that way. There were already several rats in the alley, drawn by the delights contained in the various garbage bins there. I called more to me as I walked. By the time I arrived at the back door of the pub, I had a dozen little friends waiting to greet me.

It was dark in the alley, but there were plenty of cats within range, though fortunately none near enough to frighten away my new friends. It was a moment's work to boost my night vision by linking with a nearby tabby. The light over the back door was only switched on when the kitchen staff came in and out, so all was dark. There was no one around to see me as I eased the door open, flooding the alley with light from the hallway inside. The rats' eyes shone eerily in the sudden glow.

I stepped inside, the rats at my heels, squeaking and scampering. I sent them down the passage and into the kitchen proper, while I opened the fuse box on the wall inside the door. I knew they had arrived at their target when I heard Lisa scream. A second later, the sound of breaking glass echoed down the passageway as Lisa dropped a tray of glasses. Through a rat's eyes, I saw her flee for the door that separated the kitchen from the bar, trailing rats and still screaming at the top of her lungs. I flipped the circuit breaker, plunging the whole building into darkness, and followed the rats.

I burst into the main bar just a moment behind Lisa. In those few seconds, the place had descended into pandemonium. Male voices shouted in alarm and surprise, the rats squealed and squeaked, and over it all, Lisa continued to scream. With all that going on, the noise of something heavy hurling itself against a door would hardly even have registered, except that I was listening for it.

I hurried towards that sound, grateful for the construction of the vampire's pub which didn't let in even the faintest glimpse of light from outside. If there were any shifters among the group that had been watching TV, the rats were causing enough of a diversion that their superior night vision wasn't turned our way. In a moment, someone would think to throw open the doors so they could all stop stumbling around in the dark, but until then, Lucas's activities were nicely hidden.

I arrived just as the door gave way and Lucas stumbled forward into the dark opening, barely keeping his feet. "Thanks." I put a hand on his shoulder. "You'd better get out of here now."

"You sure?" He sounded disappointed. "You never know when some extra muscle might come in handy."

"I can take it from here." It was bad enough that I'd told him as much as I had; I didn't need to drag him all the way to the underworld, too. Besides, I had no way of knowing if the ability Jake and I had to move between the worlds extended to anyone else. It might have been a courtesy Hades had only extended to us and Syl. The last thing I wanted was to drag Joe's brother into Hell and not be able to get him out again. "You go see that beautiful niece of yours and tell her Lexi says hi."

Still he hesitated in the doorway. "What are you going to do down there?"

"Better if you don't know. Now move it before someone gets the lights back on. I'll catch up with you later." *Fingers crossed.*

Reluctantly, he stepped out of the way and I shut the door in his face. One of the hinges had loosened, so I had to jiggle and shove to get the door properly closed, but I managed it. No one should even notice that it had been opened.

I took a step into the darkness. A line of light appeared under the door behind me. Someone had thought to check the fuse box. In the dim light, I could just make out a narrow staircase leading down. I felt my way down it carefully, one hand on the wall, easing my numb left foot gently onto each step. I couldn't afford to slip and break a bone, and it was pitch black by the time I got to the bottom.

At the bottom of the steps, I groped around on the wall until I found a light switch and flicked it on, revealing walls draped in great swathes of red velvet, and a grand black coffin on a plinth in the middle of the room. I almost laughed out loud. Hades had certainly enjoyed his little charade. The coffin lid stood open, showing red silk lining and the lack of any occupant.

Anyone who got this far probably would look no further, since the room was empty apart from the coffin, but I poked around behind the drapes until I found a set of smooth steel doors. At last—the elevator! I pressed the single button on the wall and the doors slid open soundlessly, revealing an interior lined with mirrored tiles.

Zeus's balls—I was filthy. It was a wonder Jeremy hadn't thrown me out. I looked like I'd been in a mud-wrestling match and lost.

I stepped inside. There were only two buttons on the panel by the door—an arrow pointing up and one pointing down, with nothing marked beside them. Fortunately, Jake had already told me that these were just for show. I rapped on the mirrored walls until I found a tile that gave off a hollower sound than the others. It took me a few moments to figure out how to open it but, eventually, I discovered a tiny indent on one side of the tile. When I got the tip of my finger into the crack, the whole tile slid aside, revealing the real lift controls. I pressed the down button and the doors slid shut.

As the elevator began to move, I sagged against the wall and contemplated my bedraggled reflection, weak with relief. I was going to Hell.

14

The elevator pinged and jolted to a stop. The doors opened onto the familiar carpeted hallway of Hades' palace, and I stepped out. I had only a moment to register a joyous barking before I was slammed to the floor by a brick wall. At least, that's what it felt like.

"Cerberus! I can't breathe. Get off me."

BOSSY GIRL BACK! WHERE MASTER? All three heads craned into the elevator, evidently expecting Hades to pop out.

I managed to struggle into a sitting position and used the front of my shirt to wipe off the dog slobber facial he'd given me. "*I'm* back? Where did *you* get to? You just ran off and left us in the middle of nowhere, yelling something about your master. What was all that about?"

He whined, a surprisingly pathetic sound considering the size of the animal it was coming from. *MUCH DANGER. MASTER GONE.*

I stood up and patted his shoulder awkwardly. "Gone? Gone where?"

Three big heads drooped in unison. *DON'T KNOW. LOST HIM.*

"But you guys have a mental connection, right? Like you and me." Only theirs was much stronger. Hades seemed to be able to direct Cerberus when they weren't even in the same world together. I'd nearly turned my brain to mush trying to do that back in Mrs Emery's cellar, and I hadn't been able to influence him at all once he'd hared off after Hades and left us stranded on the plains.

GONE, the big dog repeated mournfully. Did he mean their mental connection was gone as well, or just that Hades was gone? If their connection had been severed, that left only a couple of options, neither of which were good. Either Hades was dead or someone had managed to cut him off from his powers. Maybe there were more of these collars floating around than I'd thought. If someone had managed to get one onto Hades' neck, it would explain both Hades' disappearance and Cerberus's inability to find him.

Damn. Shadow shapers were popping up everywhere. How had they managed to find Hades after all this time? I had an uneasy feeling it might be my fault. Still, there was no use crying about spilt milk now. All I could do was keep going. The sooner we had a key to unlock those collars, the sooner we could start fighting back.

FIND MASTER NOW? Fires burned deep in Cerberus's eyes as he gazed hopefully at me. It was a little disconcerting to be the focus of such intense concentration. His tail wagged ever so slightly, as if he really wanted to put his faith in me, but wasn't sure that he could.

"I'm on it, buddy, I promise." I patted his shoulder reassuringly. "I just have a couple of other loose ends to tidy up first." Apollo probably wouldn't appreciate being called a loose end. The thought of his reaction almost made me smile. "Let's go find Apollo and Syl."

I headed down the corridor, Cerberus trotting at my heels, his hot breath ruffling my hair. Somewhere in the distance, a harp was playing, and I figured that would be a good place to start looking. When Apollo wasn't busy driving his sun chariot, he had a reputation as a pretty mean harpist.

I found them both in one of the palace's many courtyards. Apollo was seated on the low stone wall that surrounded the central fountain, the underworld's fake moonlight playing on his golden hair. The gentle pattering of the fountain formed a liquid counterpoint to the clear beauty of the harp's notes. I paused in the doorway, touched by the music somewhere deep inside. It spoke of loss and longing, and filled me with a melancholy that brought tears to my eyes. Apollo looked as if he were in a trance, his eyes focused on something far beyond the moonlit courtyard. Syl sat on a cushion at his feet, gazing up at his face with a look of such rapt attention that it made me uncomfortable to see it, as if I had intruded on an intensely personal moment. I cleared my throat and the delicate rippling sound of the harp cut off mid-note. Syl looked up, a glad smile spreading across her face as she leapt to her feet.

"Where the hell have you been?" She closed the space between us in three large strides and wrapped me in a bone-crushing hug. "I was so worried about you. How could you just run off like that? Were your fingers broken, that you couldn't even leave me a note?"

"I'm sorry. I didn't mean to be away that long—I thought I'd be back before you woke up."

She shook me a little, not hard, but enough to let me know that she meant it. "Before I woke up? You've been gone two days! And you smell like you've spent the whole time rolling in mud. Don't you ever pull a stunt like that again."

Her hair smelled of jasmine, and she had more colour in her face than last time I'd seen her. She looked more like the old Syl than the pale, withdrawn creature I'd left behind. Was there something in the air here, more than the liquid sounds of the harp? The way she'd been staring at Apollo just now …

He was giving me his usual frown. Intentional or not,

Captain Sunshine always managed to give the impression that he didn't like me. Well, if Syl was going to start mooning over him, the feeling would soon be mutual. His eyes slid to the doorway I'd appeared through then back again, lingering on my face. The frown deepened. "Where's Jake?"

Syl released me and gave me the same frowning look. Disapproval—now in stereo. Excellent. Just what I needed to brighten my already shitty day.

"Jake's been captured," I said. I began pacing as the words tumbled out, filling them in on our adventures. Syl sank down onto the wall next to Apollo, her expression dazed, as the story unfolded. Finally, I had brought them up to date and I pulled the star-metal from my backpack. "This is it. This is what we went to get for you."

I lobbed the metal her way and she caught it reflexively, still with that stunned expression on her face.

Apollo took it from her, turning it over in his hands as he examined it. "Hephaistos said a key made from this would unlock the collars?"

"Yes. Unfortunately, we're now short a metalshaper. Jake said you'd be able to make a key."

He continued to frown at the small bar of metal in his hand. The silence stretched, and my nerves with it. In the back of my mind, that clock kept ticking. How long ago did Styx tell Jake he only had twelve hours to return? I was guessing about five hours had passed, maybe a little more—but it was impossible to be sure. And Jake's life depended on getting it right. I clenched my fists, willing Apollo to give me the answer I needed.

"Of course I can make a key," he said. My whole body went limp with relief, and then he opened his mouth again. "But I'll need to consult with Hephaistos. I don't even know what this key is supposed to look like, how big it is—anything. If I had my power, that wouldn't be a problem, but without my power, I'm just a skilled metalworker. I can't work miracles."

I had to find a seat, too, as my legs threatened to give out. I sank into one of the elegant gilded chairs in the courtyard, staring at him in horror. "But it will take us a day just to get to Hephaistos. We don't have that kind of time. Jake will die."

"What do you expect of me? Without magic, no one can craft a key just like that." He snapped his fingers in illustration. "You have to make a mould, pour the metal, let it cool and harden. I need tools. A furnace." He shook the star-metal at me. "This is just the beginning. What was Jake thinking? And that's assuming there is no magic involved other than the magic inherent in the metal. But if the key needs some kind of spell laid on it in its creation …"

We were screwed. I dropped my face into my hands. Jake was screwed, regardless. Maybe Apollo would be able to make a key, and maybe he wouldn't—but clearly, there'd be no key in time to help Jake.

What *had* Jake been thinking? He must have known this, but he'd sent me back here anyway, knowing it meant his death. *Free Apollo*, he'd said, as if that was the only thing that mattered. Stupid, stupid man. How dared he throw his life away like that?

My thoughts turned to desperate rescue plans. Okay, so Apollo wouldn't be able to smite the traitorous fireshapers for me. I'd just have to come up with some other way to free Jake and get him back to the underworld in time.

Cerberus turned around a couple of times, then flopped to the ground next to my chair. His ear was soft and silky and bigger than my hand. I stroked it, thinking furiously. I could use the Helm to sneak into the Ruby Palace and free Jake …

I paused in my patting and Cerberus looked up, pushing his head meaningfully against my hand. "Can you open a way to Crosston?" I asked him. If I used the elevator to return to the pub, it was three hours' drive to Crosston and then three hours back again. If Jake only had seven hours left I needed to cut that time out of my plan.

He huffed a sigh and dropped his big head to the paving stones again, misery in every drooping line of his body. *NO. ONLY MASTER CAN.*

Damn. Why weren't things ever easy? I'd assumed that

Cerberus had opened his own way up from the underworld when I'd called him to save our bacon in Mrs Emery's cellar, but Hades must have let him through. Hades might even have been able to reason with Styx if he were here.

Yeah, well, no point wishing for what we couldn't have. I'd just have to work with what I did have. Currently that wasn't looking so hot: one grumpy god cut off from his powers, one shifter who couldn't shift, and a thief who was so tired she could barely string two thoughts together, much less come up with a brilliant plan to save the day.

Cerberus nudged me again, nearly shoving me off the chair, and I went back to stroking his velvety ear. Add one massive three-headed hellhound to the tally. Oh, and the Helm of Darkness. If I couldn't use it to free Jake from the fireshapers, maybe I could sneak up on Styx and drown the bitch. That could solve a lot of problems.

I sighed. Except, of course, that she was a water nymph—and besides which, Hades, if we ever managed to find him, might not take kindly to my running around killing his people. I eyed Cerberus. Maybe I could get him to bite her head off, the way he'd done with Mrs Emery's arm.

I stood up. Sitting around here thinking wasn't getting us anywhere, and the delay was making me twitchy. "Let's go."

Apollo and Syl stood up. "Go where?" Apollo asked.

"To see Styx. I need more time."

Apollo gave a hollow laugh. "Styx doesn't give extensions to her deadlines."

"But it's not our fault. I can't produce Jake when he's locked up in another city. If she really wants him, she'll have to be a little understanding."

"Styx doesn't do *understanding*. It's not in her nature."

I glared at him. Was being a negative arsehole in *his* nature or had he just perfected the art over the centuries? I didn't hear him offering any better ideas. "Then we'll just have to hope for Jake's sake that you're wrong."

15

Cerberus gambolled ahead of us through the Fields of Asphodel like a giant three-headed black lamb. He snapped at the occasional soul that drifted past through the misty twilight, the way a normal dog lunges at flies. He seemed as happy as I was to be moving again, convinced that I would somehow do something to find his missing master. His faith was touching, but the weight of expectations rested heavily on my shoulders. Find Hades. Save Jake. Free Apollo and Syl. My to-do list was bursting at the seams.

I stopped to wait for Apollo and Syl. "Get a move on, guys. We haven't got all day here." My left leg tingled and ached. What was the hold up? If I could keep up with Cerberus with a bad leg, why couldn't they? If there were only two of us, I would have asked Cerberus for a ride again, regardless of how much he disliked playing horse, but his back, large as it was, wouldn't fit three.

Obligingly, they lengthened their strides, marching in step as if they were in the army. Weird. I'd have liked to take Syl aside and ask her if something was going on between them, but my friend's possible romantic entanglements would have to wait, even if I thought she needed her head read for getting involved with Apollo, if that was what was happening. I'm sure he played a mean harp, and he was certainly good-looking, but every time we were in the same room together, I always ended up wanting to punch him right in his handsome face.

I tried to make allowances for the very real frustration he must be feeling. He was a god, used to almost unimaginable power. Being unable to access any of it must be infuriating. If he were free, he could shape that damn key faster than I could say "the sun god sucks". But, of course, that was the problem. He wasn't free, and therefore the key remained tantalisingly out of our reach.

He'd insisted on taking the star-metal from me, and still carried it in his hand.

"Maybe Jake wouldn't have been able to create the key anyway," I said, looking for some kind of consolation. "Metalshaping is getting harder and harder for him now that Hephaistos is dead."

"Really?" Syl looked worried. "Do you think there will come a time when metalshapers won't be able to shape at all?"

She was asking me, but Apollo answered. "I'd say that was almost certain. There are several of us who lend our strengths to the fireshapers, but Hephaistos was the only god of metalshaping. He was too jealous of his role to share it."

"So what then? Metalshaping just dies out?" I shook my head. That seemed crazy. "Can't you take over?"

"Unfortunately, it doesn't work like that. Zeus would have to create a new god for the role."

"He's created new gods before. So that shouldn't be a problem, then."

"It's not that easy, even for Zeus. He can't just elevate anyone. It would have to be someone with a special talent already. Take you, for instance." He ran an assessing eye over me, his expression making it pretty clear that he didn't find much potential there. "He could probably turn you into a god of thieves, although Hermes might have something to say to that. But he could no more make you a goddess of metalshaping than a goddess of wisdom. You just don't have the talent."

Syl gave him a sharp look. Maybe she wasn't as taken with him as I'd feared. "Lexi would make a great goddess of wisdom. She's smart and resourceful."

I grinned at Syl. *Yeah, you tell him.* She was the most loyal friend I'd ever had.

Apollo made an impatient noise. "Anyway, it makes no

difference. Zeus is missing, too, and even if he were here, it's very unlikely he would create a new god or goddess."

"Even to save metalshaping?" Syl looked incredulous.

"We gods are jealous of our power, and none more so than Zeus. There are perhaps a hundred minor godlings, but only twelve Olympians. There's a reason for that, you know. It's something great to be one of twelve. No one wants to be one of twelve hundred."

"Yeah," I said, "but now your exclusive little club is down to eleven members."

"Well, if we ever find him, you can take it up with Zeus."

Smug bastard. Were all the gods as infuriatingly self-satisfied? I clenched my fists and reminded myself that Hades had never made me want to punch him in the face.

Besides, maddening as it was, I had to admit he had a point. There was nothing we could do about it without the father of the gods, so there was no point wasting any further brainpower on it. Was Jake right, and I just liked arguing with people? Thinking of Jake and his stupid self-sacrifice made me miserable. I was going to slap him silly once I'd saved him. How could he do a thing like that? Didn't he care about me? About *us*? There I was, thinking we had a great thing going, and all *he* was thinking about was Apollo.

I fell silent for the rest of the walk across the field, hardly noticing as the shadows of fading souls slipped past among the mists. Occasionally, Cerberus's deep bark floated back to us from where he ranged ahead, but I was lost in thought, racking my brains for a way to free Jake in time. I had only just begun to wonder how much further it was when the massive laughing clown gate loomed out of the swirling shadows. It stood open and Cerberus waited beneath the huge teeth, his tail wagging encouragingly. Just down the slope on the other side of the gate was the River Styx and the wharf where Charon's ferry delivered new souls to the afterlife.

The ferry was not in evidence as we passed through the gate and headed down to the wharf. In all the myths I'd heard, the gate was meant to be closed tight and guarded by Cerberus, to ensure that none of the souls escaped back to the real world. The fact that the gate now stood open and Cerberus appeared to be free to do whatever the hell he liked suggested to me that Hades had modified his defences over the centuries. I'd never seen a soul leave through these gates once it had entered, so whatever the new system was, it was clearly working.

I walked out onto the wharf, my boots loud against the wooden planks. "Styx," I called. "Are you there?"

The mist drifted and writhed into new shapes at the sound of my voice, but nothing else stirred. There was no sign of the dark-haired nymph, and I felt like a bit of an idiot standing there shouting into the aether.

"She could be anywhere," Apollo said. "This river runs through the whole underworld."

Gosh, really? Thank goodness he was here to point out the obvious. "Do you have any better idea of how to summon her, then?" Really, that face. So punchable.

"None whatsoever."

Syl came to stand at my side. "Maybe you have to be in the water. If it's her river, she ought to be aware of everything that happens in it."

"Maybe." At least Syl was trying to be helpful, unlike Captain Obvious. "But I don't fancy getting in there. Have you seen the things that live in this river?"

There was no sign now of the writhing bodies and eternally tormented screaming faces, but I hadn't forgotten them. They'd probably still be featuring in my nightmares forty years from now, assuming I lived that long.

Maybe putting my hand in the water would be enough, though even that prospect made me jumpy as hell. "Styx! Styx, are you there?"

The mist deadened my voice, swallowing it. I sighed. It was worth a try. I pulled my knife and handed it to Syl, hilt first. "If something grabs me, stab it."

She nodded, eyes wide, and crouched at my side as I knelt down, leaning over the dark water. I managed— barely—not to flinch as I dunked my hand in the river. Nothing reached out to pull me in. Nothing bit my hand off, nor even nibbled on a finger. Still, I couldn't shake the feeling that this could all go pear-shaped horribly fast. "Styx! Where are you? We need to talk."

Silence was my only reply. I wriggled my fingers, swirling my hand through the black river. Something brushed against my fingers and I leapt back with a start.

Syl jumped, too, letting out a squawk of surprise. "Are you all right?"

"I'm fine." I felt a little ashamed of my nerves. Was I a cat to be so scared of the water? "I thought I felt something, that's all."

"Did someone call my name?" a new voice asked, and we both jumped again. It was Styx, of course, and my relief at seeing her was tempered by my annoyance at the way she'd sneaked up on us. I could tell from the smirk on her face that she'd done it on purpose. "Who's your friend? What have you done with that other gorgeous creature you were travelling with?"

I stood up and dragged Syl back a few steps, keen to have a respectable distance between her and us. "This is Syl, and he's Apollo."

She gave me a withering look. "I know who Apollo is, thank you." She nodded at Apollo, and he inclined his head in return. "I didn't expect to see you back here so early. You still have a handful of hours before your time runs out. Where is the fireshaper?"

"That's what I need to talk to you about." Her brows drew together and I hurried on. "He's been taken captive by some other fireshapers. It's going to take me a little while to free him. I need an extension on that deadline."

"Did I not do as you asked?"

"Yes, but—"

"Did I not carry you across my river when you asked it?" The water around her stirred, the surface becoming choppy with small waves. Her eyes were full of storms. "I kept my side of the bargain, and now you come to me seeking to renege on yours." The waves reached a little higher, slapping at the wooden pillars of the wharf. Syl took a wary step back.

"We'll keep your bargain." I eyed the rising water with concern. I wouldn't put it past her to sweep us all into the river in a snit. "I just need a little more time. Please."

"Ah. There's that magic word." She glared at me, eyes still stormy. "And yet I find I am completely unmoved. We had a bargain. No ifs, buts, or maybes. I kept my side of the deal, now you must keep yours."

Infuriating woman! Didn't she understand? "Jake isn't trying to skip out on his side of the deal. If you just give us a little more time to free him, he'll be back here. If you kill him just because he didn't come back at the exact moment you wanted, how does that benefit anyone? You don't get what you want, and neither do we."

Black water swirled around her milk-white shoulders, showing glimpses of the tormented souls that seemed the essence of the river. I tried very hard to keep my eyes on her face, repelled by that water. Her face settled into a sneer. "You can rant and argue all you want, but it doesn't change anything. From the moment I set my mark on him, there was no turning back. If he doesn't return at the appointed hour, he will die, and there is nothing you nor I can do to stop it. So I suggest you stop whining and get on with rescuing him." She sank down until the water closed over her head without a ripple.

I stared at the spot where she'd disappeared, rage filling my heart. If the bitch hadn't kissed him in the first place, there wouldn't be a problem. I spun on my heel and stalked back along the wharf to the shore where Apollo waited. I couldn't even look at his face—I knew what I'd see there. And if the words "I told you so" came out of his mouth, I was definitely giving in to my impulses and punching him.

"What now?" Syl said.

I turned back to her. Wordlessly, she held out my knife, and I took it, slamming it back into its sheath. Good question. I was all out of ideas.

Across the water, the mist began to boil. Was Styx returning? Had she changed her mind? Syl turned to follow the direction of my gaze.

Cerberus barked and trotted out onto the wharf, his

nails clicking on the hard wood. Out of the mists a shape appeared—not Styx; it was much too big for that.

Charon's ferry had arrived.

I stood watching as a line snaked out from the side of the ferry and wrapped around a bollard all by itself. This ferryman had no need of a deckhand. The ferry bumped to a gentle stop against the wharf and the gangway extended from the side. Grey figures began to file down in orderly lines. Cerberus watched them intently, alert for any attempt by the new souls to break away from the pack or escape their fate. I contemplated the ferry, the germ of an idea taking root in my mind.

"What are we going to do?" Syl asked as the last of the newly dead filed past and began their trek up the slope to the gate.

"Do you know Charon at all?" I asked Apollo over my shoulder.

He moved up to stand by my side. "I've met him once or twice. Seems pleasant enough. Why?"

"Do you think he'd let us borrow his ferry for a little while?"

Two sets of eyes stared at me in astonishment. "Borrow his ferry?" Apollo repeated. "Whatever for?"

I gazed down the river, though I couldn't see very far through the all-pervading mist. If we rode its tormented waters far enough, eventually we would arrive at the place where it met the Phlegethon, where Styx had built her revolting bridge of body parts. Right near the entrance to Tartarus.

"I think I know someone who might help us, but we don't have time to get there cross-country." Not if we had to go on foot, and Cerberus couldn't carry us all. Even if he could, it might still take too long. "But the river would deliver us right to his door."

"If you mean Hephaistos, forget it," Apollo said impatiently. "He can't work a physical object like the star-metal now he's dead."

"Thank you, Captain Obvious. Not Hephaistos. Someone else. Will Charon take us there if you ask him?"

"The living aren't allowed on the ferry. I don't think—"

Syl laid a hand on his arm. "Please, Apollo. Just ask him. What harm can it do?"

Apollo's face softened as he looked down at her. "All right. I'll ask him. You wait here."

"Let me mind that for you while you do," I said, nodding at the bar of star-metal he still held. He rolled his eyes, but surrendered the precious bar into my care.

Then he stalked along the wharf and up the gangway, disapproval in every stiff line of his body. I was starting to wonder about all the myths that painted him as this wild, fun-loving guy. Either he'd changed a lot or the myth writers were telling a lot of porkies.

Once he'd disappeared inside, I caught at Syl's arm. "Come on."

"But he said to wait here!"

"So? You know that Charon's going to say no. We don't have much time." Normally, the ferry cast off as soon as the last passengers were unloaded. I wasn't risking getting left behind.

Once we were safely up the gangway, Cerberus padding along behind us, I took off my backpack and shoved it at her. "Hold this."

"What are you doing?"

"Saving Jake." I pulled the Helm of Darkness from my pack and jammed it onto my head. Syl's eyes went wide as I disappeared.

I left her there, clutching my backpack, and set off to find Apollo and the ferryman, the bar of star-metal held firmly in my right hand. I moved quietly, following the sound of voices—Apollo's annoying velvet tones, and the deeper rumble of another man's voice. I'd never actually seen Charon, though I'd watched the ferry come in a number of times since I'd been in the underworld.

The interior of the ferry was filled with rows of seating, just like a commuter ferry in the real world. Maybe the familiarity was meant to calm the newly dead on their way to the afterlife. The main difference was the lack of graffiti on the walls. A staircase in the middle led up to the top deck.

I took the stairs and moved toward the bow, still following the voices. The bridge was at the front of the ferry, with windows all around giving the helmsman a view of the mist and the dark river. It was separated from the passenger section by a sliding door which stood open at the moment. That was good—Charon was sure to get suspicious if the door to the bridge started to open of its own accord. Inside, Apollo was smiling at a thin, bearded man whose long hair straggled down past his shoulders. The thin man had one hand resting possessively on the ship's wheel, and the other planted firmly on his hip.

"Absolutely not," he said. "My ferry does not divert from its course."

"I assure you, Charon, Hades would give his full approval if he were here." Apollo kept smiling the whole time, an almost irresistible, wheedling kind of smile that made me want to give him whatever he was asking for—and he wasn't even asking me. I had to admit, the smile made a huge difference to his normally grumpy face. Maybe I could see the attraction after all. It was just that he'd never smiled at me that way.

Charon, unfortunately, didn't seem to have any trouble resisting the sun god's charms. "But Hades is *not* here, is he? And I can't abandon my duty at the whim of every god who happens by."

Judging by the frustration on Apollo's face, he was out of arguments. Looked like it was my turn. I slipped into the small room with them and hit Charon on the back of his head with the bar of star-metal.

He crumpled to the floor in a most satisfying way.

Apollo leapt out of the way, confusion on his face. I removed the Helm of Darkness and the confusion cleared. "What in the name of Hades are you doing running around with the Helm? He'll skin you alive if he ever finds out."

"So don't tell him." I stuck my head out the door and called for Syl.

Apollo shook his head, staring down at the felled ferryman. "Did you have to hit him so hard?"

"No, of course not." I knelt down to check Charon's pulse. It was still strong, thank goodness. He'd only have a headache to show for this little adventure. "Only if we didn't want to take the ferry."

Syl appeared, breathing hard, and gazed down at Charon. "Is he dead?"

"No thanks to your friend here if he was," Apollo snapped. "Is she always this …"

"Unpredictable? Violent? Resourceful?" Syl grinned at me. "Yes. Yes, she is."

I looked up at Apollo, enjoying his outrage. Clearly, he thought plebs like me had no business going around bopping divinities on the head. It didn't fit with his worldview at all. "So, what do you reckon?" I asked Syl. "Tie him up or just chuck him overboard?"

She nearly choked, but quickly recovered herself and pretended to consider it.

"You can't throw him overboard!" Apollo roared. "He is Charon the Ferryman, son of Nyx, the Goddess of the Night!"

"I guess you'd better tie him up, then."

And that was how the great god Apollo came to be trussing Charon the Ferryman like a chicken being prepared for roasting while I eyed the control panel of the fabled ferry of the dead and hoped like hell I could back it away from the wharf without taking out the whole structure.

"Any last words?" I muttered to Syl as the deck beneath me began to vibrate with the throbbing of the great engines. She seemed in a much better mood, even humming to herself as she stood at my side, watching the grey world swing past outside as the ferry began its ponderous turn. Must have been the prospect of finally getting her collar off that made her so chirpy.

"You're doing great," she said. "Full speed ahead, and watch out for pirates."

I snorted. Where we were going, pirates would be the least of our troubles.

16

Gradually, my fingers unclenched their death grip on the ship's wheel as the ferry moved down the black river. Syl was right—I had this. I could drive a car, and this was no different. Easier, in fact. All I had to do was point the bow in the direction I wanted to go.

Syl stood beside me, scanning the mists outside. Apollo had carried Charon into the main passenger area and laid him out across a row of seats to make him more comfortable. Or at least as comfortable as anyone can be whose hands and feet are securely tied with one of their own ropes. Charon was not going to be a happy camper when he woke up, but that would be Apollo's problem. I had enough of my own already.

Right on cue, one of them reared its ugly head.

Syl stiffened beside me. "What the hell is that?"

A wall of water had risen in front of the ferry, and

though the engines were still working, we weren't moving. A figure appeared at the top of the wall, balanced on the pulsing slope of water as if it was solid ground. It was Styx, of course. She had been a pain in my backside since I'd met her. Why should now be any different?

"Hold this." I shoved Syl in the direction of the ship's wheel, and stomped outside onto the open deck. "What are you doing, Styx? Get out of the way." I had to shout to be heard over the noise of the water, as the wave constantly renewed itself while other parts of it succumbed to the lure of gravity.

She showed those pointy teeth in a vicious smile when she saw me. "I thought it was you. What have you done with Charon?"

"What makes you think I've done anything with Charon?"

"Because Charon has been ferrying the dead across my river here since before history began and, in all that time, he has never once diverted from the normal course. You can't take this ferry. How will the dead find their way to the afterlife without it?"

"The dead might just have to take a chill pill and wait a little while. What does it matter? They're dead, for God's sake. Where else are they going to go? Charon can get back to business as soon as we finish our errand."

"I forbid it."

"Dammit, Styx! Do you want Jake or not? I can't get him for you unless I borrow this ferry."

"My oath to Lord Hades—"

"Has nothing to do with it," a new voice cut in. Apollo stalked out onto the deck, favouring Styx with the glare he usually reserved for me. "You swore to guard the borders and facilitate the passage of souls across the river. Nothing more."

She grinned in triumph. "Exactly. And how are those souls meant to cross the river without the ferry? You cannot take it."

Apollo drew himself up to his full height. Even without access to his power, he cut a pretty impressive figure. "I require the use of this ferry for the next several hours, after which I shall see it is returned to Charon's care. Souls are only brought across the river once the ferry has a full load. Since it has just made a trip, it won't be needed again until I'm finished with it, so its absence will make no difference. Now let us pass, or you will stand in breach of your own oath to Jacob Steele."

She frowned, a sudden wind blowing her hair back from her face and whipping the water beneath her into a dark froth. "How so?"

"You made a deal with him, and he agreed that the punishment would be death if he failed to keep his end of the bargain. If you now thwart him from keeping his promise, you have effectively murdered him. And everyone will know that the word of Styx is no longer to be trusted."

Ooh, low blow. Styx's whole reputation was built on the "my word is my bond" thing. She couldn't afford to let a story like that get around.

There was a long silence while Styx digested this. "I bow to my Lord Apollo's will," she said at last. If looks could kill, Apollo would have dropped dead on the spot. I didn't care about Styx's hurt feelings. She'd just have to suck it up. Not even a goddess always got her way.

The wave subsided, taking Styx with it. In a moment, the river was as flat as a mill pond, albeit the darkest, most foreboding mill pond in existence.

I grinned at Apollo. "I always thought you'd come in handy for something if we kept you long enough."

He rolled his eyes and stalked back inside. I followed as the ferry began to move once more.

"Nice job," Syl said as we came back onto the bridge. "Do you want to take the wheel again?"

I waved a hand at her. "You can have it. I might try to grab a nap before we arrive." It felt like years since I'd slept. This saving people thing really took it out of you.

"Where exactly are we going?" Apollo asked.

"We're heading for the point where the Styx meets the Phlegethon." I glanced at Syl. "You'll know it when you see it. It's a river made of fire."

Her eyes widened. "We don't have to sail on it, do we?"

If any ship had a chance to sail the River of Fire and survive, Charon's was probably it. Fortunately, we didn't have to risk it. "No, we won't get too close. We'll be disembarking there."

Apollo's gaze went vague, as if he was mentally reviewing a map of the underworld. I could tell the instant he realised where we were going, by the expression of horror that came over his face. "Tartarus? You're taking us to Tartarus?"

"I'm afraid so."

"May I ask why?" His tone was frosty.

"Because we need a master smith. Someone with metalshaping powers, who can whip up the perfect key for us before we run out of time."

"No," Apollo said, folding his arms across his chest. "You can't."

Syl glanced uneasily from me to Apollo and back again. "She can't what? Who are you talking about?"

I ignored her for a moment, trying to stare Apollo down. There was no way I was losing this argument. It was the only chance Jake had. "He was Hephaistos's assistant for centuries. He's probably the greatest living smith in the world." In either world—the underworld or the real one.

"No, absolutely not." Apollo shook his head decisively. "I forbid it."

"Then I'll shove you overboard and you and Styx can

forbid each other things until the cows come home. But I'm breaking him out of there. It's the only way."

"Breaking who out?" Syl asked.

"She's talking about Brontes," Apollo growled, never taking his eyes from me. "One of the cyclopes, thrown into Tartarus by Zeus. Never to be released," he added pointedly.

"Well, as you said yourself, Zeus isn't here anymore. We have to work with what we've been given."

"He won't help you anyway," Apollo said. "The cyclopes all hate me. He'd probably be thrilled to hear I've lost my powers."

"Then I won't tell him it's for you. Why does he hate you, anyway?"

"It's a long story," Apollo growled. Ha. I'd used that line myself on Lucas just recently. It usually meant the speaker had been involved in some dodgy stuff and didn't want to incriminate themselves.

"Fine. Keep your secrets." It hardly surprised me to hear that someone hated Apollo, but I couldn't see a better way. Someone had to make that key, and there were no other metalshapers in reach. "Do you want that collar off or not?"

Apollo made a noise of frustration and flounced out.

"Are you sure about this?" Syl asked. "You're not just jumping in without thinking it through because you're worried about Jake?"

"You think we should sacrifice Jake because Apollo *might* be able to make a key to get the collars off eventually? Are you willing to wait around, just keeping your fingers crossed it will all work out? Or would you rather we took action?"

"No need to get all fired up at me. It sounds like a big risk, that's all. I want to be sure there's no other way."

"I think the biggest risk is to do nothing. The gods haven't been winning too many rounds lately. If they're not careful, the shadow shapers will land a knockout blow while they're stuffing around waiting for someone to save them."

She sighed. "Fine, whatever. I suppose since we've already stolen the ferry there's not much point turning back now. But *you* get to explain it all to Hades."

❦

A hand on my shoulder shook me awake. Syl was leaning over me. "We're here. Nap time is over."

Already? Surely I'd only closed my eyes a moment ago? I struggled upright, rubbing my back where the hard ridges of the row of plastic seats had stuck into it. "What time is it?"

Syl pretended to consult her bare wrist. "I make it a hair past a freckle." She gave me an exasperated look. "Even if I had a watch, it wouldn't work down here, but I reckon you were asleep for two or three hours."

Two or three hours! I forced down the panic that threatened to rise into my throat. It was a damn sight quicker than the journey over land had been, but I was ever conscious of Jake's dwindling time. If Syl was right, he only had a couple left now. I glanced out the window of the ferry, but the level of light outside told me nothing, as this part of the underworld existed in a permanent twilight. There was no time to waste, however. I rubbed the sleep from my eyes and headed for the bridge with my backpack.

Apollo turned as I entered. "Good. You're awake. The harpies are massing. They'll try to stop us leaving the ferry. What's the plan?"

The ferry had come to a stop beside the riverbank. The confluence with the Phlegethon lay ahead, the orange glow of the River of Fire giving the whole scene an eerie look. Overhead, harpies circled, and several had landed on the rocky ground between the ferry and the yawning red-lit cave that led down to Tartarus. They glared suspiciously in the direction of the ferry.

"At least they haven't started throwing rocks at us," I said.

"I'm sure they recognise the ferry," Apollo said. "They were once my sister's followers, so they will know me, but I doubt that will hold much sway over them. They belong to Hades now."

"That's all right. I have this, remember?" I pulled the

Helm of Darkness from my backpack and settled it on my head. "Run out the gangway."

Syl pressed a button on the console. "Good luck."

I went downstairs and headed back through the main cabin, with both Syl and Apollo trailing me. Outside on the open deck, the smell of harpy was strong. If any of the winged horrors had bathed in the last millennium, I'd eat my own Baseball Cap of Supreme Sneakiness. I nearly gagged on the stench of rotting meat that clung to them like flies to a corpse.

Three harpies landed on the gangway, effectively blocking it. They fluffed their black feathers and spread their wings menacingly as Apollo and Syl stepped outside to meet them. I moved to one side so as not to get trampled.

"Son of Zeus," one said, stepping forward. "What are you doing here?"

"I've come to inspect the prison," Apollo said.

"Our master told us nothing of this." Suspicion was in every haughty line of the harpy's face. "Where are his orders?"

Apollo tapped his forehead. "In here."

"Not good enough. No one is allowed into Tartarus without written permission from Lord Hades." She cackled. "Unless, of course, you wish to become a resident."

Apollo gave her that regal sneer of his. "I am a god. How dare you defy me?"

"I would defy Zeus the father himself," she said, rattling her feathers as her companions hissed their displeasure. Looking closer, I discovered what made the rattling sound—the long feathers of her wings were tipped with steel that gleamed razor sharp in the orange light. "No one may pass without a decree from Lord Hades."

Cerberus, I called silently. There was no way I could sneak past the bird women. That would be a good way to get myself sliced to ribbons, invisible or not.

Cerberus emerged from the depths of the ferry. He began to growl as soon as he saw the harpies, the hackles on the back of his necks rising.

Get 'em, boy!

Cerberus didn't need to be told twice. He leapt forward with a deep bark, and the harpies scattered, screeching and cursing. I wasted no time in following him down the ramp to shore.

I hurried up the slope toward the cave mouth, grinning to myself as Cerberus continued to harass the harpies. None of them were stupid enough to come within range, but that didn't stop him from leaping into the air, all three heads snapping with gusto at any harpy that looked like it might even be thinking of getting close enough to bite. A harpy was perched on a rock beside the cave mouth, presumably meant to be guarding the way, but she, too, was distracted by Cerberus's antics and the outraged cries of her sisters. I slipped past without her ever knowing I was there.

Inside, I inched forward into the demonic red glow. My connection to Cerberus sharpened my night vision somewhat, though it wasn't as good as being linked to a cat. Still, beggars couldn't be choosers. It was certainly better than standard human-issue vision.

The ceiling of the cave lowered toward me, and the walls closed in until I was walking in a tunnel which sloped gently down. Faint whisperings echoed up to greet me, murmurs of protest and hissing sounds, with the occasional scrape of claws on stone or a clinking of chains. Darkness pressed in around me and my steps slowed. I must be crazy to even think of entering this place. As if someone had read my mind, a low chuckle issued from somewhere down the tunnel. It was not a happy sound.

I forced myself to continue, step by reluctant step. Gradually, it became easier to see as the red glow brightened, lighting the tunnel's rough stone walls. There were no doors or side passages, only this one tunnel that continued inexorably to sink further below ground. I was just starting to wonder how far I would have to walk before I found anyone, when the first door appeared on my right. It was made of steel, and the bolt that secured it appeared to be rusted in place. Surely there could be nothing alive inside? Yet as I passed, something big hurled itself against the door, growling in a way that sent shivers down my spine. I moved a little faster, anxious to put some distance between me and whatever lurked on the other side of that door.

The tunnel rounded a bend, and suddenly, a vast space opened before me—a huge pit, its bottom lost in darkness. The path I'd been following now became a ramp which spiralled around the edges of the pit. I could barely see the other side through the gloom. I started down, keeping close to the wall. The ramp was wide enough for three or four to walk abreast, but there was no railing, and I had no wish to find out exactly how deep the pit was. Further down, where the ramp curved away from me, were some barred openings. Mindful of my experience with the locked door further up, I made sure not to get too close to the bars as I approached the first cell. I didn't want anything inside getting hold of me. I peered into the darkness, but nothing moved. The cell appeared to be empty, unless the inhabitant was as invisible as I. After a moment, I moved on. The cell was too small to hold even an invisible cyclops. The one-eyed giants were not known for their diminutive size.

A noise like a giant chewing rocks rose from the depths of the pit, and I shrank against the wall, heart pounding. Silently, I drew my knife. Maybe it wouldn't be much use against the denizens of Tartarus, but it made me feel better to have it in my hand, ready to strike if needed. After a moment, the rock-grinding noise faded away and I continued down the ramp.

My eyes were getting better adjusted to the low level of light. In the next cell, I could make out the figure of a man curled up on the floor. He didn't move, and I couldn't tell if he was asleep or dead. In either case, he wasn't a cyclops, so I forced myself to keep going. I couldn't free everyone here. Indeed, I would be a fool to try. Zeus might have imprisoned some of the inmates with little cause, but many of them had well and truly earned their eternal punishment. It would be the height of stupidity to release them because of a misplaced pity for their condition. And whatever Apollo's opinion to the contrary, I wasn't stupid.

The next cell held a cyclops. Finally!

"Brontes," I whispered, trying not to make too much noise. "Is that you?"

The cyclops lifted his head and blinked once, a ponderous movement of his giant eyelid, but he didn't answer.

I tried again. "Brontes, servant and apprentice of Hephaistos, is that you?"

The cyclops hauled himself to his feet, sniffing the air suspiciously. He stepped up to the bars and I backed away, just in case. The great eye swivelled to one side and then the other as the cyclops searched for the source of the voice.

"I'm a friend of Hephaistos," I said.

The cyclops threw himself against the bars, howling. Startled, I leapt back, and nearly managed to throw myself into the abyss. The cyclops got one massive arm out between the bars and scrabbled at the hard stone of the ramp. With horror, I noticed the deep scores in the floor, showing just how many times before he must have done the same thing. I shuddered and moved on, hoping that this wasn't Brontes. The howling faded into a keening sound behind me.

I continued down the ramp. Brontes would be no use to us if he was in that condition. What would I do if that had been him? I shook my head, trying to shake loose the gloomy thoughts. Hephaistos had said there were several cyclopes locked up here. Brontes *would* be sane when I found him. He *would* be able to help us. I'd come this far; I just had to keep the faith a little longer. It couldn't all be for nothing. Jake was depending on me.

The next cell held something that huddled in the darkness against the back wall. I couldn't really make out its shape but it was too small to be a cyclops, so I left it in peace. This could take longer than I had hoped. Apollo would just have to hold off the harpies without me for a while longer. At least he had Cerberus to provide enthusiastic assistance.

The rock-crunching noise started up again in the depths of the pit and I shuddered. Whatever was down there, I had no desire to meet it. I marched on through the darkness, completing a full circuit of the pit before I reached the next cell. At least this one contained a cyclops. I checked the floor outside the cell; there were no scratch marks. That was a good sign.

Mindful of my last experience, I took up a position well to the side, safely out of reach. I had no desire to dice with death on the edge of the precipice again. "Brontes? Is that you?"

The cyclops in the cell hauled himself to his feet. He was more than twice my height. He clenched the bars in his massive hands and rattled them.

"Brontes, servant of Hephaistos," I repeated, in a louder voice. "Is that you?"

"Who calls?" a deep voice responded from further down the ramp.

At last! I hurried down the ramp, the cyclops behind me still rattling the bars of his cell. The next cell had no bars, only a heavy wooden door set into a blank stone wall. There was a small slit in the door at eye level, and I peeked through. A cyclops sat on the floor, with his back against the wall. Even seated, he was a good head taller than I was. How on earth had he even fit through that door? His single eye squinted suspiciously into the darkness toward the slit.

"I do. I've come to offer you a bargain."

"Show yourself, spirit." The cyclops lurched to his feet and approached the door. "Or am I finally going mad like my brothers?"

"You're not going mad." At least I hoped so. I could

certainly do without any further complications. I took the baseball cap off and shoved it into my pack, revealing myself to the imprisoned giant. "My name is Lexi. I'm a friend of Hephaistos."

Bloody hell, but he was big. It was all I could do not to back away as he bent down to bring his eye level with the tiny opening in the door. If he didn't turn out to be friendly, we were in serious trouble. "Are you real? What is this magic that brings a human to the Pit?"

"It's called having friends in high places," I said. "Hephaistos told me all about you."

"I haven't seen Lord Hephaistos since I was sent to this miserable place. He tried to speak for me, you know, but Zeus wouldn't listen."

"I know." Zeus sounded like a right charmer. Maybe it wasn't such a bad thing that he'd gone missing.

"Did Lord Hephaistos send you here?"

"Kind of." Not really, but I figured it would only help my case if he thought so. "Lord Hephaistos told me of your great skill with metalshaping, and I'm in desperate need of a good metalshaper."

He regarded me gravely from that single eye. "You must be, to come into a place like this. What do you want of me?"

"My friends are trapped in magic collars, and I need someone to create a key that will unlock them." It felt odd to refer to Apollo as my friend, but I didn't want to name any names.

I shifted from foot to foot, impatient to have this over with—impatient to get to the part where I rushed outside and liberated Apollo and Syl. One step closer to saving Jake. But the cyclops seemed in no hurry.

He frowned. "Why come to me? Lord Hephaistos is far more skilled than I will ever be. If you are such great friends with him, why did he not create this key himself instead of sending you here?" He shook his head in wonder. "It has been so long since a mortal found their way into the underworld. Can you really be true, or are you but a dream?"

I reached through the slit and prodded his cheek. It was like poking a rock. "I'm as real as you are, buddy." I sighed, not wanting to tell him the truth, but I could see no way around it. "But I'm afraid Lord Hephaistos was in no position to help me." I paused. Damn. How did I put this? Best to just rip through it and get the pain over with. "I'm afraid he's no longer in the land of the living." There, I'd said it.

Brontes' frown only deepened. "But … What do you mean? You make no sense, mortal. Truly, this is a confusing dream."

"I'm sorry to have to tell you this, Brontes, but Lord Hephaistos is dead."

"Now I know you are a figment of my imagination. Begone, dream woman. Lord Hephaistos is a god. He cannot die."

"And you are the son of a god, and yet you are buried in this living tomb. A lot has changed upstairs since you last saw the sunlight, and it turns out gods aren't quite as bullet-proof as everybody thought. There's a new game in town, and it's called 'let's kill the gods and steal their powers'. Hephaistos is dead, and so are several minor godlings. Hades is missing. Zeus is missing." Not that I expected that to bother Brontes, considering Zeus was the one responsible for his imprisonment. "And my friends are cut off from their power by these collars I mentioned. Hephaistos would want you to help them. He *did* want you to help them. That's why he told me where to find you." Maybe that was embellishing the truth a little, but I didn't care. And I'd managed to get all that out without once mentioning Apollo's name.

Brontes slammed a massive fist against the door, which barely vibrated under the blow. It must be ridiculously thick—guess it would have to be to keep a cyclops locked away. Unlike the other cyclopes' cells, his didn't have any iron bars. Trying to keep a metalshaper locked up with metal would have been a fool's game. There was a padlock on the outside of the door, but that was beyond his reach.

"Even supposing I believed you, little figment, how can

I help you? There is no metal here for me to work, and a little thing like you will never get this door open."

"I have metal." I'd left it in Apollo's care—it hadn't seemed like a smart idea to bring the precious bar of star-metal into Tartarus. "If you promise to help me, I can get you out of there."

"And then what? There are guardians of this hell that you haven't seen yet. Shall you free me just to see me die? You will die, too."

Apollo hadn't mentioned anything about guardians. Surely he'd have told me if there was anything to worry about.

"You'd rather stay here for the rest of eternity? Come with me and make the key, and then you can join Hephaistos in Elysium." He'd be thrilled to have his old companion back.

He gave a bitter laugh. "Are you a god, to promise such a thing? Hades will send me straight back to Tartarus."

"He won't." Hopefully. Surely he'd understand? "I'll explain it all to him." Besides, Hades wasn't here anyway. By the time we found him—if we found him—no one would remember a lone cyclops who was living somewhere he shouldn't be. I knew Hephaistos wouldn't say anything. And Apollo would be so grateful to have the damn collar off he'd promise anything. He, at least, would support me. "Swear to help me, and leave the details to me."

He sighed, a great gusty noise of resignation. "I must be mad, but if you are indeed more than a figment, it would be good to breathe the free air again before I die. I swear to aid you in your quest."

Hallelujah. I hoped he wasn't expecting much in the way of free air. All I had to offer was the type that was laden with the smell of sulphur and the stench of angry harpies. But even that might be welcome after a few thousand years inside Tartarus.

"Then stand back." I pulled Jake's safecracking gizmo from my backpack. I'd been carting this thing around forever, just waiting for an opportunity to use it. Finally, the big moment had arrived. It was small, no bigger than my fist, and shaped like a slightly squished egg. I attached it to the padlock—it was magnetic—and offered up a silent prayer. *Please work this time.* It had failed when I'd been trying to crack Mrs Emery's safe, because it relied on Jake's magic to function, and Jake had been wearing one of the collars at the time, cut off from his power. I just hoped that the fact that we were in the underworld and Jake wasn't wouldn't cause a similar problem.

I pushed the button down and stepped smartly away. Fingers crossed. I counted down from thirty, my whole body taut with tension. *Please.*

At seventeen, it went off like a firecracker in a flash of white light so bright it blinded me. There was a metallic clank as the padlock hit the stone ramp. I darted forward to free the bolt. It took me a couple of tries, as the bolt was stiff and my fingers were shaking, but I got it loose at last and pushed the heavy door open. The hinges squealed as the door scraped across the stone floor of Brontes' cell, and I glanced around uneasily. We were making a lot of noise.

Brontes dropped to his knees and crawled through the opening. His shoulders only just fit through the doorway. As he climbed to his feet, a bell began to toll somewhere deep within the pit, loud and frantic, as if a drunken bell ringer was hanging on the rope.

Brontes hunched his massive shoulders, as if he thought he could make himself small enough to hide. The creatures in the other cells began to shout and throw themselves against the bars. We stared at each other in horror. There'd be no sneaking out of here now.

"Run," I said.

17

We pounded up the ramp and back through the tunnel. I took two strides for every one of Brontes', but the cyclops was no athlete, and his condition wasn't improved for having been locked in a tiny cell for the last umpteen-hundred years, so I kept up with him easily, despite my injured leg. The monster in the first room inside the tunnel roared and hurled itself against the door again as we passed, but there were no other signs of life, and I began to relax as the opening to the cave came into view. We were almost there! I'd been terrified that we'd get here and find the opening blocked, but the way was clear. We burst out of the cave, skidding on the loose rock outside, and the panting cyclops drew in his first breath of free air.

"Lord of Chaos!" the cyclops cried. "What is happening?"

The scene before us made no sense. The ferry lay at anchor in the Styx where I'd left it. There was no sign of

Apollo or Syl, but Cerberus was on the shore, barking all three of his heads off. Not at the harpies, who were circling en masse in the sky overhead, and making enough noise of their own to wake the dead, but at the Phlegethon.

The River of Fire had grown a giant lump, which was writhing its way into the sky, spitting fire in every direction. It was like an enormous bubble that refused to burst as it grew bigger and bigger, until it towered over the ferry, making it look like a child's toy.

And then the bubble stretched and grew a neck, with a horned head atop it. The head swung in our direction, and a mighty foot slammed down on the ground as something too big to comprehend heaved itself from the river.

It was a dragon. Made of fire.

"Zeus's balls," I breathed. "Where did *that* come from?"

"It's the guardian," Brontes said. "I told you we would die."

He didn't even sound upset, just resigned, as if death were a foregone conclusion. Well, not on my watch, buddy. I quested outwards, feeling for the mind that animated the enormous beast. It might be made of fire, but if it were even remotely animal, it should respond to me.

It was even stranger inside the dragon's head than inside Cerberus's. I looked out through its glowing eyes at the giant hellhound, and he looked like a toy, his barking a tiny sound, less significant than the buzz of a mosquito. I saw myself, burning like a dying star, and I planted a powerful suggestion inside the alien consciousness. *Stop. Turn away from the tiny humans and their yipping dog. Blast those harpies from the sky instead.*

The dragon shook its head as if trying to shake me off, scattering droplets of molten lava everywhere. The rock sizzled where they landed. Its will was strong; it had been created to be the last line of defence for Tartarus. Its whole purpose in life was to prevent anyone leaving without authorisation, and the tolling bell called to something deep inside it. *Ignore these people,* I urged it. *The harpies are the ones you need to destroy.*

The dragon snarled, and its voice was like rock shattering. Was this the sound I had heard deep in the pit? I poured my will into my efforts, fists clenched, my whole body shaking. The dragon *would* obey me.

It heaved itself fully onto the land. It wasn't scaled like a normal dragon, but coated in molten lava. Huh. That was cute—a "normal dragon"? Since when had dragons been normal? My whole life was the very definition of "abnormal" these days.

I gathered my will, determined to stare the bastard down. Like staring into the sun, it hurt my eyes to look directly at it for too long. I squinted into its fiery light, tears leaking from my stinging eyes. The great creature roared again and the earth shook beneath us. The harpies were screeching, urging it on. Two of them dived toward us, vicious claws outstretched. I had nothing but a knife. *Kill them,* I urged the dragon. *They are your enemies.*

Brontes picked up a rock the size of my head and lobbed it into the sky, trying to bring down a harpy. His aim was off, but he merely found another rock and tried again. Despite his conviction that we were doomed, he didn't seem inclined to simply lie down and accept his fate. The dragon roared in a final act of defiance, and then turned to obey me, snarling. My head felt as if it were about to explode, but the sight of the enormous tongues of flame shooting into the air from its mouth went a long way towards soothing my pain.

Some of the harpies were lucky enough to see it coming, and managed to swerve out of the way in time, but most of them were not. Nothing but ashes rained down from the leaden sky. The dragon's flame was so potent that nothing else remained of the dozen or more harpies caught in the inferno of its breath.

The remaining harpies fled the scene. They weren't stupid enough to try to stand against such a force. The dragon sent a bolt of fire blasting after them, but they were too far away to be singed.

"Come on," I said to Brontes. "Let's get to the ferry."

Brontes looked at me as if I were crazy. "Are you in such a hurry to die? That monster will kill us."

Of course, Brontes had no idea what had just happened. All he had seen were random acts of violence from the biggest monster in a world full of them. "It's all right," I said. "I've got this under control. The dragon won't harm us."

I staggered out into the open. The dragon's blazing head turned to watch me, its will still straining to be free. My head was pounding in time with my overtaxed heart. I wasn't quite as confident as I was making out. If the dragon slipped my control, we were all dead. I gestured to Brontes to follow me. "Come on!"

We needed Apollo's help. *I* needed Apollo's help. I had a feeling only a god with full access to his powers could hold this beast for long.

Brontes hurried after me, the expression on his face making it clear that he expected to be charred to a crisp at any moment, but I didn't care, as long as he was moving.

The dragon snarled and took another step closer. It felt like someone had just opened an oven door right next to me as the heat from its massive body swirled across the baking rocks. I ran faster, staggering every time my numb left leg threatened to give way on me.

"Guys!" I screamed, my voice hoarse. I'd have given anything for a beer right then, or even just a long cool drink of clean water. "Get down here! We need the star-metal."

Cerberus bounded towards me, his hackles raised,

barking for all he was worth. Clearly, he meant to defend me from the fiery menace stalking across the plain. It was a nice thought, but I doubted even a hellhound would stand a chance against the dragon. Its body was halfway to the ferry, but it was so big that the end of its tail was still immersed in the River of Fire. No wonder the harpies had fled once it had turned on them. No one could hope to take on such a creature and live.

Apollo appeared at the top of the gangway, Syl at his side. I could hear her shouting, but I couldn't make out the words over the crackling of flames. The dragon was getting closer. It appeared to be made of flame and molten lava, its surface shifting and its shape changing as it moved, but the ground shook with every step it took, so there must be some substance to it underneath the fiery exterior. How long had it lain hidden at the bottom of the River of Fire, waiting until it was needed? It was a thing of impossible beauty, but as my legs strained and I fought for breath in the superheated air, I was in no mood to appreciate its charms. It was also an unstoppable killing machine and its will writhed against mine, straining to be free.

I staggered again and would have face-planted onto the rocky ground except that Brontes swooped in and hoisted me up without breaking his stride. He threw me over his shoulder and ran for the ferry as if his life depended on it. I was starting to think it did—I couldn't hold the dragon's will much longer. My vision was blurring and all I could see was fire, flames dancing in front of my eyes wherever I looked.

Syl rushed to my side as Brontes laid me on the stony ground with surprising gentleness. "Are you hurt? What's wrong?"

"Give the star-metal to Brontes," I gasped, my chest heaving. My head was spinning, as if there were less and less oxygen in the air. I couldn't pass out; I would lose the dragon the minute I lost consciousness, and then we were all dead. "I'm trying to hold the dragon. Hurry."

I didn't see much of what happened next; I was too busy lying around gasping like a fish out of water. Apollo handed Brontes the bar of precious star-metal, and the cyclops crouched down to inspect the collar around Apollo's neck.

"This is beautiful work," Brontes said. "I recognise Lord Hephaistos's hand in it."

"Hurry up," I moaned as the seconds ticked past, every one drilling a new lance of pain into my skull. This was not the time for admiring the craftsmanship of the collars' maker.

Brontes glanced across at where I lay, half-supported by Syl's arms. "Hush, Figment. I need to listen to the metal."

Sweet baby Hermes, as Jake would say—how could he hear anything with all this racket going on? The dragon was making more noise than twenty bonfires, between the flames crackling all over him and the shuddering thunder of each step. The remaining harpies circled the peak of the mountain, screeching insults and threats. Beneath all that lay the regular hisses and pops of steam venting all over the blasted landscape. My head was pounding fit to explode, the noise battering against me like a physical assault. It was a wonder Brontes could hear himself think, never mind anything the metal could tell him.

I started to giggle, imagining the little bar of star-metal actually growing a mouth and chatting to the giant cyclops. *Yeah, Brontes, I've had a pretty crazy time since I arrived on this planet. Haven't had much chance for sightseeing, unfortunately. Been locked up in some weird forge pretty much the whole time. It's a shame; I was really hoping to get out and try the seafood down here—I hear it's awesome.*

"Lexi!" I could hear Syl's voice calling me, but it sounded a long way away. "Lexi, stop it! You're scaring me."

Well, of course she was scared. Syl was always scared of something—such a scaredy cat. That set me off again. Scaredy cat.

Inside my head, something was pushing at me, searing me with talons of fire. I knew I was supposed to push back, but I could no longer remember why. Maybe I could stop soon? I was so tired. If only Syl would stop shaking me, I could go to sleep right here, even though whatever I was lying on was so damn uncomfortable.

"Hurry!" Syl shouted, and someone shouted back, a deep rumble of a voice that sounded like it came from a giant. My head was about to burst. The pressure was too much. Little by little, something was tearing free, but I couldn't find it in me to care anymore. The sweet siren song of unconsciousness beckoned, and I sank gratefully toward it. Something heavy and wet slapped across my face, and I had the sense of people rushing around, but it all felt like it was happening somewhere far away.

A golden light pierced the fog surrounding me, silencing the noise in my head. All at once, the pressure eased, as if it were a bubble that someone had popped. I opened my eyes in time to cop a faceful of tongue as Cerberus licked me again.

"Get off!" I flailed at him with both arms, but for some reason, I was flat on my back, and it seemed to take an enormous effort to move. One head yipped in excitement, while another bent down to administer another enthusiastic licking before someone shooed him away.

Was that Apollo? I shaded my eyes with one hand. The golden light was coming from him, bursting forth as if he really were the sun. It hurt just as much to look at him as it had to look at the dragon.

The dragon! Memory came rushing back, and I fought my way into a sitting position, looking wildly around. Where was the dragon? What was going on?

Syl appeared, crouching down beside me. Tears streamed down her cheeks, but a smile of pure joy lit her features as she grabbed me in a fierce hug.

"Syl! You're free!" The collar was gone. I squinted over her shoulder at Apollo. His neck was blessedly bare, too. "You did it."

Apollo smiled down at me. "No. *You* did it. You have my eternal gratitude."

My eyes were watering in the glare coming off him. "You're welcome—but do you think you could turn down the special effects?"

"Sorry." He had the grace to look abashed. The light emanating from him dimmed as he and Syl helped me to my feet. "You gave us a bad moment there."

"I thought you'd died." Syl hovered anxiously as I wobbled. "You started laughing and raving, and the next minute you went limp and the dragon was coming for us like a steam train."

"Something seemed to slow it down for a few moments," Apollo said. "Just as well, or it would have been on us before Brontes could remove the collars. We were lucky."

Very lucky. And *I* was lucky that Apollo hadn't seemed to figure out what—or rather, who—had slowed the dragon for those vital seconds. He obviously hadn't heard me tell Syl I was trying to hold the dragon.

"Sorry I kind of blacked out on you there."

"Don't apologise," said Apollo. "You did more than any mortal I've ever known could have. You have the heart of a lion."

Wow. This was so weird. Apollo was actually being nice to me.

Behind the cyclops towered the dragon, its blazing eyes fixed on Apollo, head bent in submission. Flame hissed and crackled across its skin in a beautiful light show that I could finally appreciate now that I wasn't responsible for stopping it from killing us all.

"Go now, Phlegethon," Apollo said. His voice had that deep thrum underlying it again, that I'd first noticed during his brief moment of freedom in Mrs Emery's cellar. It resonated through my body; I could almost taste the power. "You have done your duty, and answered the call of the alarm. Go back to your river and sleep until you are needed once more."

The dragon inclined its mighty head in a graceful bow, then turned away. We watched in silence as it re-entered the flaming river, sinking down, becoming one with the molten lava until it disappeared. I couldn't have said whether it had sunk beneath the surface or dissolved and become part of the river. Either way, I was glad to see the last of it. Now we had only the harpies to deal with.

Not that they seemed keen to approach our little group, even without the dragon to contend with. Two of the braver ones had alighted at the cave mouth, and watched us warily. The rest still circled high above the volcano's peak, unwilling to come any closer to the newly resurgent god. Their raucous voices had fallen silent.

Brontes stood behind us, his face like thunder. The two collars dangled from one enormous fist, and in the other hand was a silvery key that looked tiny enough to open a mouse's treasure box compared to the hand that held it. His fists were clenched so tight the key seemed in imminent danger of being snapped.

"You're Apollo," he ground out through gritted teeth. "I didn't recognise you in time, without your glamour, or I would have left you to rot." He turned his blazing gaze on me. "You lied to me, Figment."

"I didn't. I said my friends needed help." Calling Apollo a friend was a bit of a stretch, but it wasn't precisely a lie. "I just didn't give you their names."

"Then you tricked me."

"I *saved* you. I broke you out of Tartarus. Maybe you had to help someone you don't like in return, but it seems a fair trade to me."

"You made me help the killer of my brother's sons, and that seems fair to you, does it? He's a bigger monster than anything locked inside Tartarus."

Holy shit. Now his bitterness made sense. Apollo had killed his nephews? I stared at the god in shock. He hadn't mentioned *that* little fact when he'd been trying to talk me out of coming here.

Apollo made no attempt to deny the accusation, which only confirmed his guilt as far as I was concerned. To think I'd almost started to warm to him. "The question is what to do with you now. I cannot let you leave the underworld."

The giant drew himself up to his full height. "Then you mean to kill me? The figment said I could join Lord Hephaistos in Elysium if I helped her. Was that a lie?"

"It most certainly was not," I said hotly. "And my name is Lexi."

Brontes ignored me, his challenging gaze resting on Apollo's face. I had a feeling he knew perfectly well what my name was anyway. *The figment?* Syl mouthed at me, and I shrugged. I'd explain later, once the showdown was over. If Apollo didn't stop glaring at the cyclops like that, I'd put that damn collar back on him myself.

"That seems acceptable," Apollo said at last. "Give me the collars and the key. Elysium isn't far from here. Do you know the way?"

"I do." The cyclops threw the collars and their precious key onto the ground at Apollo's feet, though the look on his face said he'd have thrown them into the Phlegethon if he dared defy the god. "But what's to stop those devils up there from trying to haul me back into the Pit once you're gone?" He nodded at the two harpies glaring at us from their posts outside the opening to Tartarus.

"I will order them to leave you be."

Yeah, right. As if the harpies would take any notice once he wasn't there to enforce his orders. They were already staring at Brontes as if he were a giant chew toy and they couldn't wait to start playing tug-of-war. I dug into my backpack.

"I have a better idea." I held the Baseball Cap of Supreme Sneakiness out to Brontes.

Looking doubtful, he took it in his massive hand. "What am I meant to do with this?"

"It's a hat. You put it on your head."

"It's too small." Nevertheless, he lifted it to his head. The cap grew larger as it approached his head, transforming itself to the required size. By the time he settled it on his head, it was the perfect fit, and they both disappeared.

"Mother of Chaos! What magic is this?" He reappeared, cap in hand, and examined it with a keen interest, his quarrel with Apollo momentarily forgotten.

"It's the Helm of Darkness. I believe you may have had a hand in its original creation."

"Indeed I did." He put it back on, took it off, and put it back on again, like a child with a new toy. "Though it has changed marvellously since then."

"Hades likes to keep up with the times," I said. "You

should be able to evade the harpies with that. Ask Hephaistos to keep it safe once you reach him. Oh, and tell him I said hi."

"I will." He glared once more at Apollo, then he jammed the Helm on his head and winked out of existence, though his heavy tread could be heard receding into the distance.

I heaved a great sigh of relief, and Syl turned to me anxiously. "Are you sure you're all right? You seem kind of wobbly."

"About that …" I flicked a sideways glance at Apollo. "I got speared by a ghost centaur on the way to find Hephaistos. He said I needed a fireshaping god to burn the rest of the poison out of me." Not before time, either. The numbness had spread all the way back up my leg again, and I was heartily sick of stumbling and tripping everywhere I went.

"Allow me," Apollo said, taking my hand. He said nothing more, but a soothing warmth began to flow from our joined hands up my arm, spreading through my whole body. Jake's delivery method had been more fun, but I was glad I didn't have to swap saliva with the sun god.

It was different to when Jake had done it in other ways, too. Jake's fire had burned—not unpleasantly, but like the burn of a good whiskey sliding down your throat. Apollo's fire felt like lying out in the sun on a warm day. I could have closed my eyes and nodded off as the feeling of well-being filled me. I wiggled my toes in satisfaction. It was the first time I'd been able to feel them all properly in forever.

Apollo withdrew his hand from mine. "Better?" he asked.

I balanced on my tiptoes and took a few steps, then bent into a deep squat. My legs felt fine—better than fine; they felt great, as if I'd had a good night's sleep or a relaxing massage. I guess there was a reason gods outgunned shapers. I felt as good as new.

"Much better." I suppose I should have thanked him, but I wasn't feeling too charitable towards him at the moment, still rocked by the cyclops's revelation. I mean, I knew gods had the power of life and death over everyone, so, in theory, it was no surprise that he'd killed a few people in his time. But I couldn't help feeling betrayed. I'd liked the giant cyclops, and it had stung to see him look at me with such disappointment.

"What now?" Syl asked. "Do we have to go back to the palace?"

"No need," Apollo said. "There's a gate here that we can use, and I can make sure it opens into Crosston for us."

Another benefit of having a god on your team. I guess I had to take the good with the bad. My personal dislike of Apollo meant nothing, as long as he helped me save Jake. The little knot of anxiety in my stomach loosened somewhat. Jake's time was still limited, but we were getting closer. "And once we're there, you can free Jake from wherever the Ruby Adept's got him locked up, right?"

"Of course. Wait here. I'll release Charon from his bondage before we leave." He strode up the gangway and disappeared inside the ferry.

I put the collars and their key into my backpack, keeping a wary eye on the harpies outside the entrance to Tartarus while he was gone.

One of them rattled her metal-tipped wings at me. "Lord Hades will punish you when he hears of this, mortal."

"Good luck finding him," I muttered.

Before she could work up the courage to move from threats to action, Apollo returned.

"Ready?" he asked.

I nodded. "Let's go kick some fireshaper butt."

18

We arrived at the Gate of Dusk much more quickly, it seemed, than when Jake and I had been running from the harpies.

"Stay here, Cerberus," Apollo said.

Cerberus whined and nudged me with one of his heads, nearly knocking me right through the gate. I stroked a velvety ear soothingly. "He was pretty handy against the shadow shapers. Can't we take him?"

"He was wonderful," Apollo agreed, reaching up to pat another head approvingly. "But I'm back at full strength, and I won't need any help to discipline a few fireshapers. Best if he stays here. The gods aren't a secret, but we like our anonymity. There's no point parading a hellhound around unnecessarily."

He *was* kind of hard to miss. I stood on tiptoes and reached up to get my arms around one of his necks. "We'll be back before you know it, buddy."

I was rewarded with one of those enthusiastic licks. I was going to need a long, hot shower when this was all over.

Apollo held out his hands, one to me and one to Syl, and together we stepped through the gate. This time, there was none of that disorienting sensation we'd experienced on the way to Hephaistos's forge. Clearly, there were advantages to travelling with a god. The world simply flickered as we passed under the arch, and when I set my foot down, it touched a smooth, tiled floor.

The floor belonged to a great, vaulted space, cool and dim. Above us, a dome soared. In the centre of the enormous room, directly beneath the dome, a fire burned brightly in a circular pit. Radiating out from the central fire were the rays of a golden sun, inlaid into the tiled floor.

"Where are we?" breathed Syl.

Apollo let go our hands and smoothed his shirt a little self-consciously. "Welcome to my temple in Crosston."

Syl's eyes widened, and she looked around with renewed interest. "This is the Great Temple of Apollo? Cool! I've never been here before."

"Me neither," Apollo said, glancing around with a critical eye. "It seems adequate. Could do with a little more light."

It *was* pretty dark for the temple of the sun god, but the ring of windows that circled the bottom of the great dome above us showed a night sky. It would be brighter in the day time. Obviously, no expense had been spared. An enormous gold statue of Apollo stood against the wall, almost as large as the one in the Plaza of the Sun, though this one had no horses and chariot. Here, Apollo was depicted as the music lover, golden head bent over his harp strings. It must have cost a fortune.

"Really? You've never been here?" Syl asked. "But the temple has been here for nearly three hundred years."

Apollo shrugged. "Just because a god *can* appear in any of his temples doesn't mean he *will*. I have better things to do with my life than pop up like a genie every time some mortal wants a question answered or a boon granted."

Well, there were no mortals here now except us. Presumably, Apollo's priests and other devotees were at home in bed.

"Let's go," Apollo said. "The Ruby Palace is just down the road."

He led us through an archway into a smaller foyer. The door that opened to the outside world was still twice the height of a man, but he pulled it open with ease.

"Don't they lock this at night?" I asked.

Apollo shot me a sidelong glance. "Why do you ask? Professional curiosity? What is there to steal in my temple? It would take fifty men to get that statue out, and they're welcome to my holy fire."

We stepped out onto the pavement and I knew where we

were straight away. He was right; the Ruby Palace bulked on the other side of the street just a little further down. Two men in gym clothes jogged past it. It wasn't quite as dark as the glimpse of sky from inside had made it appear—it looked like dawn was approaching. Compared to the misty gloom of the underworld, the streetlights made it feel almost as bright as day. Apollo pulled the massive door gently closed behind us.

"Maybe so," I said, "but vandals could get in and spray paint 'Apollo sucks' all over the walls."

His mouth twitched in a reluctant smile. "And if they did, they might receive a personal visit from me. I doubt they'd enjoy the experience."

"How are we going to do this?" I asked as we headed down the street to the palace. Already, I was reviewing everything I knew about the interior layout, the patterns of the guards' movements, and the placement of every security camera.

"The easy way, of course," he said.

Okaaay. This should be good.

I reached out with my inner sight, checking for allies within the building. A family of mice scampered around the ground floor, keeping mainly to the kitchen and eating areas. Cockroaches scuttled through the dark places—there were always cockroaches—and the odd spider hid in a corner. I also found the Ruby Adept's cats ensconced in his private suite, but since his door was shut and they couldn't get out, they were no use to me. I didn't imagine Jake would be locked up in the Ruby Adept's bedroom. I sent my new troops scurrying through the building in search of my favourite fireshaper.

The gates were made of heavy wrought iron and barred for the night. Just inside them stood a small gatehouse. The lone guard on duty there regarded us with only mild curiosity as we stopped outside the gates.

His curiosity changed to alarm when Apollo laid a hand on each gate and tore them open.

"Tell your masters their god is here for an accounting," he said.

"Like hell I will. No admittance after hours." The guard hurled a weak fireball as he came out of the gatehouse at a run, but Apollo didn't even blink. He brushed aside the man's pitiful flame with a blast of his own that left only a blackened corpse in its wake.

"Shit." Syl stared at the charred body in horror. "Did you have to kill him? He was only doing his job."

"Then he should have chosen a different employer," Apollo said.

"But …"

"Come on, Syl." I grabbed her arm and towed her along, following Apollo. I didn't want to get left behind—if he was going to stir up a fire storm, the safest place to be was right behind him, where he could protect us. A siren started wailing somewhere as we strode up the driveway towards the Palace.

"Is he going to kill everybody?" Syl's face was pale. Apollo had probably seemed so meek and gentle when he wore the collar, when he played the harp for her and comforted her. She was seeing a different side to him now, and I couldn't help a tiny feeling of satisfaction. This should kill off any hint of romance that might have been blossoming between them. I guess that made me a bad friend, but I had never liked Apollo as much as she obviously had, and I thought she deserved better.

"I guess he'll do whatever needs to be done to save Jake," I said. I didn't share Syl's soft heart. As far as I was concerned, these guys had it coming. They wanted to play with the big boys? Then they had to be prepared to face the consequences.

Apollo reached the grand front doors of the main entrance just as they burst open and a wall of flame surged out. A fireshaper would have thrown up his own wall of fire in return. I'd seen Jake do it enough times to know. But Apollo merely waved a hand and the flames turned back on the shapers behind them, consuming them. Apollo didn't even break stride. I liked his attitude. Maybe he wasn't so bad after all.

"This is a nightmare," Syl muttered as I steered her past the smoking bodies.

"Not much longer," I said. Maybe we should have left her back at the temple. I was surprised she hadn't turned cat by now—that was her usual response when life as a human got too hard to cope with.

"I'm okay," she said, as if she knew what I was thinking. "I wanted to see them punished for what they did—I just didn't expect the punishment to be quite this extreme."

I gave her a quick hug. "Fireshapers never do anything by halves. You know that. Gods are like fireshapers on steroids."

She nodded, the memory of our first introduction to the methods of fireshapers flickering in her dark eyes. All those people screaming, trapped in the burning building. Then she squared her shoulders and marched after Apollo. "Come on, we've got a friend to rescue. And I don't trust you to manage it without me. You seem to get hurt every time I leave you alone."

We hadn't been able to rescue our friends back then, but this time was different. We'd both come a long way since then. I was proud of her bravery.

"Right." I checked back in with my cockroach spies, who were on the level below our feet. It seemed the most likely place to keep a prisoner. I refused to consider the possibility that Jake wasn't here. There was no other building in the whole city that was more suited to hold a fireshaper of his powers. This place was crawling with fireshapers. Apollo destroyed another couple who had tried to set up an ambush around the corner of the corridor.

"Maybe don't kill them all?" I suggested. "We should question a few and find out what they know about the shadow shapers."

"I must teach them not to defy me."

"Then you'd better leave a few alive or there'll be no one left to learn the lesson." I tugged him down the corridor. "This way. The stairs to the lower level are over here."

The alarm continued to blare, louder now that we were in the building with it, as we hurried down the stairs. I wiped sweat from my eyes—all this flame getting thrown around made the place feel like an oven, even though Apollo protected us from harm. At least it was elemental flame and not the garden-variety kind, or the whole building would be going up like a torch. Elemental flame had the advantage of being able to be turned on and off like a tap at the shaper's whim.

This lower level was nearly as big as the ground floor, but my trusty cockroaches had covered a lot of the ground already. As I directed Apollo down the branching corridors, a cockroach showed me what I most wished to see. I couldn't restrain a whoop of joy.

"Found him! He's this way." Apollo gave me an odd look and it occurred to me that he didn't know about my powers, and it was probably best to keep it that way.

Hastily, I added, "I mean, this is where they usually keep their prisoners." He knew I'd studied the floor plans before I'd broken in to steal his ring. We'd never explained exactly how I'd managed it, and he hadn't been interested in the details.

We hadn't seen a guard in a while. Either Apollo had roasted them all or they were massing somewhere to attack us. I could just imagine the panic on the top floor as they raced to protect the Ruby Adept. Not that anything could protect him from the wrath of his god. Funnily enough, that thought didn't bother me at all.

Besides, I had better things to think about. We arrived at Jake's door. It was no dungeon; the corridor was just as well-lit as the rest of the building, and the parquetry floor as clean and polished. The door was locked but that made no difference to Apollo—he merely had to touch the metal handle and the door swung open. How had they managed to keep Jake contained?

Jake rose from the bed he'd been sitting on as we entered. He was fully dressed—the noise of the alarm must have woken him—but his skin had a yellow tinge and he moved like an old man.

A smile broke across his face. "My Lord! You're free."

Apollo smiled back. "And so are you, now."

Jake grimaced. "I think it may be too late for me." He sank back down onto the bed, his whole body trembling.

A cold fury began to burn inside me. What had been in that injection they'd given him? "Have they mistreated you?"

He shook his head. "I don't feel well, but I think that's Styx's doing. I've been getting chills for the last hour and I can't seem to stop shaking. It feels like something is inside me, chewing on my organs. How long is it until her twelve hours are up?"

Renewed hatred for Styx burned in my heart. I laid a hand on his forehead, and he was burning up, despite his talk of chills. How dared she poison Jake with her kiss? What had he ever done to her?

"I don't know." If I could kiss him better, he'd be fighting fit in no time. Hopefully, there'd be time for that later, but right now, we had to focus on what was important—getting him out of here and back to that pointy-toothed bitch. I didn't even want to think about what would happen between them after that. The main thing was just keeping him alive. Fear fluttered inside me. He looked half dead already. "I don't even know what time it is now, or when we made the deal. Probably a couple of hours at most. I get the feeling that there's not much time left."

"I get that feeling, too," Jake said.

"Then let's move," Apollo said, herding us all back out of the small room. Jake leaned heavily on me.

"I don't know how much help I'll be," Jake said apologetically. "I can't feel my power anymore."

"Don't worry about it," Apollo said. "I've got this."

He led us back along the corridor and up the stairs. Jake seemed to have trouble with them; he had to hold on to the handrail. I bit my lip and said nothing, hovering close enough to catch him if he fell. Syl and I exchanged glances, and she moved to his other side as soon as we gained the top of the stairs.

Apollo strode ahead, leaving the two of us to support Jake. He managed to keep putting one foot in front of the other, but the effort was clearly costing him.

"It's not far," Syl said. He looked like he needed all the encouragement he could get. He shouldn't be this sick, should he? Maybe my guesstimates of how much time had passed were wrong. How long did he have? I'd like to run that bitch Styx over with the ferry. I hated her for doing this to him. "It's just down the street."

Nobody challenged us as we followed Apollo through the empty halls, the alarm still wailing its warning. We passed the bodies of the fireshapers he'd killed just inside the front entrance. They were still smoking. If Jake noticed them, he didn't comment. It appeared to be taking every bit of his energy just to keep moving.

Apollo glanced up the grand staircase. "I need to find the Ruby Adept and the other councillors."

"Not now," I said, indicating Jake, who was hunched over as if every movement pained him. "We don't have time."

His gaze swept over the trembling fireshaper and his face darkened. "True. House-cleaning will have to wait. Stay here a moment."

He stepped out the front door into the dark, while we waited obediently. The sound of automatic rifle fire split the night, followed by the whoosh of an enormous fireball. The reflected light of the flames played on the wall opposite the door. For once, I felt no urge to peek outside, happy to keep my head down.

Apollo stuck his head back inside. "All clear," he said. "Let's go."

The carnage in the dark garden was impressive. It looked like a whole squadron of guards had decided to try human weaponry instead of magic against Apollo. Did they have no idea who he was? Who could possibly have imagined that guns could defeat one of the Olympians? They must have assumed he was another fireshaper. I guess that made sense, considering how little the gods had had to do with the world lately. No one knew what he looked like, and he wasn't doing his godly glowing thing. I averted my eyes from the smoking bodies as we hurried past, though I couldn't avoid the smell of charred meat. Syl looked positively green.

Apollo glanced back at the palace, his face like flint. "The Ruby Council and I are going to have a long chat very soon."

His expression made me glad I wasn't a councillor. It also made me feel more charitable towards the sun god. Finally, we had something in common, even if a mutual hatred of traitorous fireshapers might not normally be considered a great basis for a relationship. But if he intended to whoop the Ruby Adept's arse, we'd be best friends forever.

Despite all the noise we'd made, there was no one else in the street. Residents of shaper cities learned to make themselves scarce when shapers squabbled amongst themselves. If they didn't, they often became collateral damage.

Jake stumbled and would have fallen if Syl and I hadn't managed to catch him.

"Apollo," Syl said urgently.

He turned and took in the situation at once. He swung Jake up and over his shoulder in a fireman's lift as if the tall shaper weighed nothing at all. "Let's move, ladies. Our friend doesn't have much time left."

He took off running down the street, and after a moment of stunned surprise, Syl and I bolted after him. I had a horrible feeling that he was right.

Time was running out for Jake.

19

I had to admit, I liked this new, decisive Apollo much more than the whiny guy who'd sat around with a face as long as a wet week because he was trapped in the shadow shapers' stupid collar. He stormed back into his own temple, his boots ringing hollowly on the marble floor.

An old Chinese man, his white hair no more than a few wisps on the sides of his head, knelt by the sacred fire, praying. He looked up in surprise as the door banged open and creaked to his feet, carefully rearranging his long robes. His eyes narrowed as he took in our no-doubt disreputable appearance and the unconscious man draped over Apollo's shoulder.

"What do you want?" Clearly deciding we were a bunch of undesirables, he flicked his wrists and fire appeared on his fingertips. His flames were weak, but they would have been enough to deter the average temple vandal. "The temple doesn't open until nine o'clock."

"What time is it now?" I asked, dreading the answer.

"Just before six," he said. Shit. If my calculations were correct, that meant we had less than an hour to get Jake to Styx. "Please leave."

"What are they teaching you people these days?" Apollo asked. "What kind of priest doesn't recognise his own god?" The room filled with a golden light that put the warm glow of the sacred fire to shame. The light, of course, emanated from Apollo, who was now almost too bright to look at. Show off.

The old priest fell to his knees with an enthusiasm that made me wince as they cracked against the tiles, and prostrated himself on the floor.

"A thousand apologies, my lord," he mumbled into the tiles. Then he raised his head a little, squinting into the glare. "But you don't look much like your statue."

It was true; the statue's curly locks didn't match the shaggy look Apollo was currently sporting, and the nose was a different shape. Apollo sighed, and his hair rearranged itself to match the statue's. The old priest beamed and bowed his head again. Ah, the power of a good haircut—Tegan would have been proud.

"How may I serve you, my lord?"

"No serving necessary … ah …"

"Winston," the priest supplied helpfully.

"Winston. We're just passing through." Apollo juggled

Jake into a more comfortable position on his shoulder and thrust one hand out to Syl. "Grab hold."

Syl took his hand and I tucked mine into the crook of his elbow on the other side, between his arm and Jake's limp body. Together, we took a step forward ... into the misty gloom of the underworld. The Gate of Dusk cast its shadow over the stony ground in front of us. When I looked back through it, there was no sign of Winston or the glittering temple we'd just left.

"That's a neat trick," Syl said, as we hurried from the gate down the rocky slope toward the river. "Can you teleport anywhere in the world like that?"

"No." He wasn't even breathing hard, though Jake was no lightweight. "We can move between worlds at will, using our temples as take-off or landing points, but if I wanted to get from Crosston to somewhere like Berkley's Bay—that has no temple—I'd have to drive like anybody else."

"That's a shame," Syl said. "You need more temples."

He grinned at her. He cast a little light of his own here in the underworld, brimming with returned power, and the mists cleared around him as he walked, as if the darkness refused to cling to him. "It was certainly easier in the old days, when there was a temple to Apollo in every little one-horse town. Still, it could be worse. At least I still *have* temples. I could be Hestia or one of the minor godlings, with no worshippers left. Their travel options are severely curtailed."

I listened with only half an ear, keeping an anxious eye on Jake's pale face. Syl babbled on, keeping up a flow of conversation with Apollo. I doubted she was really that interested; I caught her glancing at me once or twice, checking up on me, and I had the feeling the conversation was more her attempt to distract me from Jake's perilous situation than any true desire to dig into the secrets of the gods.

We reached the black waters of the Styx at last. The ferry still lay at anchor where we'd left it, though there was no sign of Cerberus. Perhaps he was on board sleeping.

Apollo laid Jake down on the rocky ground beside the river. "Styx!" he called. "Jacob Steele is here to fulfil his side of your bargain. Come and release him from your spell."

Styx's dark head broke the water soundlessly. Oh sure, she popped up on command, like a weasel out of its burrow, the minute Apollo called. No having to shove his hand into the water to get her attention and get the crap scared out of him the way I'd had to. I would have loved to give her a piece of my mind, but I had enough sense not to irritate her when Jake's life was hanging in the balance. I clamped my lips shut and swallowed the anger that threatened to spill forth.

"Just in time," she said brightly. "I was starting to think

that dear Jacob wasn't going to make it. You *are* cutting it a little fine."

I knelt on the riverbank, hovering protectively over Jake. His eyes opened and the smallest of smiles flickered around his lips as he gazed up at me. He lifted a shaking hand to stroke my cheek, though I could see the effort it cost him.

"Don't look so worried," he said. "I'll be back before you know it."

I caught his hand and pressed my face against it, feeling the unaccustomed sting of tears. What the hell? I didn't cry over guys. I must be overtired. Nevertheless, I breathed deeply of his familiar, smoky scent, so frightened for him that my pulse hammered uncomfortably in my throat.

"That's right." I glared at Styx. "It's only for one night. That's what we agreed." It wasn't as if we were married or anything. Hell, we hadn't even been on a date. Why should I care what he got up to with another woman? As long as he lived, that was the main thing. I'd make her sorry if she hurt him.

"From sunset to sunrise were the exact terms," she said, a small smile playing around her lips.

"What?" Apollo sounded horrified. "That's it? Just 'sunset to sunrise'?"

I gazed up at him in alarm. "What? What's the matter?"

"That's outrageous," he said flatly, favouring Styx with a glare every bit as vicious as my own. "You have no right."

I glanced at Syl; she looked as confused as I felt. I jumped up and caught Apollo's arm with a mounting sense of dread. "What's wrong?"

Styx laughed. "On the contrary, sun god, I have every right. It's not my fault if people aren't careful enough."

"It's unconscionable."

She laughed even harder at that. "Why, Apollo! Have you grown a conscience at this late stage in life? How droll."

I tugged at Apollo's arm. He looked down at me, and the defeated expression in his eyes sent chills down my spine. "Jake agreed to stay with her from sunset until sunrise."

"And?" I could hardly squeak the word out, consumed by dread.

"And that's not specific enough. He should have said sunset to sunrise in the world above." He waved a hand at the misty greyness surrounding us. "There *is* no sun in the underworld. When will there ever be a sunrise here to release Jake from his vow?"

Now I *really* wanted to kill Styx. Manipulative bitch. "But by that reasoning, there's no sunset either, so Jake never has to go to her."

Apollo sighed. "That's true, but I'm afraid it would be a hollow victory indeed if he didn't. If I'm not mistaken, he only has a few moments left to live. The only way to undo the curse that Styx has placed on him is to fulfil his side of the bargain."

"But that's not fair!"

"No, it's not, but that's what Jake agreed to."

"There must be some way out of this," Syl said, ever-pragmatic. "You're the sun god—can't you make a sunrise?"

"I am the sun god in the world above, not in the underworld. It has its own rules. I'm afraid I don't have that kind of power."

"Can't you force her to release him, then?" I asked.

"*I* can't, no. Hades could do it, or Zeus."

But both of them were missing. God dammit. Jake's eyes had closed again and his lips were a frightening shade of blue. I fell on my knees beside him. "Jake!"

He didn't respond, even when I shook him by the shoulders.

"If you're done discussing it, perhaps we could get on?" Styx said, as if bored with the whole thing. "I'm afraid dear Jacob is about to expire."

"Take him, then." Apollo's face was bleak.

Styx drew closer to the riverbank in a swirl of dark water. "He must come to me voluntarily. I can't take him."

"For fuck's sake, he's unconscious, you crazy bitch!" I screamed. "Take him before he dies or I'll jump in there and wring your scrawny neck."

Her dark eyes glittered with malevolence. "You were involved in the bargain. You can give him to me."

Syl crouched down beside me, her hand a reassuring weight on my shoulder. "Let me help you. Hurry."

She took his legs and I grabbed him under the armpits. Together, we heaved him into the river, though I could barely see what I was doing through the tears of rage in my eyes. The splash as his legs hit the water nearly broke my heart. I would get him back. I *would*. And I'd make this pointy-toothed bitch sorry she'd ever been born.

Styx jerked him from my grasp, giving me a smile of poisonous sweetness. "There. That wasn't so hard, was it?" She bent her head and fastened her bloodless lips to his. As if someone had flicked a switch, Jake came alive in her arms and began to struggle. "Relax, handsome. I promise I'll take good care of you."

She pulled him down into the depths, and the last thing I saw of Jake was the terror in his eyes as the black water closed over his head.

20

I stepped out of the elevator with a heavy heart, Syl on my heels, and the doors whispered closed behind us. Apollo had headed straight back to Crosston to administer a divine smack-down to the Ruby Council, leaving Charon to ferry the two of us and Cerberus back to the wharf near the main entry. Charon hadn't said anything about my knocking him out and stealing his ferry, but his silence had spoken volumes. That was okay—I was in no mood for talking anyway.

I couldn't get that look on Jake's face out of my mind. He hated water, and now he was trapped in the scariest damn river I'd ever seen, relying on that lying bitch to keep him alive. It was a nightmare, and it made me sick with horror. I wanted to smash something, but there was nothing to do and no action I could take to save him. So I sat helpless, fists clenched, and brooded all the way back to the wharf.

From there, it had been a short trudge back through the laughing clown gate and across the misty Plains of Asphodel to Hades' palace. Cerberus had been unhappy at being left behind again, and six mournful eyes had watched pleadingly until the elevator doors had closed on him, but I was adamant. Sleepy Berkley's Bay wasn't ready to meet the hellhound. Until I could find someone to unleash him on, he was better off where he was.

The lights were on when we opened the door into the bar, though there were no customers. Someone was whistling out the back, but otherwise we had the big room to ourselves. I eased the door to Alberto's private quarters shut behind us, then Syl and I moved quietly towards the outer doors.

We were almost there when Harry came in from the kitchen. He gave a small shriek at the sight of us, and clutched a hand dramatically to his chest.

"Holy hell, girls, you shouldn't sneak up on a man like that. You nearly gave me a heart attack."

"Sorry, Harry. Didn't mean to scare you."

He smoothed his hair back carefully. "What are you doing in here, anyway? You know we don't open until midday."

"Just … ah … looking for Alberto. You haven't seen him, have you?"

One perfectly plucked eyebrow rose. "Not much point

looking for him at ten o'clock in the morning, darling. Even if he was here, he wouldn't be up and about in daylight."

Damn. That was a bad slip-up. "So he hasn't been back?"

Harry sighed and slumped onto one of the bar stools. "Haven't seen him in days. I don't know what we're going to do if he doesn't come back soon. Can't keep this place running indefinitely. I mean, who's going to pay the wages?"

"I'm sure he'll be back soon." I'd certainly be doing my damnedest to find him.

"You're doing a great job," Syl said bracingly, and Harry sat a little taller.

"You think so?"

"I'm sure Alberto will be very grateful, when he gets back."

"Let us know if you hear anything, okay?" I said. Harry nodded and I gave him a little wave before pushing through the double doors to the outside world.

God, it was glary. I'd forgotten how bright real sunlight could be—it seemed like years since I'd seen it.

It might be years before Jake saw it again.

The warmth went right out of the day with that cheerful thought, and I followed Syl across the street to our apartment lost in gloom again. We didn't make it all the way, though. Tegan saw us through the window of her shop and burst out into the street, still clutching her scissors.

"Lexi! Where the hell have you been?" She enveloped me in a bear hug—or tiger hug, I suppose. Either way, I could barely breathe, as she seemed determined to crush all the air out of my lungs. Just when I thought I was about to expire, she let me go. "And who's this?"

"Syl," I said. She'd never actually seen Syl in human form before—or if she had caught a glimpse of her in the big showdown with Anders, Hades must have wiped it when he stole her memories of that battle.

Syl immediately got the same hug, then Tegan thrust her out to arm's length, beaming joyfully. "Oh, let me look at you—aren't you gorgeous? I was starting to think something awful had happened to you two. You won't believe what's been going on around here while you've been gone." She punctuated her sentences with wild gestures of the hand holding the scissors, and I stepped back smartly.

"You're going to cut somebody's head off with those things if you're not careful," I said.

"Oh." She looked at the scissors as if she'd forgotten she had them, then shoved them in the pocket of her apron. Little snippets of hair clung to the long white sleeves of her low-cut blouse. You could usually follow Tegan by the trail of bits of hair she left behind her—it was an occupational hazard of being a hairdresser. "There've been shapers all over the town, looking for you. The Master of the North himself turned up with a warrant for the arrest of that gorgeous local councillor of ours." She dropped her voice in a conspiratorial way—which, with Tegan, only meant she went from a loud roar to a slightly softer one. "I have no idea what he'd done, but the fireshapers were in a lather over it. You two wouldn't happen to know anything about that, would you?"

Should we tell her? Tegan was absolutely useless at keeping secrets, but I had a feeling Apollo wasn't going to be too discreet about cleaning out the nest of vipers currently inhabiting the Ruby Palace. Everyone would soon know that the gods were still alive and kicking—most of them, anyway. And the ones who were in danger, like Hades and Zeus, wouldn't be helped by our silence. I looked at Syl and she shrugged, as if to say, *What difference does it make now?*

"Why don't you come upstairs with us?" I said. "We probably shouldn't be discussing this in the middle of the street."

Tegan's eyes positively glowed—she could sense a juicy story coming. She hustled us up the stairs faster than you could say "gossip time". Hopefully, none of those haircuts were urgent.

We made so much noise that Joe and Holly's door opened as we reached the landing.

"I thought that was you!" Joe cried. "Honey, Lexi and Syl are back."

Obviously, he still had most of his memories intact. Probably Hades had only removed the part where he'd revealed his true identity. He dragged us into another round of hugs and a baby began to cry in the apartment behind him.

"For goodness' sake, Joe, you've woken the baby," Holly scolded, but she was smiling as she came to the door. "Come in, come in. We've been so worried about you— especially since Lucas arrived. What on earth was all that sneaking around the pub in the middle of the night about?"

She opened the door wider, practically dragging us inside. Lucas rose from the couch as we entered, putting a mug of coffee down. It looked like they'd been eating breakfast together.

"Hello again," he said. "Did you get wherever you were going in time?"

I smiled at him over Holly's shoulder. When she'd finished hugging and exclaiming over us, I dragged Syl over to meet him. I'd already told her about the part Lucas had played in getting the star-metal to the underworld. "Yes, I did. This is my friend, Syl. Syl, this is Lucas, Joe's little brother."

She craned her neck to look up at him and grinned. "Not so little. Nice to meet you."

The big werewolf looked down at the tiny cat shifter and smiled a slow, warm smile. "Nice to meet you, too."

"I hear you ride a bike. What make?"

His eyes lit up at her interest, and they started talking bikes, so I left them to it.

With six of us in it, the little room felt super crowded, but Holly ordered people around with her usual ruthless efficiency, and soon everyone was settled on couches, though I noticed Lucas had managed to manoeuvre things so that he was sitting next to Syl. Joe was dispatched to the nursery to retrieve his wailing daughter.

"Would you like a coffee or tea?" Holly asked, filling the kettle in the tiny kitchen area. "Or something stronger?"

"Sit down," Tegan ordered her. "I'll do that. You feed Mireille."

"You called her Mireille?" I asked. "That's such a pretty name."

"It means miracle," Joe said, walking back in with a tiny bundle. "Because her birth was a bloody miracle."

"Her middle name's Alexis, after you," Holly added, a little shyly, "since she wouldn't even be here without you."

Oh, my gosh. I put a hand to my heart, tears pricking at my eyes. "I don't know what to say. I'm honoured."

I didn't tell them my full name was actually Alexia. That didn't matter at all—it was the intention that counted. I was so touched I could hardly speak.

"Meet Mireille Alexis," Joe said. "Mireille, this is your Auntie Lexi."

Mireille's red face was scrunched up as she focused on demonstrating just how much noise such a small person could make.

"She'll be more sociable when she's had a feed," Holly said, laughing as she took the baby from Joe. "Come here, my darling. Don't worry, Mama knows exactly what you need."

Holly settled in the armchair with the screaming baby in the crook of one arm. She pulled up her top, and the minute Mireille found her breast, all noise stopped, as if someone had flicked a switch. One little arm waved aimlessly in the air until Holly caught the tiny fist in her own and kissed it. She gazed down at her contented daughter with such love in her eyes that it nearly melted my heart.

"She's a good eater," Joe said, watching his wife and daughter with a fond smile. "She'll make a fine, strong wolf."

"I'm surprised you're home," I said. "Shouldn't you be at work?"

Joe laughed. "It's Saturday. You must have been on a real bender if you can't remember what day of the week it is. Tegan, you'd better make her coffee a strong one."

Tegan handed out coffees, then settled herself on the couch next to Joe. "All right, start talking. What have you two been up to?"

I took a sip of coffee and launched into the story, leaving nothing out. Well, almost nothing. There were a couple of kissing parts that I kept to myself. I figured nobody needed to hear about my love life, even if Tegan probably would have liked that part the best.

I did feel a little guilty at blowing Hades' cover after all these years, but secrecy did nothing to help him now. We needed all the help we could get. If he was really pissed with me over it, he could always zap their memories when this was over.

Hmm. I paused for a sip of coffee. It looked kind of suspicious that there were all these gods around with holes in their memories—not to mention my own situation—and there was Hades, with his convenient river of forgetting. But no, I wasn't going down that path—I'd go mad if I had to suspect everyone around me. Besides, Cerberus wouldn't be so convinced that his master had met foul play if he was the evil mastermind behind this whole mess. The hellhound was incapable of deceit. That thought cheered me up immeasurably.

By the time I'd finished, my voice was hoarse and my coffee had gone cold. Little Mireille had long since finished her feed, been burped, and gone back to sleep again. Everyone else looked stunned.

"Wow," said Tegan. "You *have* been busy."

"I can't believe the gods are actually real," Holly said.

"Even though Lucas told us what you'd said to him at the pub. I mean, I always just thought of them as some kind of spirits watching over us, not actual people who bicker with each other like we do."

"And serve beer at my local pub," Tegan added.

"Your story explains one thing, at least," Joe said.

"What?" I asked.

"Why a brand-new four-wheel drive turned up on my doorstep this week. The guy who delivered it said that Jake Steele had paid for it, but that was all he could tell me."

"Really? When would Jake have had time to order a new car?"

"Maybe the night he went topside with Hades," Syl said. "The night before you two took off looking for Hephaistos."

"That was the night that Hades disappeared. Did any of you see him that night?"

They all shook their heads. "Rosie saw him, but they only chatted for a moment and then he left," Joe said. Rosie was his ex. "He never came back, because Lisa was complaining the next day about being the only one behind the bar all night."

"What did he and Rosie talk about?" Maybe their conversation would give me some clue.

Joe shrugged. "She didn't say."

I let my head fall back against the couch as I cradled my cold coffee. What could have happened to Hades? Where had he gone? Most likely, he'd been caught by the shadow shapers—and if he'd had his avatar on him at the time, that meant he was already dead. What a depressing thought. Surely Charon would have mentioned it if he'd given his boss a ride lately. It was kind of important, even if he was pissed with me about the ferry.

I had no idea what Hades' avatar was; I'd never asked him, which seemed a stupid oversight now. I missed him—and besides which, if he were here, he could put that bitch Styx in her place and get Jake back.

I sighed. How did the damn shadow shapers keep getting close enough to kidnap gods, anyway? I could understand it at first, maybe, but surely the gods were all on their guard now? Whatever the killers were doing must be pretty damn sneaky.

"What are you going to do now?" Holly asked.

Good question. I refused to abandon Jake—and I couldn't have gone back to work at the bookshop as if nothing had happened anyway, since my employer was missing. But I was kind of stumped. I had to find Hades—but where did I start looking?

"I'm not sure," I admitted. "I'll have a talk to Rosie, and see if she can shed any light on Hades' disappearance. I need to find him. Or Zeus. Either of them could force Styx to free Jake." And there was also my personal interest in discovering what had happened to my friend, of course, and saving him if he needed help. I couldn't abandon Hades. Plus, finding those two would put a powerful crimp in the plans of the shadow shapers, which was definitely a bonus. As far as I was concerned, the shadow shapers' little war on the gods had become personal. "I guess I'm basically mounting a one-woman campaign to stop the shadow shapers."

"No, you're not," Syl said. "Not a one-woman campaign. Definitely at least two."

"This might be a good time to find yourself a less dangerous friend."

"Ha! As if you'd get anywhere without me."

I smiled gratefully at her. She'd always had my back.

"I know a few werewolves you can count on, too," Joe said.

"And a tiger." Tegan never wanted to be left out of anything. "I'm not letting you lot have all the fun without me."

I looked around at their earnest faces, and all of a sudden, I wanted to cry. Again? Clearly, I needed more sleep. It wasn't like me to be so weepy. "Guys, I really appreciate this." More than I could ever say. "But this is serious stuff. It's dangerous. I can't let you risk yourselves for me."

"Oh, get over yourself," Syl said cheerfully. "You know they don't even like you, right? They just put up with you for my sake."

"And for Hades'," Holly added, straight-faced. "We like *him*."

"That Jake's a pretty stand-up guy, too," Joe said. "He bought me a new car!"

Then they all burst out laughing. They made so much noise that the baby woke up and started fussing again.

"You should see the look on your face," Syl said.

I sighed in contentment, happy to be back among my friends. If only Jake were here with me.

"Tomorrow." Holly was still grinning as she jiggled little Mireille and patted her soothingly. "Think about it tomorrow. You can't save anyone until you've had some rest. You look like you're dead on your feet."

I felt it, too. "I reckon I could sleep for a week."

Tegan stood up. "Then go home and sleep. I'd better get back to work." She gave Joe a sly look. "*Some* of us have to work on Saturdays."

Lucas rose, too. "I'm staying at Mum and Dad's. I might hang around for a while in case you need another ride."

He might have been talking to me, but he was looking at Syl as he spoke. And she was smiling an enigmatic smile that I recognised, even though I hadn't seen it for a while. Uh-oh. Lucas's life was about to get very interesting.

Syl and I said goodnight, even though it was the middle of the day. I had every intention of sleeping the clock around. I'd been running for so long on so little sleep, and now the bill was coming due. I staggered into my bedroom and collapsed onto the bed, fully clothed.

I shut my eyes, feeling blessed unconsciousness beckon.

Tomorrow. I would save the world tomorrow.

THE END

Don't miss the next book, coming soon! For news on its release, plus special deals and other book news, sign up for my newsletter at www.marinafinlayson.com.

Reviews and word of mouth are vital for any author's success. If you enjoyed *Rivers of Hell*, please take a moment to leave a short review where you bought it. Just a few words sharing your thoughts on the book would be extremely helpful in spreading the word to other readers (and this author would be immensely grateful!).

ALSO BY MARINA FINLAYSON

MAGIC'S RETURN SERIES
The Fairytale Curse
The Cauldron's Gift

THE PROVING SERIES
Moonborn
Twiceborn
The Twiceborn Queen
Twiceborn Endgame

SHADOWS OF THE IMMORTALS SERIES
Stolen Magic
Murdered Gods
Rivers of Hell

ACKNOWLEDGEMENTS

Thanks to Mal, Jen and Connor for your speedy beta reading, and for your enthusiasm for this story and this series. A special thank-you to Mal for all the dinners you've cooked while your wife has been busy writing. Love you!

ABOUT THE AUTHOR

Marina Finlayson is a reformed wedding organist who now writes fantasy. She is married and shares her Sydney home with three kids, a large collection of dragon statues and one very stupid dog with a death wish.

Her idea of heaven is lying in the bath with a cup of tea and a good book until she goes wrinkly.

CPSIA information can be obtained
at www.ICGtesting.com
Printed in the USA
BVHW03s1928110718
521408BV00001B/14/P